Editing by Natalie Cammaratta

Proofreading by The Fiction Fix

Cover art by MoonPress Designs | *www.moonpress.co*

Artwork by CeNedra Sunni Rae

Artwork by Céline Lavën

❦ Created with Vellum

THE FIRST LOSS

J.D. LINTON

CONTENTS

BEFORE YOU READ...

As much as I wish every story could have a happy ending, this one simply couldn't, and you already know why.

This is a story I ripped from my heart, word by word, piece by piece, and it's not an easy one. It's not merely a love story—rather, a **tragedy.**

Please take this as a warning. Read this when you are _ready,_ not a moment before.

<u>Content Warning List:</u> explicit sexual content, loss of a loved one/spouse, watching a traumatic death, murder, discussion of parent death, parent lost to illness, parents lost to sudden accident, implied domestic violence (spousal and parental), profanity, grief, anxiety, panic, vomiting, and blood.

A LETTER

Goddess, please hear me.

The years pass faster and faster while somehow each day feels slower, and I am slipping... Into what or who, I'm not sure, but I'm alone—surrounded by people and utterly alone.

Please send me someone, someone who understands this feeling, who could possibly understand me.

Send me love, platonic or otherwise.

Send me happiness so that I may banish this fear from my heart. It's dark and hard, each day harder than the last, and I'm so tired—overwhelmingly tired—and I fear my love's soul may be too.

Send someone to fill me with light so that we may breathe again.

Send me the one whom my soul craves day and

night, because while I don't know them yet, I miss them incessantly.

I do not ask this of you lightly. Rather, I beg.

Please.

PART I

THE BEGINNING

"Being her friend is the most reckless thing I've ever done."

1

FOUR YEARS AGO

Elora

Spring had always been my favorite—the changing of seasons, the signal of life, hope, and renewal. As nature woke, it reawakened hope in me as well. The warm swell in my chest lifted my spirits with the promise of *more:* more to come, more life, more happiness and sun and green and spring showers.

I strolled over the hill, my gaze falling to the apple grove tucked away in the valley below, echoed on all sides by hills covered in glowing forests. With a growing smile, I adjusted the basket in the crook of my elbow before continuing down the dirt path, my long skirts swishing around my ankles.

Goddess, I love the color of spring, especially here.

The orchard was notoriously Fae-owned, and I'd come to the conclusion that the land was steeped in magic, as it produced both blooms and fruit year-round, each tree impervious to the season and in their own stage of growth.

Even now, the apples were red against emerald green leaves, the blooms a soft pink that complimented spring's rainbow of flowers at the bases of their trunks. All of the trees in and around it were vibrant beneath the sunshine, rays beaming through the foliage and falling to the lush ground.

It was beautiful in a way no other season could ever hope for.

The orchard was encircled by a small white picket fence, aged and falling apart in some places, but it had its charms. Its gate was perpetually propped open, forever inviting any passersby.

As I strolled through the entrance, I bit my lip and glanced around before setting the basket down to unlace my boots and pull them off. With boots in hand, I walked toward the nearest tree, the grass thick and soft under my bare feet as I held my face to the sun. A breeze wound through the grove and wrapped me in the scent of apple blossoms, caressing my exposed skin and rustling the leaves as I placed my shoes at the base of a tree. I took a slow breath and wiggled my toes in the grass; the coolness revitalized my tired soul.

Scooping my basket from the ground, I continued through the trees, searching for the best fruit. I was making *another* apple pie for Alivia, the daughter of my adoptive father—and my best friend. I, personally, felt like apple pie was an autumn staple, but she and our father craved it year-round, and I was happy to oblige. There was something so...magical about the way food affected people; the darkest of moods could be sweetened by a good dessert, even if only slightly.

I loved it, touching people's souls with nothing more than a bit of sugar.

Hums slipped past my lips as I lowered the basket to my hand and swung it with each step. I strolled for a few minutes, longer than needed, before reaching up to pluck an apple from its stem. After examining it, I dropped it in the basket and picked another, then another.

My basket filled quickly, but I didn't want to leave just yet. The day was too nice, too beautiful to leave so soon.

Instead, I sat beside my boots at the base of the tree and tucked my legs beneath me as I picked an apple from the basket, wiping it on my dress before taking a bite. With my free hand, I dug through my satchel until I felt the worn leather and smiled to myself, pulling out the book.

Thick, fluffy clouds rolled over the sun as I reclined against the tree, taking another bite and cracking the book open, but they released the light soon enough, and warm rays fell to the old pages.

Then, I read, falling in love with yet another story—one of epic love and longing and tragic loss.

* * *

Vaelor

I had come to paint spring in a new light, to capture nature's rebirth, but I stayed for *her.*

With long strands of auburn sparking in the sunlight and eyes the color of pure blue skies, she could have been the embodiment of the season itself. When she pulled her shoes off, leaving them under a tree to stroll across my orchard barefoot, she only confirmed it. Now, as she sank beneath a tree with her heavy basket and pulled out a book, I felt my breath leave me.

I watched nature itself fall in love with her—the sun's rays reaching for her, the breeze kissing her pale, freckled skin, the flowers leaning into her as they swayed. Even the butterflies flew close. One landed on the knuckle of her finger, and she laughed, cocking her head to look at its brilliant orange wings. The sound carried over to me—a glorious sound I didn't think I'd mind hearing again, hearing a thousand times.

In another life, I would have gone over to her. I would have introduced myself and told her of her beauty, for I believe one would love to hear how fully she has enraptured another. I could have at least stayed to paint her—the slope of her cheekbones, the curve of her full, red lips, her long hair the color of leaves in autumn—but I feared there would be no way to ever truly capture her, and anything less than perfection would have been an insult.

I could have done a lot of things that day, but I couldn't bring myself to disturb her peace. She was too happy, too beautifully content.

Instead, I silently packed my easel and canvas, tucking them under my arm as I threw my bag of paints and brushes over my shoulder.

With one last glance at the goddess across the orchard from me, I turned and followed the path away from her.

In another life.

2

Elora

The carriage hit yet another bump in the road, and my heart lurched. I gripped the seat so tightly, my knuckles were white, my fists shaking. The cushions did nothing to ease the jarring. With closed eyes, I reclined my head and took a deep breath, releasing the seat.

Alivia groaned and braced her hand on the door for reasons entirely different than mine. "You'd think with as traveled as this road is, it'd be smoother."

"Not everyone is lucky enough to travel by carriage," I teased halfheartedly, opening my eyes to find her a bit greener than she'd been moments ago.

"That's true, I suppose," she said, tugging at her tightly-laced corset. "But still—I think riding on the grass would be smoother than this."

I'd much prefer grass. Hell, I'd take walking.

I shifted my gaze to the window as the sun sank on the horizon, perfectly framed by twin mountains. Tucked away at the base of those two peaks was a valley, one I had waited a very long year to return to.

It was where we were headed now. Not the valley per se, but the estate near it—one of many our family-owned, close to the Ravaryn border and bought for this exact reason: the annual peace treaty meeting between Ravaryn and Auryna.

"Not much longer," I said.

"Thank the Goddess. I don't think I could manage much longer. This ride is agitating my motion sickness to no end." Alivia cupped her forehead before following my line of sight to the window, and a curious smile curved her lips. "Are you excited?"

"Yes, very," I replied, but not for the reasons she thought.

This was my first year being allowed in the meeting room where the treaty would be signed once again, and while I was excited to lay eyes on the elusive King of Ravaryn, I was much more excited, albeit anxious, to return to this place for other reasons—all tied to one carefully folded letter, tucked in my corset, burning the skin above my nervous heart.

"He's quite handsome, you know, the King." Alivia wiggled her brows as she sat up, leaning forward on her elbows. The carriage hit another hole in the mud-soaked path, and Alivia pressed her lips into a flat line, biting back her nausea with a deep sigh.

"I've heard."

Rumors of the kind King Vaelor circulated to every corner of the realm—the handsome king who refused to take a wife, keeping his circle small and his love life smaller.

"I wonder why he's not married yet. He doesn't have the countenance of a rake." Alivia reclined in her seat, twirling a loose curl around her finger, her gaze following the passing trees through the window. "Do you think he's impotent?"

My eyes cut to her, a surprised laugh bubbling from my chest. "Alivia!"

"What?" She threw her hands up. "There must be something wrong with him. Why else would a king not marry? He'll need heirs if nothing else."

"I guess that's true." I tilted my head to the side, lifting my brows in consideration. "Perhaps he prefers the company of men."

"I..." Alivia's mouth fell open, like the possibility had never occurred to her, but she snapped it shut again as her hand went to her chin. "But if that were the case, why would he not take a husband? Why refuse to marry entirely?"

"Hmm... Quite the mystery, that one."

"An overly attractive mystery." Her mouth ticked up in a grin.

I laughed, rolling my eyes. "Liv, do you *like* the King of Ravaryn?"

"Oh, no. None of that." She waved a hand through the air in dismissal. "But would that be so unreasonable? The man could have been carved by the Goddess. Perhaps that's why he doesn't marry: he was sent to our realm with the task of showing us what we *could* have but never will. Perhaps he is our punishment...the punishment to our loins."

"Or perhaps he was sent as a gift—a gift to bless our eyes and feed our midnight activities."

Alivia's laughter burst from her, echoing off the walls of our small carriage, and I couldn't contain mine either. When Alivia snorted, I laughed so hard, no sound would come—a silent laughter that had me clutching my abdomen as my belly burned and tears fell.

"You haven't even seen him yet." She wiped beneath her eyes and took a breath, slumping back in her seat as she smoothed her skirts absentmindedly. "You just wait and see how accurate that statement truly is."

Her hands always fell into some kind of movement when she was thinking, and as they ran over the fabric, I realized she was wearing one of her nicer gowns: blacker than midnight with silver embroidered stars.

My eyes trailed over her, following each constellation until I reached her face. I lifted a brow, and she did the same as we locked eyes. "Liv, are you wearing your nice gown in hopes of catching his attention?"

"I mean, honestly, I don't know why you didn't. He could lay his eyes on one of us and fall madly in love."

I chuckled, glancing down at my attire: a simple, dusty blue dress, but it had its charms. It hugged my form in all the right ways, accentuating my bosom. "I'm not the kingdom's princess."

"Well, not technically, but—"

"But nothing. I don't have the obligation to outshine everyone around me—which, by the way, you could do with nothing but a potato sack, Alivia. You're beautiful, regardless of what fabric adorns you." She shook her head, opening her mouth to argue, even as a deep smile set in. "Besides, I rather like blending into the background. It gives me free rein. No one bothers with a second glance in my direction."

The humor slid from Alivia's face a fraction, her eyes going distant as her mind drifted to whatever dark place it frequented when she spoke of such topics. "Privacy is not something I'll ever be afforded." Clearing her throat, she brought her attention back to me, sitting straighter as she smoothed her already-smooth dress—sliding her mask of royalty back on. "But that's a trivial sacrifice I make for my kingdom."

My heart sank, my brows furrowing, and I reached forward to place my hand over hers. "It's not trivial. It's a massive sacrifice —one our people may not understand—but know that you are all the braver for it. Selfless, in a way no one else could ever understand."

"Thank you, El." She nodded, but her eyes remained nearly sad as she turned back to the window.

"You're welcome." I squeezed her hand and sat back. "Now, back to your mysterious lover—"

"*Not* my lover." Her eyes cut back to me, her mouth falling open. "Although I wouldn't be opposed, I guess. He would be much better than any other suitor my father's council has proposed, even if he is a bit closed off. Anything would be better than that damned lord's son. What was his name?"

"Oh Goddess, the one with a mop of red hair and an ego the size of the moon?" I cringed and waved my hand. "No, your father would never *let* you marry him, much less force. He's insufferable; even Godrick's eye twitches with restraint in his presence."

"Well, let's hope. Could you imagine? Living with someone who can only hold a conversation if it involves his steeds, his '*unmatched*' archery skill, or Goddess forbid, he makes me sit through another conversation about his damned books. He thinks he's so superior because he reads nothing but the '*classics*' in the old language."

"Why is it that the most average men have the most outrageous egos?"

As much as my heart ached for her—and it did because Alivia was a lion trapped in a bird's cage—I couldn't deny the subtle relief that flowed through me knowing the council would never argue for control of my marriage. I wasn't sure I even wanted to marry, not for a long while yet at least, and I'd realized the silver lining of my situation years ago. As an orphan unofficially adopted by Godrick and Emma Stirling, my presence held no true weight, despite that they were the king and queen of Auryna. My hand in marriage would gain no favors.

I wasn't royal blood, so in the eyes of the world—if the world *had* known of my existence—I held no true value, and I let those who did know of me believe so. They could view me as Alivia's maid or lady in waiting or even a simple companion, because it didn't truly matter which role they placed me in within their minds; they all gave me the ability to hover in the background, nothing more than a fly on the wall, allowing me to lead the life I wanted. I could slip through the shadows and passageways with ease, and Godrick and Emma allowed it. While Emma worried, I thought Godrick secretly encouraged it as it gave me some semblance of freedom, and he loved me in that way, loved Alivia and me both in that way. He wanted us to taste and understand freedom in any way we could.

I knew Godrick would never force Alivia's hand—not to this imbecile, not to anyone. He was her father before her king, and he wouldn't sacrifice her for something as simple as alliances or favor.

"But Lyren..." I started, the smile creeping back into my face.

"What of him?" Alivia asked nonchalantly, but her growing blush gave her away.

I narrowed my eyes at her, and she averted her gaze. "Spare me. You, the girl who has never liked riding, have suddenly started going on daily rides, and when did that start? Oh, that's right—when he was hired as the stable boy."

"He's a stable boy, Elora. Nothing could ever come of it, regardless of our feelings."

I leaned forward and cocked a brow. "Maybe not, but he could be...fun, for now, if you allowed it."

She tipped her head to the side, returning her gaze to the sinking sun, but her stifled smile was still visible in her profile. "Perhaps."

"Kidding aside, if this mystery king is as handsome as you say, he wouldn't be a completely nonviable option, right? No matter what dress you wear, you'll undoubtedly bring the poor man to his knees."

She rolled her eyes, a genuine laugh escaping her.

"And if he still doesn't, then I fear he may be hopeless—utterly and regrettably hopeless."

"You may be right, but my dress for tomorrow is even *better:* red silk with a plunging neckline." She wiggled her brows. "Truly, one of my favorite gowns I've ever seen. Anyone who wore it would stand out, especially among the elders we'll be surrounded by at the meeting."

I knew the exact gown, as I'd been there the day she bought it. "Anyone else would be lost in it."

It took a special kind of person, a special kind of confidence, to wear a gown like that, but Alivia had been raised as royalty, and she had the self-assurance that only a princess could. Beyond that, every bit of her looked as royal as she was. With long, blonde hair, chocolate brown eyes, soft skin untouched by labor, and voluptuous curves formed by the rich food at court, she gave the dress life.

"Not just anyone could wear that," I added.

"Well, then perhaps King Vaelor will be so enamored that he'll end his refusal to marry right then and there, demand my hand, and end the council's fervent pursuit of my marriage."

"That's the spirit," I said, sinking back in my seat.

"But while King Vaelor looks to be carved by the Goddess, he's as stoic as a statue, too. He may as well have been carved from stone. Every time I've seen him, his conversations were dry and solely centered around his kingdom. Nothing more. Maybe that's why he hasn't married—he only has enough love for his throne and has none left to give to another."

"Or maybe no one has accepted his proposal." I covered my mouth, stifling a giggle.

"Maybe every potential spouse has died of boredom or fled for their lives."

I scrunched my eyes when I burst into laughter, muffling the sound with my hand. "We're horrible."

"The meanest," she managed between gasps, clutching her side.

Taking a few breaths, I wiped my eyes and pulled my legs up to cross in my lap—a particularly stubborn habit to break. "I suppose that does make him an admirable king, but how will his line of succession work without an heir?"

"I don't know," she said. "Maybe the customs are different in Ravaryn, though. Who knows?"

I shrugged, turning back to the window as we neared the estate, merely a small, black silhouette against the burning orange sunset from this distance. Despite so much beauty, however, my gaze honed in on the small valley behind it—the one that held the orchard.

3

THREE YEARS AGO

Vaelor

I hadn't come back to see her again—or rather, that was what I told myself—but as the sun dipped on the horizon, disappointment sank in my chest.

I'd brought supplies to paint something, anything, but nothing seemed to strike inspiration, not like I knew she would, even from a distance. It had been a full year since I'd seen her, but her memory was burned into mine: her flaming locks of auburn, eyes the color of the clear skies I so frequently clouded.

I had told myself she wouldn't be here. I had told myself I was coming to paint the orchard as I had every year before I saw her. Her presence hadn't changed anything. I still painted. I was still the King of Ravaryn, and she was just...a woman—a simple, human woman who liked apples and reading, who liked to take her shoes off and hum to herself as if she was the only person in the world.

She didn't change anything, and yet, she changed everything.

I didn't know anything else about her. I didn't even know her name, but it was as if each passing moment led me back here to this damned orchard, one I frequented every year but was now tarnished by something much more important; I just wanted to *see* her. I wanted to know she wasn't a tea-induced hallucination or a dream of temptation sent from the Goddess herself, because I was starting to think perhaps she was.

The sun set the great expanse aflame with its brilliant light, but it didn't last. As the disappointment rolled in, so did the clouds, the ones that followed my sadness, an echo of the emotion inside me.

I slowly packed my supplies: the blank canvas, the paints, the untouched brushes. They all sat where I put them this morning when I arrived, waiting for the inspiration that never came. Once it was all packed neatly in the bag, I stood and glanced around with a deep sigh.

The clouds were a deep gray—a fitting setting, I supposed. When the sun disappeared entirely, the world was thrust into darkness as my storms blotted out the moon, leaving the self-lit torches sporadically placed along the orchard as the only light.

This is for the best.

Why would I need to speak to a woman, a human at that? My kingdom needed my full attention, and I didn't need anything or anyone else. I had my small family, and that was enough. It had to be.

My kingdom, my father, Iaso, and Ewan.

They were all I needed. Anything or anyone else would be... a distraction. An alarming, inconvenient distraction.

So, why did it feel like I was leaving something overwhelmingly important behind as I strolled down the path, my feet moving as slowly as they possibly could like she would suddenly step from the shadows?

"Ridiculous," I muttered under my breath.

* * *

Elora

I noticed him as soon as I arrived and hid before he could see me, but I couldn't tear my eyes away from him. He was... different—a Fae man, impeccably tall and lean.

It was his face that gave me pause, though.

He was ethereally handsome in a way that didn't belong here, not in Auryna, not in this realm. While he looked to be in his mid-forties, the air about him seemed ancient and graceful —unlike any man I'd ever seen. There were no rough edges, no harshness or insecurity in his movements. He was gentle, a painter.

In a sea of men, he would undoubtedly stand out like lightning among clouds, utterly unmissable, mesmerizing. There was no other way to describe it.

He demanded my attention effortlessly, without intention, and he didn't even know I existed. As I stared, studying every inch of his face, I realized his features, while stunning, were marred by something deeper—disappointment, maybe? Every few minutes, he would glance around, peeking over his blank canvas and through the trees before his chest would rise and fall in a sigh.

He was clearly waiting for someone, perhaps a lover. He was handsome enough to have one—to have anyone he wanted.

This mysterious person must be otherworldly to have such a man on the edge of his seat waiting for them.

As curiosity got the better of me, I plucked an apple from a tree and took a seat at its base, settling in my hiding spot. I had no other plans for the day, so I resolved to wait for his love to appear, if only to see who could enrapture such a man so thoroughly.

My heart ached for him when they never arrived, and as the storms rolled in, spitting a slow, miserable drizzle, he glanced around one final time before packing his things and strolling from the orchard.

I stared after him long after he disappeared over the hill, pouring over the possibilities that were *him*. Was he as kind as he was graceful? Was he as ancient as he seemed? Was he heart-broken by the absence of his awaited?

The questions carried me back to the estate alongside the image of his face, the disappointment on his features lingering in my gut.

A perfect stranger, and yet, I was captivated.

4

Elora

"Let's just go." Alivia tugged on my hand. "It'll be fun."

"I don't think Godrick would appreciate us leaving after explicitly asking us *not* to leave," I said flatly, resisting her pull. "And Goddess, imagine how Emma would react if she found out."

"She's asleep, and besides, this would normally be *your* idea." She held my hand to her chest and gave her best pleading look. "Please. For me? I can't go alone."

I rolled my eyes with a groan. "Fine, but I swear to the Goddess, if we get caught, I'm telling him you forced me."

She squealed and bounced up and down, her dark cloak falling back to reveal her blonde braid. "Fine, yes. Let's go."

She pulled her hood back over her head as she turned and opened our chamber door. Peeking her head out, she glanced left and right before giving me the thumbs up and slipping out the door.

"This is such a bad idea," I muttered before following behind her.

The night air was crisp as we snuck through a seemingly unnoticed door and stepped into the back courtyard, the moon our only light.

"You know I'm normally all for going to the tavern, but Godrick asked us to stay in this night for a reason. The meeting is tomorrow, which means Fae are roaming the towns."

"So? When did you become such a scaredy-cat?" Alivia whispered, peeking over her shoulder. "We're here for the *peace* treaty resigning, which, in case you didn't realize, means they're *not* looking for a fight, El."

"I'm not scared. I was respecting Godrick's wishes," I mumbled.

Godrick took me in as an infant when my parents, his childhood friends, died in a tragic accident, and Emma accepted me with open arms. Together, they'd raised me alongside Alivia, treating me like their own daughter, and had always been so, utterly kind. I loved them for it and wanted to show them the respect they deserved, the respect they'd earned.

Although, if Fae *were* roaming around tonight, maybe there was a chance *he* would be there. A spike of adrenaline shot through me, and I took a slow breath, pulling my cloak tighter around my shoulders.

Her steps slowed and stopped when we came to the dirt road. She looked left and right before turning to me. "Do you... happen to know where the tavern is?"

I glared at her, my mouth pressed into a flat line, but she shrugged her shoulders and widened her eyes as she threw her hands up.

"Well?" she asked.

With a deep sigh, I pointed a finger down the path. I knew exactly where it was because I passed it every year on the way to the orchard I loved so dearly; if not for the darkness of night, we'd see the trees from the tavern's entrance, massive and green, speckled with shining red apples. She grinned, giving my shoulder a quick squeeze before taking off in that direction.

We made it to the tavern within the hour, finding it alive with people and music. Patrons came and went steadily, the golden light from inside pouring from the open doors and windows. A slight breeze blew, and the scent of cyser drifted along with it—their sweet apple mead.

I inhaled deeply, reveling in it before Alivia looped her hand through mine and tugged me forward. When we walked in, I scanned the room and bit at the inside of my cheek, stifling the uncomfortable feeling in my gut. They were only humans.

Alivia jumped up, waving a hand as she spotted Evander in the corner with a few other soldiers. Evander's face lit up when he saw us, and we waded through the packed tables to them.

"Didn't expect to see you two here," he said, his eyes shifting from Alivia to me and lingering.

"Well, while we're here..." I grabbed the whiskey shot from the table in front of Evander and downed it.

His brows shot to his hairline, but he lifted another small glass in offering. With a grin, I took it too and relished the burn. As bad as I felt for disobeying Godrick's one request, we were already here, the tavern was lively, and I knew the liquor would be bought with the crown's coin.

Might as well enjoy the night.

* * *

"Final round!"

My head spun with alcohol and anticipation, my heart thundering, but no one beat me in Coins, Evander included, and he wasn't going to now. The goal was simple: bounce the coin into the cup and chug the mead.

I could barely contain my giggle as Alivia counted down from three.

At two, I shimmied my shoulders, and Evander nudged me with his, giving me a sidelong glance. At one, I zeroed in on my mug, the smile sliding from my face, and at "go," I bounced the coin and landed it on the first try. The tavern erupted in cheers as I snatched the cup and downed the mead in a few gulps before slamming it back down.

Evander grinned, arms crossed over his chest and eyes on me, not bothering with a second toss of his coin as I destroyed him. He didn't look upset, though. Another emotion lingered in his eyes, in his smile, more than mere happiness. Humor didn't quite cover it, either. Pride, maybe? But that didn't make any sense at all. My brows furrowed, and he opened his mouth to speak but didn't have a chance to say a word before Alivia threw her arm around my shoulders.

"Atta girl!" Alivia gave me a quick squeeze and swiveled me to our table, Evander following behind.

I plopped down in an old chair, my hands jerking out as the wood creaked under my weight, and I paused in fear it would give way beneath me. When it didn't, we burst into laughter again, our drunken euphoria a welcomed feeling, but then, seemingly out of thin air, a deep brown hand set a vial in front of me.

Our laughter died off as my gaze followed the arm, climbing each band of gold, each emerald to the person it all belonged to, and found the most beautiful woman to have ever existed—I was sure of it. The memory of *him* waiting for his mysterious lover flashed in my mind, and I couldn't help but wonder if this was her, because she was as beautiful as he was handsome.

"This will prevent a hangover," she said, her voice smooth, ancient. I met her gaze, and her irises were an unnatural amber —*Fae,* a voice whispered in the back of my fuzzy mind. I couldn't see her ears as they were hidden beneath voluptuous curls, highlighted with small golden beads that matched her rings, but I knew. I could feel it in my bones.

"I don't think we're supposed to take things from strangers." I chuckled awkwardly and peeked at Alivia. She was as mesmerized as I was, her attention glued to the woman, but she shook her head faintly.

"You can trust me," the Fae woman said, and for some unfathomable reason, I believed her. She handed another vial to Alivia before a man joined her side. With short, brown curls and deep, blue eyes, he was attractive, but not in the way this woman was, not in the way my Fae friend was.

He didn't suck the air from the room with his devastating appearance like the other two, but he did look kind and wholesome, his skin tanned from years in the sun, and his ears... My head tilted to the side as I stared at them. They were eerily similar to a human's but pointed where they should be rounded.

Fae, then. They're definitely Fae.

He looked at the woman, and I knew, without a doubt, he was hopelessly in love with her. I had a knack for seeing these things, and it was as clear as day in the way his eyes warmed as he neared her. His features softened, and when she peeked back at him, he smiled, a dimple appearing in his cheek.

"Come on. Let's get back," he said, tilting his head toward the door.

She nodded, returning his smile before she turned back to me. "Be safe, and take your cures, all right? I have a feeling you'll thank me in the morning."

With that, she looped her arm through her friend's, and they strode out the front door without another word.

Alivia and I glanced at each other, pausing for a moment before lifting the vials and examining them closer.

"I don't think I'm going to take this," she said, unsure. "I don't trust people enough for that."

Maybe it was the alcohol deciding for me, but I trusted her, so I popped the cork off and swallowed the bitter liquid. When I finished, Alivia and Evander's wide eyes were on me, their faces fallen in shock.

Alivia placed a hand over mine as she leaned in. "That could be the most foolish thing you've ever done."

"Oh, it absolutely was," Evander said as he jerked a chair out and sank into it. He took my face in his hands and his eyes flicked left and right between my own, as if to check for any signs of impending death.

I pulled my face from his grasp. "I'll be all right. I trust her."

"You didn't *know* her, El," Alivia said. "She was a stranger *and* a Fae. How do you know that wasn't a spell or magic or just plain old poison? You can't ingest things from strangers!"

Under normal circumstances, she'd be right, and maybe she was even now. Maybe I wouldn't make it until morning, but I did know that right now, in this moment, I could feel my head clearing and my stomach settling with each passing second.

It could be my mind playing tricks on me, wanting to believe I made the right choice, but I didn't think so. "No, I think it's working."

Alivia sat back in her chair with a sigh, concern pressing between her brows. "Yeah, all right. Well, I'm going to keep whatever wits I have left and choose not to take a strange liquid from a strange woman."

I rolled my eyes and swiped her vial before holding it out to Evander, giving it a light shake.

"You really believe this will prevent a hangover?" He took it and held it up to the light, watching the small bits of herbs floating inside. "You don't feel like you're going to drop dead at any moment?"

"Yes, I do." I stifled a laugh and shook my head. "And no, I don't."

With a deep inhale, he popped the cork off. "Aw, hell with it. If you say so."

He tipped it back, and Alivia groaned, slapping her hand on her forehead. "You two better not die on me."

"No promises." I winked at her, and her mouth fell open, but she chuckled and swatted my shoulder. "Are you ready to head back? I believe it's already well past midnight."

She sipped from her mug of mead one last time before answering, "Yes, I need sleep. Immediately."

Standing, I formally extended an elbow to her, and she grinned, dipping into a curtsy before sliding her arm through mine. A comforting warmth settled in my chest as I led her through the tavern toward the exit, heated by alcohol, contentedness, that strange tonic, or a potent combination of all three. Whatever the cause, it pulled the corners of my mouth up, etching what seemed to be a permanent smile on my lips.

As I opened the door, we waved over our shoulders and shouted simultaneously, "Goodnight, Evander."

"Goodnight, princesses," he shouted as we stepped out into the night, his voice carrying over the remaining patrons with a humorous lilt.

My face jerked back to him with a glare, even as I suppressed a small laugh, but he only winked and lifted his mug to me. I rolled my eyes, shaking my head as the door closed with a soft click, cutting him from view and ceasing the tavern chatter.

He knew I hated being called that.

I was *not* a princess, nor did I ever want to be.

5

TWO YEARS AGO

Elora

I wasn't entirely sure I was going for the apples. No one had asked me for our traditional spring apple pie yet, but it didn't matter much. Baking was how I showed my love when words weren't enough, and this year was no different.

Whether they ask or not, they're going to eat the damn pie, stolen apples and all.

With a deep sigh, I ran a hand through my hair. It seemed the aggravating bundle of nerves that had settled in my gut was bleeding into all parts of me—my heart, my movements, even my thoughts.

"I'm just here for apples," I whispered, rolling my shoulders and adjusting the basket in the crook of my arm.

The walk to the orchard was pleasant this spring, the sun warm and the air only slightly chilled, the breeze soft and birds' chirping lively—the kind of day that offered promise and relief, but not even it could settle me, as much as I wished it would.

"Why am I so on edge today?"

The question was moot. In the very back of my mind, I knew

it was, even as I fervently tried to convince myself otherwise, but the dress clinging to my form and matching bow tying half my hair back was answer enough. The soft blue fabric dipped low on my chest to reveal what little cleavage I had and hugged my curves while still allowing me to move, the color bringing out the blue in my eyes. At first glance, it may not look like much, but I wasn't too humble to admit it complimented me.

Fidgeting with the sleeve, I released another sigh, hoping this one would release the tension from my chest. At this rate, between it and the corset cinching my waist, I was liable to faint before I plucked my first fruit from the stem.

My visits to the orchard had started over a decade ago. I stumbled upon on it by happenstance, and it stuck with me, pulling me back year after year. I found comfort in nature's silence there, and I was hopeless to resist. Even Godrick encouraged my visits, claiming the apples were sweeter, the pies better; he did not, however, know they were stolen. In my defense, he never asked, and I never saw anyone to pay.

It was always empty.

Always.

Until it wasn't.

Last time, I had seen a person, and not just any person: a Fae man, one I fully believed could be a god among men.

Was it not the same orchard I'd been to a dozen times? Was it different now? Had it lost its feeling of solitude? I knew other people frequented it. It was owned and maintained by someone —probably a few someones—but I had never *seen* anyone, so it had somehow felt like mine. It had become my special secret I could escape to, but now, I *had* seen someone else there.

It wasn't my solitude. It was...ours?

He'd been alone too, albeit waiting for someone, but they never showed.

I winced, running a hand down my face. Was I really doing

this? Was I really kind of...happy his love never showed, even after seeing the disappointment and hurt on his face as he stalked away in the rain?

I'm a horrible person.

None of that mattered though, me being happy or sad or empathetic, because he wouldn't be here. I knew that. I had told myself that repeatedly, but it somehow wouldn't get through my thick skull. Truly, what were the odds that we would both return on the same day, a full year later?

Nonexistent. The odds were nonexistent. Wearing my favorite dress to an orchard was idiotic. Having hope of seeing someone who so clearly belonged to another was foolish.

Having hope of seeing a man I saw once, a year ago, was foolish.

Why did I even care?

"I don't," I murmured. "But if a man like *that* comes here, I might as well wear my best dress. It seems an insult to nature herself to have me in anything less than my best with that perfect specimen in the vicinity."

My feet paused when the end of the trail came into view. The small dirt path didn't actually end, but as it dipped over the steep hill, it appeared that way. I could see the back half of the orchard from here, and even that stopped my heart.

What if he is there? I swallowed hard and lifted my chin. *So what if he is? I was here first...I think.*

I dropped my eyes, looking at my feet with a newfound confidence that didn't quite register in my pounding heart. *Move.*

They didn't.

"Move."

They still didn't. It wasn't until a twig snapped behind me that my feet finally left the spot they were anchored to. I jumped and swiveled, my hand flying to my chest, only to find a deer watching me—a doe.

I stared back at her, her eyes brown and warm. She eyed me curiously, without fear or hesitation, her head lifting into the air, sniffing. She didn't seem to be spooked at all; she even took a small step closer.

I leaned forward a fraction. "*You* scared *me*. I think it's supposed to be the other way around."

At my words, she bounded off in the opposite direction, disappearing into the thick foliage, taking some of my anxiety with her. Her presence, calm and steady, had bled into me, and I was grateful for it.

Smiling slightly, I turned toward the orchard and strolled along, over the hill and down the path. The small white gate was already unlatched and propped open, dozens of white daffodils blooming along the base of the picket fence. I quickly unlaced my boots and set them in front of a post before sighing. The cool, plush grass under my feet would never not be one of my favorite feelings.

With a mixture of hope and anticipation, I walked forward, keeping my eyes glued to the trees. I didn't come here to look for him, and if he was here, I didn't want to fall into his unintentionally-laid trap again, as the sight of him would undoubtedly ensnare me.

Apples, I reminded myself. *Just apples.*

Spying the perfect one, round and red, shining with a glint of sunshine, my smile deepened, and I strode toward it. It was a bit high for me, but I reached regardless, extending my arm and standing on my tip toes as much as I possibly could. My fingertips missed it by an inch or so. With a slight grunt of frustration, I tucked my hair behind my ears, took a deep breath, and reached again, this time for the branch holding the damned fruit.

My fingertips grazed the bark, but not enough.

Just when I was about to turn to find a stump or stool to

stand on, another hand reached around me, and I froze, utterly still, not even daring to breathe.

His arm—undoubtedly a man's—was lean and tanned, his corded muscle revealed by his white sleeve messily rolled up to his elbow. When my breath finally returned, my cheeks flushed with heat as I inhaled the intoxicating scent of ocean, leather, and...rain?

How does anything smell like rain?

The hand plucked the apple, and I turned, following it as he pulled his arm back, only to be met with a solid chest clothed in the white button-up. My gaze slowly slid up, noting the top few buttons undone, and finally landed on his face.

My lips parted in a gasp, and he didn't miss the small movement. His eyes, as gray as the deepest storms, swirling with near-imminent rain, flitted to my mouth before lifting back to meet my gaze.

Him. My heart screamed—in excitement, in satisfaction, in fear, in hope.

The corner of his mouth lifted into a lopsided grin, revealing adorably crooked white teeth. "I think this is yours."

His voice... Oh dear Goddess, his voice. I couldn't begin to imagine how many people had fallen to their knees just because he had asked them to do so.

He cocked a brow, tilting his head, and I finally realized he was holding the apple out to me. The flush in my cheeks *burned.*

"T-thanks," I said, hiding my wince at the unsteadiness in my voice, which only deepened his smile, revealing a dimple in his right cheek. Lifting my hand hesitantly, I wrapped my hand around the apple, and our fingertips grazed.

Grazed wasn't the right word.

Collided? Tilted the world on its axis? Sparked? Could skin spark at the contact of another?

Because I believed mine just did.

* * *

Vaelor

Neither of us moved. Nothing moved. Not even time.

Everything stilled as our fingers touched, hers dainty against mine, and there was a current, a tangible electrical charge, a warmth that spread from her into me, racing up my arm and into my heart, into my damned soul.

And there she remained, settled in my chest, consuming every bit of air in my lungs and replacing it with a fire that caught me viciously off guard, like her red and orange strands were actual flames. Perhaps they were. Perhaps she had magic. Perhaps...

Time resumed. My heart lurched, then raced. My breath left me in a whoosh. Everything moved too fast, especially my thoughts.

I stumbled back a step, jerking my hand away from hers.

Perhaps this human was my mate.

My mate?

I swallowed hard.

This woman, the most beautiful I've ever seen, the one I've been obsessed with for years, *is my mate?*

My eyes flicked to hers, and they swallowed me whole, like I was falling through the sky—into the sky.

She *was* my mate.

There wasn't an ounce of doubt, not as I held her gaze. I could feel it, could feel her, wanted her, *needed* her more than anything else. I had never needed *anyone* so badly.

But the desire was nearly matched by a fierce wave of fear.

I had wanted to speak with her for years, her face a steady image in my mind, piquing too much curiosity. I had simply wanted to meet her, to see if her voice was as sweet as she looked, but a mate? That was too much.

That made her dangerous.

Goddess be damned.

I clenched my jaw, averting my gaze against the overwhelming urge to hold her expectant one, because her eyes, as beautiful as they were, were a carefully laid snare, specially designed by fate to entrap me of all people.

A mate bond meant...

My head swam.

Leave.

Leave before the damage is done.

Walk away and never look back, never think of her again.

My mind screamed at my body, but no part of me moved. My heart ached, and it was far stronger than rationality. She was a human for Goddess' sake; they died faster than anyone.

My gut twisted. I'd outlive her for multiple human lifetimes.

No, I could not—would not subject myself to that.

Why did I come here? Why was I even looking for her in the first place? This was foolish, so fucking foolish.

And then, like venom, a thought seeped into my mind: was it the mate bond calling me back here to her? For some reason, that didn't settle well with me. I hadn't wanted to fuck her into oblivion...at first, but now, doubt rolled through me.

Was that truly why I was here? Was it the mate bond holding me hostage?

I wasn't entirely sure what I hoped to find with her, but it wasn't lust—that much I knew. Maybe a friend, maybe more, if I was honest with myself.

But in every scenario I'd ever imagined with her, absolutely *none* of them ended with her being my damned mate.

I took another wide step back. I should take another and another. I should turn away from her and stop looking at her, stop drowning in her blue. I should leave her here. The deep-rooted fear clawing at my chest demanded it, a clear warning I *would* heed. She was already too carefully wound through my being for me to remain here; any additional second was dangerous.

Then why wasn't I leaving? With love came loss. Not that that was what this was, but a mate bond signified one thing and one thing alone: children. It paired souls that would produce the strongest offspring, and *that* would be a love lost I wouldn't survive.

After five hundred years in this realm without a mate, I had thought I was in the clear, but here she was, the embodiment of temptation.

Everyone dies, I reminded myself with a hard swallow, a millisecond from bolting, but then, she giggled—softly, but it was enough to give me pause.

She clutched the apple to her chest, her face lit with amusement. "Sorry, I didn't mean to spook you."

"Spook?" I couldn't stop the surprised chuckle that slipped past my lips. "You didn't spook me. You…"

She tilted her head, studying my face as I studied hers. It dawned on me in that moment as I took in her relaxed expression, happy and unbothered, a hint of mischief in her eyes. She didn't feel the bond, and I didn't think I liked that, not one bit, even if I didn't intend to act on it.

"I what?" She twirled a finger through her hair, and my eyes fell to the strand wrapped around her finger, momentarily jealous of the absentminded movement.

I wanted to touch her hair, to see if it burned my skin like the flames it resembled. *Burning in her fire wouldn't be so bad*, I thought. *Not if she burned with me.*

No. I took several steps back, preparing to turn away once and for all, giving her an apologetic look. "I'm sorry. It was—"

The breeze blew then, at quite possibly the worst moment. It enveloped me in her sweet cinnamon vanilla scent, anchoring my feet to the ground, and I inhaled slowly, letting her fill every crevice of my body, which reacted *immediately.*

A wave of sparks spread under my skin, rushing to my hardening cock, a low moan rumbling in my chest.

I'd heard of the lust induced by the mate bond, but this? This was much more than I expected. This was not simple want. This was torturous, demanding *need.*

"Are you okay?" She laughed, snapping me from her trance.

I blinked rapidly, shaking my head. "I'm fine." *In complete shambles, but fine.*

Her eyes flashed, and she nodded incredulously, strolling closer with an innocent smile, her hands clasped behind her back. I stiffened as she got closer and closer—too close for how volatile this bond made me feel.

"Are you sure?" She bit her lip, suppressing a giggle. "Because you seem like you might be...in pain, if I'm honest."

A loud laugh escaped me, and she jumped in surprise, her smile widening. I *was* in pain, but her playfulness popped the bubble of lust I was in with a needle of humor. I wasn't sure what I expected her to say, but it certainly wasn't that; regardless, it was exactly what I needed. I released a breath of relief and raked a hand through my hair.

Lifting a brow, I leaned down until my face was a mere few inches from hers to whisper, "It's not me you should be worried about, little *human.*"

Her face fell slightly, her spine straightening, but the flush in her cheeks deepened to a heated red—a sight I was decidedly fond of.

"Elora," she said in a rush before clearing her throat and regaining her composure. Her easy smile returned. "My name is Elora. And for the record, I may be the human here, but I still think it *is* you we should worry about. I'm not the one who looks like I'm about to faint."

I suppressed a groan. Of course, her name was Elora.

"Figures," I said with a chuckle, stepping away from her, but my eyes dropped to her feet when she matched my step with one of her own. My lips twitched, fighting back a ridiculous grin; she was barefoot, the little nymph.

"What does that mean?" she asked.

"Elora means sun." I strolled to a nearby tree to pick another apple for her. She took it without hesitation and dropped it in her wicker basket. Turning back to the tree, I plucked two more. "Sun ray, specifically."

She didn't answer at first, her silence mildly intriguing, but when I turned to hand her the fruit, she asked, "But why did you say figures?"

I stared for a moment, suddenly realizing she was still here with me. She could have left. Hell, she could have been terrified —a human woman alone with a Fae male. She...trusted me, for some odd reason, at least enough to not hurt her, and she wanted to *talk* to me. I couldn't decide if that made her sweet or reckless.

And because of that, for a split second, my reasoning slipped. I stepped closer and tucked a finger under her chin to tilt her face to mine. She gasped at the contact as if I had shocked her—maybe I had, either catching her by surprise or my magic running rampant. I could feel it sparking under my skin; I wouldn't be surprised if it escaped into hers.

Her red lips parted, but she didn't pull away. She didn't even tense. No, it seemed she nearly melted as my eyes flitted back and forth between hers. *Not good. Not good at all, but fuck, she made it so easy.*

"I said figures, because your eyes are such a bright blue that if you told me you held the clear skies right there in your irises, I would believe you. It's only fitting that your name would mean sun, to accompany the sky you carry."

"The sky?" The words were barely a whisper on her breath. "In *my* eyes?"

"Do you need me to repeat that? Because I have no quarrel doing so."

Her smile appeared then, so sudden and genuine that I couldn't help but return it. She shook her head as she took a step back this time. "What is your name?"

I blinked once. Twice. She didn't recognize me—not that she should have; she was human, but most did. This could be my chance to be someone other than the King of Ravaryn. I could just be...me without the pretenses or crown or reputation.

Hopeful excitement sparked in my chest. Could I allow myself today and then walk away, never to return? A small twinge of guilt dulled the excitement for what I knew I was about to do, but would my name really matter if she only knew me for a few hours?

This was anything but smart—foolish, idiotic, self-destructive, dooming, selfish—because I *knew* that once I said these words, I would stay, at least for the rest of the day.

After an abnormally long minute, I cleared my throat and looked back to the branches as I answered somewhat honestly, "Wryn. My name is Wryn."

My childhood nickname was Wryn, so it wasn't entirely a lie.

I plucked another apple and handed it to her without pulling my eyes from the tree. She took it, and I glanced down at the sound of her biting into it with a loud crunch. She sat at the base of the tree, nestled perfectly among the blooms, and reclined against the trunk with a contented sigh.

Damn. It. All.

After swallowing, she asked, "Pray tell, what does Wryn mean?"

I couldn't stop the ironic chuckle that left my lips. Who allowed me to be king? I clearly didn't have a wit about me. I should have known she'd ask that question next. "Funny enough, it means little ruler."

A laugh burst from Elora, and I whipped around to face her, another apple in hand. Her gaze was already on me, as warm and full of mirth as the delicate sound bubbling from her lips. Her laugh was infectious, though, a sweet disease, and I found myself thoroughly infected and laughing along with her.

"And what do you rule, Wryn?"

So many things, my sweet sun ray. More things than I would like. I paused, tapping my finger on my chin as if I was actually mulling it over, before shrugging and throwing my hands out to the side. "This orchard, I suppose?"

She sat up straighter, her eyes widening. "You own the orchard? How—what?" Her smile slid from her face, and she slapped a hand over her mouth before giggling into it. "Oh, I've been stealing your apples for years."

I gasped in mock outrage, placing a hand over my chest. "Years?"

She laughed harder and nodded. *So very easy with her.*

"Oh, dear Elora, I do believe you owe me, then."

"What do I owe you?" she whispered.

Nothing. I should *say nothing. She doesn't owe me anything.* I should have left when I had the chance, because this question opened a door I hadn't seen at first.

I should have done a lot things, but I wanted more with her: more smiles, more laughs, more time, more...words.

"Write me."

Am I a masochist? I must be.

She froze, clearly not expecting those words. "Write you?"

"You do know how to write, yes?" I cocked a brow, the corner of my mouth tipping up in a smirk.

She scoffed, rolling her eyes. "Of course, I know how to write."

I took a seat beside her and leaned back on my hands, stretching my legs out, feigning nonchalance when I felt anything but. "Then it should be easy enough. Write me a letter for every apple you've taken."

She shook her head slowly. "Why do you want me to write you?"

Confusion furrowed between my brows. "Why?"

"Yes, why? You don't know me. Why would you—"

"Because I *want* to know you." My heart skipped a beat as the words left my mouth before I had a second to consider the truth in them.

But it was exactly that—the truth. I wanted to know who she was, down to her core, the very essence of her person. I wanted to know her *soul,* because fate had decided ours would be powerful together, and I wanted to know why.

She still hadn't answered me, which only made my heart race painfully. She eyed me curiously, and I suddenly felt like I might explode if she didn't reply soon.

When I couldn't take it any longer, I gently asked, "Would you like to know me, Elora?"

For some unfathomable reason, I needed her answer. I needed to hear her say she wanted to know me too.

With a thoughtful smile, she finally replied, "Sure."

With that, she slipped a hand into her basket, pulled out an apple, and tossed it to me. I lurched forward, catching it with one hand, and brought it to my mouth, but stopped mid-bite when she said, "You seem like you could use a friend."

I chewed and swallowed slowly.

* * *

#1

Wryn,

Can I be completely honest? I've written this letter at least ten times, but none of them have felt... substantial. I'm just rambling.

What am I to say in these? I haven't a clue what I'm supposed to write you, but since you want to "know" me, I've decided on this:

My favorite color is blue, if that wasn't made apparent by my choice in clothing.

My favorite hobby is baking, specifically apple pie (I promise I'm not laughing while writing that).

My favorite season is spring.

There's your start. I expect the same from you in your reply.

Sincerely,
Elora

P.S. I've decided we should number the letters. I'll be odd, and you even (although you should be odd, for obvious reasons).

PPS. That was teasing. You're not that odd... Well, maybe just a tad, but aren't we all?

* * *

#2

Elora,

Ramble if you wish. I'll read it all regardless.
As for your request...

My favorite color, oddly enough, is also blue. I prefer the ocean to land. Perhaps that's why.

I haven't really thought about which of my hobbies would be my favorite. I enjoy creating in general, but if I had to choose, I would say painting. There's something so satisfying about changing a blank canvas to something colorful and meaningful.

My favorite season is autumn. The waning colors are so warm—much like your hair.

For your next letter, tell me of your dreams. Any kind of dreams: sleeping, life, goals, anything.

Like I said, I'll read whatever you choose to send me. My days are dull, so excite me, Elora.

Sincerely,
Wryn

P.S. I like the idea of numbering our letters. I'll let you be odds, for obvious reasons.
P.P.S. Indeed.

6

Elora

"Spring?" Livvy scoffed, tightening a thick shawl around her shoulders. "More like winter. It's frigid, and my head is pounding. An utterly miserable combination."

The morning was colder than normal. A light frost had settled over the outside world, and the chill seeped into the estate, despite every lit fireplace.

"It'll warm up," I said, looping my arm through her elbow.

"Goddess, I hope so," she muttered as we strode through the hallway.

The estate was old but nice, the hallways lined with an intricate carpet, the walls decorated with sconces, flickering with small flames. The floor creaked under our steps—a sound I'd always found comfort in.

We passed few people as we made our way to breakfast, but as we rounded into the room, Godrick and Emma greeted us, already seated at the table, their plates full and smiles bright. The early morning sunshine bathed the room in warm yellow, its light sparkling off the ice visible through the large windows.

"Morning, girls," Godrick hummed, lifting his mug to his lips.

"Morning." I snagged a piece of toast from the plate as I walked around to take the seat beside him.

Alivia shuffled around Emma and sat next to her. "I'm cold."

"It is quite chilly this morning." She peeked up with a satisfied gleam in her eyes. "But ice is a good omen. It means the meeting will go smoothly. No heated heads today." She clicked her tongue before taking another sip from her steaming mug.

With that, she nodded once and went back to eating her multitude of pastries. How the dainty woman could eat so many cinnamon rolls, I would never know, but it was one of many things I loved about her. She could eat, and she had never been shy about it—had never let us be shy about it.

Alivia reached for the silver kettle and poured a cup of tea, the light scent of peppermint wafting over. After taking a hesitant sip, she sighed and sunk into her chair, hands wrapped around the mug.

"El, are you nervous about your first meeting with *the* King of Ravaryn?" Godrick asked, wiggling his brows before shoveling another bite of eggs in his mouth.

I rolled my eyes, a smile curving my lips. "You say that like I don't live with *the* royal family of Auryna."

He nudged me with his shoulder, Emma laughing.

"You are part of the royal family," she said. "That doesn't count."

Warmth flooded my chest. That statement never ceased to fill me with a sense of comfort, because I knew she truly meant it. She had always treated me like a daughter; she held me, read me to sleep, braided my hair, and laughed and played until our bellies burned. She raised me alongside Alivia without hesitation or complaint or favoritism.

But most importantly, she taught me how to bake, as her

mother taught her, and hers before that. Our recipes spanned back hundreds of years, and I had craved that connection. When I whipped up a cake, it wasn't just a cake; it was a woman from a hundred, three hundred, *five* hundred years ago guiding my hands.

"Although..." Emma continued, her eyes dipping to my bodice. "Should we wear something more appropriate?"

My brows furrowed as her mouth ticked up in a suspicious smile.

"What are you up to?" I asked slowly.

She shrugged her shoulders, grinning down at her plate, but Alivia and I both stared at her, waiting.

When she didn't reply, Alivia groaned. "Well? What is it?"

"Oh, you two spoil everything," she sighed. "It's just a dress. I had a dress made for each of you."

"Thank you." My eyes burned, and I blinked the sting away, swallowing hard. "I can't wait to see."

"Of course. This is a special day for you." The second the words left her mouth, she paused, her eyes flitting to Godrick, but it was replaced with her usual mirth so quickly, I almost questioned if I had imagined it.

She sipped her tea again, her eyes falling back to her plate as Godrick cleared his throat and reached across the table. He grabbed the biscuits and a small jar of honey, the golden substance inside catching a ray of sunshine.

Suddenly, an image of the beautiful Fae with amber eyes from the night before flashed in my mind, and my eyes darted to Alivia. She was pecking at a dry piece of toast, her breakfast barely touched.

The cure worked. I felt fine—no nausea, no headache, no parched mouth, and no death. I was alive. Hell, I was better than alive. I felt great like I'd gotten the best sleep of my entire life. I smiled to myself and turned back to Godrick to find him pouring gobs of honey onto his biscuit. Then, he turned and stirred a heaping spoonful into his tea.

"And this is why I call him honey," Emma said, pointing at him with her fork.

"I do believe I was a bee in a past life." He lifted the biscuit to his mouth and moaned as he took a huge bite.

"Or a bear," I muttered with a chuckle and took a gulp from my mug filled to the brim with warm coffee.

Alivia snorted, her eyes flashing to her father. "Definitely a bear. I think your past life lingers even now. That's probably why you're so hairy."

Godrick's warm brown eyes found hers. "It seems you've inherited that."

Coffee came out of my nose. I covered my face as I choked on a laugh, my sinuses burning. Emma released a sound halfway between a cackle and a scream, and Alivia gasped dramatically. Then, like the true spitfire she was, she launched an entire boiled egg at her father, the King of Auryna.

It hit his forehead with a slap, and he stilled, his fork halfway to his mouth with another bite of biscuit. The egg bounced and rolled under the table, but no one moved for at least ten seconds.

Hysterical laughter erupted from every single one of us. The room overflowed with the sound of pure merriment—echoing down the hollow halls, I was sure, as it did every time we sat down to eat a meal together.

"In all seriousness," he said, gasping for breath as he leaned under the table and scooped up the damned egg. He tossed it back to Alivia, and she caught it, smiling ear to ear before setting it on an empty plate. "If we *did* have another life, I wouldn't be a bee or a bear. I believe I would've opened a tavern or an inn, or maybe both. I've actually thought about this quite a lot, what we would do if I hadn't been born a king."

The smiles around the table shifted from humorous to soft as he continued.

"I imagine that in another life, one where we didn't bear such heavy responsibility, we'd have lived a small life, cozy and safe."

"What would you have called this mysterious tavern-inn?" Emma asked with an amused lilt in her voice. She peeked over her mug at him as she sipped from it again.

He grinned, meeting her gaze as he took another obnoxiously massive bite. "Honeyed. I would name it Honeyed, as everything would be sweetened just to my liking."

* * *

THE DRESS WAS MORE than beautiful, soft pink and delicate, the sleeves two matching pieces of lace swooping over the top of each arm. The corset was white, speckled with pink flowers and laced with rose-colored string.

It wasn't something I would normally wear, but it was so feminine that I felt...womanly, which was odd, because I had never felt anything different. This dress made me want to run barefoot through blooming fields and sing songs with a group of girls; I suddenly needed to braid a crown of wildflowers, as it would suit it perfectly.

No, not just wildflowers.

The soft pink reminded me of apple blossoms.

I dropped my gaze to the corset, leaning down to study the flower. They *were* apple blossoms. My cheeks flushed warmly, and I stood straighter.

"It's beautiful," Emma whispered. "*You're* beautiful."

"Thank you, truly," I said, glancing once more in the mirror. "I love it."

Wryn would've loved it, too. The flush in my cheeks deepened furiously, and I quickly turned away from the mirror, taking a slow, deep breath as I strolled to the shoe rack. I skimmed my fingers over the few pairs of boots and sandals, feigning indecision. "What does Alivia's look like?"

"Similar, but where yours is pink, hers is blue."

I peeked at her, my mouth agape, one eyebrow raised. "Are you sure you didn't get the dresses mixed up?"

She smiled gently and closed the distance between us, taking my hand in hers. "No. This one is yours." She lifted a strand of of my auburn hair, hanging past my waist. "You know I love you in pink. It suits you, brings out the color in your cheeks."

I nodded, giving her hand a quick squeeze. "I know."

A knock sounded on the door.

"Ready?" Godrick's voice sounded from the other side.

My eyes flitted from the door to Emma and back, my brows furrowing. "What—"

"Yes, she's ready," Emma replied as she lifted my hand to her mouth and kissed the back of it. Her eyes were brimming with unshed tears, and my heart leapt in my throat.

"What? What am I ready for?"

Godrick opened the door slowly, peeking in before opening it fully. He stopped short when he saw me, a fatherly grin on his face, but when his eyes also went misty, my mouth fell open.

"What is going on?" I asked with a slight chuckle, but it sounded hollow as confused trepidation undercut it. "Why are you two getting all emotional on me?"

He extended an elbow to me and tossed his head toward the door. "Come on. Why don't I show you?"

I nodded and slid my arm through his, even as adrenaline poured through my veins and my thoughts raced through every possibility.

Was the dress a part of this suspicious surprise? The peace treaty meeting wasn't for hours, so we couldn't be going there.

Then, he led me outside. The air had heated tremendously, the sun high and warm on my exposed skin. I closed my eyes and titled my face to the sky, letting Godrick lead me away from the estate.

"Where are we going?" I finally asked. "Can't you at least tell me that much?"

"I suppose..." He sighed dramatically, but his wide smile revealed his teeth, off-white against his thick beard. *A bear for sure.* "The orchard. We're going to the orchard."

I tripped over my feet, stumbling a step, and he caught my elbow. My heart thundered, my pulse nearly painful, my throat tight.

"W-what? Why are you taking me to the orchard?"

"Nervous, are we?" He wound my arm back through his, as if worried I'd trip again, but then he paused. "Aw, no, did someone spoil it for you?"

"No one has told me anything at all," I said, a bit of exasperation bleeding into my tone. I slid my arm from his and planted my hands on my hips, attempting to act like I wasn't about to explode on the inside. "But you are. I'm not going another step until you tell me what is going on!"

He sighed, running a hand down the side of his face. "I told him you didn't like surprises."

This wasn't just a surprise. It was teetering on my most kept secret, one I did not care to unveil today. "It's not—" The words stopped in my throat as I processed what he'd said. "Him?"

"Yes, he wanted to plan this all for you." He motioned for me to continue, but I stayed put, holding his gaze. I had half a mind to deny him and refuse to take another step in any direction. I didn't know who *he* was, but I knew someone who loved the orchard as much as me.

I slid my arm back into Godrick's in a slight daze, allowing him to guide me forward.

There was no possible way it could be Wryn, though. Godrick didn't know him, nor would he have particularly liked the idea of me spending time with a strange man alone.

There was no way, and yet...

My heart sped up for a different reason—a hopefulness I knew would only lead to painful disappointment because it wasn't going to be Wryn standing at the end of the path waiting for us.

My mind knew that, but my heart clearly didn't.

With each step closer, my heart pounded harder. If it went any faster, I feared it might beat right out of my chest, but it was when I noticed the sun directly above us that it nearly burst—high noon.

My stomach clenched, and I wasn't sure if I wanted to run toward the orchard or away from it. It had to be Wryn. It *had* to be.

It was noon, the exact time he asked to meet.

He would be here.

Godrick glanced down at me with an arched brow. "Figure it out, did you? I knew you would." He released a deep sigh. I opened my mouth to correct him, but before I could, he continued, "Evander would be such a good match."

My skin went cold, the foreign feeling that bottomed out in my stomach *painful,* deafening, and I had to strain to hear Godrick's next words, even though I desperately didn't want to.

"His family would make a good ally, great even. They're wealthy, honest, and have had a long-standing relationship with the crown, long before we were around." He shook his head with an audible exhale. "But you know, I... I don't really care about that. I should. As the king, I should have given your hand, but I could never do that to you. The only reason I gave my permission for him to ask is because he's kind and you two are friends."

A roaring started in my head at some point, a numbness in my extremities creeping into the rest of my being.

"I want you to understand that this is your decision, Elora. I won't force you, but..." He raked a hand through his bushy, brown hair. "He comes with financial stability. He may not be the oldest of his brothers, so he won't carry the family title, but he does carry a torch for you." He stopped walking and turned me to face him, taking my hands in his. "Look, you are my daughter, and I am your father, blood be damned. You've been a part of our family since the day I brought you home."

A single tear slid down my cheek.

"But the rest of the world doesn't see it that way, and Evander..." Godrick's hands tightened around mine, his mouth pressed into a flat line.

I knew what he needed to say but didn't want to.

"He's the best proposal I'll ever get," I whispered.

Godrick's eyes met mine, and they were brimming with pity. His mouth opened and closed before he finally said, "I need to know that you'll be taken care of wherever you end up, whoever you end up with. I need to know that you'll live the rest of your days in comfort and splendor with someone who is truly kind. I need to know that you'll be *safe*, Elora. He can give you that. He can give you a full life of ease."

Ease. I nodded numbly and forced a smile. He wiped my cheek, his smile mirroring mine, but his was much more genuine.

"But this is your choice. I would never take that away from you, and Evander doesn't expect me to. He knows you, knows that hard head. He merely asked for my permission to ask, and I granted him that."

"I know," I whispered and steeled myself with a deep breath.

Running a hand over my hair and down my dress, I swallowed hard and rolled my shoulders back.

Today was the day I was supposed to finally get some answers. A sound slipped past my lips, halfway between a chuckle and a sob. I was certainly getting *an* answer, but not one I ever expected or sought.

I wanted to make Godrick proud, though, more than anything. I wanted to be as selfless as Alivia, and this would give Godrick and Emma peace of mind. It was time I acted like a part of this family and shouldered the responsibility that came with it.

Would it truly be so bad? I had known Evander most of my life. He *was* kind and one of my closest friends. Alivia, he, and I'd had several nights of laughter, our friendship spanning back nearly longer than I could remember.

This could be a suitable marriage, even if it wasn't a love match—although, most matches weren't for love, right?

They were for advantage, based on logic. This was logical.

Why, then, did it make me feel like I was being stabbed in the chest with a white-hot poker? Wryn's face flashed in my mind with that same heartbroken expression he wore as he strolled off the first day I saw him.

No.

I swallowed hard and stalked toward the hill leading us to that familiar white fence.

Wryn was a dream, an exhilarating ghost I rarely saw—one I had to stop chasing.

He wasn't a husband.

Evander could be. He was steady and predictable. Safe, if only for Godrick's sake.

And Godrick mattered more than my feelings because they were just that—mine. They could be felt and handled and managed by me, without ever hurting those I loved, but to know

I let Godrick down, that I caused him worry or, Goddess-forbid, disappointment would be enough to end me. I couldn't bear it.

I wouldn't, which was why I descended the hill with my chin held high, shoulders rolled back, and Godrick on my heels. I saw him then, Evander, leaning on the open gate with a bouquet of crudely plucked flowers.

Apple blossoms, I realized. *Wryn's* apple blossoms.

7

ONE YEAR AGO

#301

Wryn,

Is that number right? I checked and rechecked the last work of art you sent to make sure, but 301 feels wrong...right? Are we sure we've sent 300 letters already?

We should enter some kind of contest, because truly, I think we may have set a record for most letters sent in the shortest amount of time. Although, I'm not sharing the prize with you. You can enjoy it from afar, way over there in your cozy corner of Ravaryn.

Speaking of, don't forget the paints and canvases, but know I am being utterly serious when I say no laughing. Under any circumstances. Are we clear?

My hands are skilled in the kitchen, all right?
You can laugh at me when I see you bake a
perfect cinnamon roll.
   <u>*No. Laughing.*</u>

                                    See you soon,
                                    Elora

P.S. Is it odd that you're my closest friend,
even from hundreds of miles away? Odd or interest-
ing? Don't answer that. I'm choosing the latter.
   P.P.S. Don't ever tell Alivia I called you my
closest friend. She'll have both of our heads on
spikes. Separated. The horror.

* * *

Elora

I fidgeted with the basket in the crook of my elbow, running my other hand over my hair for the hundredth time, the butterflies in my stomach growing stronger with each step closer to the orchard.

Wryn would be there. He'd be waiting, and I was taking my sweet time, feigning interest in my surroundings when my mind swirled around one thing—one person. At some point, I had paused to smell a patch of flowers, feeling a tad ridiculous. I had actually stopped to smell the damn roses.

The orchard was just over that hill, but my feet had slowed until they stopped entirely, still on the path that would lead to Wryn.

Biting my lip, I adjusted the basket again and rolled my shoulders back. With a swirling pit in my stomach, I nodded and took a step forward, then another and another. When I crested the hill, my heart hammered so hard, I thought I might take flight—or faint, whichever came first.

But the breeze blew then, rolling the clouds away from the sun so its warmth kissed my skin, along with the orchard below, and I saw him.

He stood at the gate, leaning back on the small picket fence, tossing an apple in the air. He looked to the forests, his gaze slowly scanning over the trees, moving toward me. I remained where I was, my heart beating harder with each passing second. My chest rose and fell faster as his gaze inched closer, but I couldn't move. I could do nothing but wait for him to find me.

Then he did.

The apple paused in his hand, a broad grin stretching across his face, bright and brilliant and...Wryn's.

The nerves left my body in an instant, and I suddenly couldn't remember why they were there in the first place. A smile of my own pulled at my lips as we locked eyes for a moment before I dropped the basket, grabbed my skirts, and ran down the hill. His mouth opened in a laugh I couldn't quite hear, and he tossed the apple behind him, turning to me with open arms. My feet didn't slow until I reached him, throwing my arms around his neck like he was my oldest friend.

His warm chest vibrated with a hum as he wound his arms around my waist and lifted me, my feet dangling. His voice was as soothing as I remembered when he said, "Hello, sun ray."

He sat me back on my feet, and I released him, stepping back to look upon his face—so familiar, yet I'd only seen it once before. "Hello, Wryn."

* * *

Vaelor

Elora was lost in her work when I chuckled into my hand, peeking over her shoulder.

"I said no laughing!" She elbowed me in the gut, and I released a gruff laugh. "I told you I wasn't very good."

Standing straighter, I tilted my head and stepped closer. "Art can't be 'not good.' It's all subjective." My arm reached around her to slip a hand over her paintbrush. I pretended not to notice the way her breath hitched as I moved her hand, still holding the brush over the canvas, and layered dark green to shadow the lighter leaves she'd already painted.

She glanced up at me, not even bothering to watch the small strokes we added to her canvas with her own hand. I stifled a laugh, feeling her lingering gaze before I finally looked down to find her pale, freckled cheeks flushed, her soft lips redder than normal.

I wanted to bite them, to break the skin and taste her.

Mine, a faint voice whispered from the back of my mind.

I tore my eyes from her and stepped back.

My friend, yes, but not mine. *Not in that way.*

She smiled, turning back to her canvas. She cocked her head to the side, bringing the wooden end of the paintbrush to her lips. "That does look better. More..."

"Dimensional?"

"Yes!" She swiveled around and pointed her brush at me, her forearms and cheeks smudged in various shades of green. "Dimensional. That's it."

I tilted my head, looking over her shoulder as she turned back to her canvas. "I just helped you add a little shadow."

"Hmm," she said, the end of the brush back between her lips. "I guess shadows are important, then, because it was a green mess before."

"Shadows are always important. Shadows tell us we're here, that we exist, that everything around us exists. If there were no shadows, it would mean there was no light, and what kind of world would that be?"

When she didn't answer, I pulled my eyes from the canvas to find her mouth had fallen open in a slight smile, her eyebrows raised.

"Do you just...think like all the time?" she asked.

"Like what?" I arched a brow of my own.

"Like a poet."

My cheeks flushed, and I looked back at the canvas. "Not always."

She was still staring. I could feel her gaze, studying, gauging, reading. It felt as though she saw straight into my mind, my soul. Maybe she did.

"I don't know if I believe that." She tapped her brush on her lips again. "I think... I think you see everything through an artist's eye, and so everything becomes...more, somehow. You're an artist, Wryn, through and through."

Warmth spread through my chest, and I inhaled slowly, her soft cinnamon scent filling my lungs before I released a breathy laugh. "I am an artist."

"You are, but there are those who make art as a hobby, as a stress reliever, or just because they like it... And then, there are those who create because they must. Because not painting or sketching or writing would be like asking the rain not to fall or the sun not to rise. They do it because it's a necessity of their existence, and you, Wryn, are the latter. You paint like you breathe, like you sleep and eat. You paint because you have to. You paint because if you did not, you might not exist."

I didn't know when my eyes fell to her lips to physically watch the words leave her mouth, but I couldn't look away, not even when they ceased talking and curved into a soft smile, the delicate kind she bore so often.

No one had ever articulated the feeling so exactly.

To everyone else, I was not an artist. I was a ruler, a king. When one held such a role as that, there wasn't enough room to be anything else in the eyes of the world. It became them, swallowing whoever they were before.

But she saw *me*.

I couldn't stop the words that left my mouth, barely a whisper, albeit an urgent one. "Are you an artist, Elora?"

She had to be. How else would she know the feeling?

Her eyes warmed, the blue in her irises a comfort I hadn't realized I'd missed until this very moment.

Iaso's tonic must be wearing off.

This was the mate bond doing what it did, drawing me to her, but I couldn't bring myself to care. Not right now. Not as she leaned in closer to place a small hand on the center of my chest and whisper back, "No, but I know one."

I couldn't answer her. There wasn't a single thought in my brain to relay to her. For the first time I could ever recall, I was rendered speechless. All I could do was stare—until she patted my chest and started to pull away, and I caught her hand. Her smile faltered, her eyes locked on where my hand held hers.

Hesitantly, she lifted her gaze to mine.

"If I'm an artist, you're one of the Goddess' soldiers."

A scoff escaped her. "Oh, shut up, Wryn."

She pulled her hand, and I let her go. As she turned back to her canvas, tapping that damned paintbrush on her lips again, I leaned on the nearest tree trunk and crossed my arms. "Her soldiers are not those who wield swords and spill blood. They do not fight or search for glory or vengeance."

She peeked over, her blue eyes catching in the sunlight, her brow cocked, and lips tilted up in a teasing smile.

"Our Goddess is one of love. She created everything under her stars and moon—us, the realm, the land and seas and trees and creatures—every single thing made with her love, in the hope of creating a world that bathed in it, thrived in it." Her smirk fell, the paintbrush pausing its infernal movement. "And you, Elora, love. That is what you do. Despite every dark and painful thing this life holds, you wear the most fragile part of you, your heart, right on your sleeve for the world to see, because you're brave—brave and selfless enough to truly accept people into your soul, to feel things deeply and wholly without fear or hesitation. You're a lover, Elora, and *that* makes you her most valiant soldier."

She was still as stone, her eyes round. She didn't move for a few moments, left as speechless as I was, before the color in her cheeks deepened, spreading down to her chest. She blinked rapidly and cleared her throat.

"Poet," she muttered with a shaky laugh, turning back to her canvas like nothing had happened.

I felt her eyes, though, peeking over at me as I did the same, lifting my own brush to dip the bristles in burnt orange. "Soldier."

Then, like some strange stamp of approval from the Goddess herself, the wind blew, and a shower of apple blossom petals fell around us, swirling and dancing along the breeze. Elora closed her eyes and tilted her face to the sky, a few pink petals snagging in her hair as it blew around her form. When the strands stuck to the wet paint on her canvas, a soft giggle poured from her, mingling with the sounds of nature. She carefully pulled the stuck hair and lifted the ends to find them painted green.

I stilled, an ache forming in the back of my throat. The smile slipped from my lips, pulled down by the sinking feeling in the pit of my stomach.

She might be brave, but I was not.

She shifted her gaze to me, her face still smudged with color, her hair messy and wind-blown, now tipped with emerald and flecked with pink, but her smile... Her smile was so damned happy, so at ease, so *genuine,* that my chest physically hurt.

Because that smile, that sweet, sweet smile, was directed at me.

Being her friend is the most reckless thing I've ever done.

8

SIX MONTHS AGO

#421

Wryn,

Look, I like to consider myself a patient woman. A kind one. Understanding, even.

But as the sun is setting and I have yet to receive any kind of gift, I'm beginning to think perhaps I'm not so patient after all.

I expect begging. Lots of begging. And chocolate, flowers, perhaps a new apron, or actually, now that I think about it, I would like another sketch—of you this time. Maybe even us. Perhaps of the orchard.

All of them. I want all your sketches, the entire sketch book, wrapped with a nice bow.

Oh, are you confused? It's my birthday, you asshole, and it seems you've forgotten. The physical distance between us doesn't count as an excuse either, because you're my closest friend, remember?

I suppose I could forgive you... Only because I'm in such high spirits. Alivia and I somehow managed to find the perfect gown for tonight's festivities, and to be truthful, it's a damned shame you'll miss it. Better yet, best you did. I believe you'd find yourself standing in a puddle of your own drool.

Well, I'm off to drink and dance the night away.

I hope you sulk in the orchard, thinking of all the ways you'll make it up to me.

See you in 6 months,
The Birthday Girl

P.S. I miss you, Wryn.

* * *

Elora

"Oh. My. Goddess." My mouth fell open at the overwhelming number of people in the ballroom, all dressed in their best attire. Every person sparkled or glowed, their metallic masks catching the candle-light with every swirl on the dance floor.

From the balcony, the long gowns created a dark sea of swaying gossamer and silk against the black and white tiled flooring, the room dimly lit by the sconces and chandeliers.

Between the masks and heavy shadows, everyone became anonymous, which seemed to cut any hesitation. People danced and chattered, laughed and drank—and the night had only just begun.

The musicians were stationed in one corner, lifted atop a small stage, while the opposite wall was lined with every sweet treat imaginable, including some kind of... My eyes widened incredulously. "Is that a fountain of mead?"

"Caramel mead." Alivia nodded to my right, her elbows leaning on the rail.

"We outdid ourselves, I must admit," Emma said to my left.

"I'd say so," I chuckled.

"All right, well, I have a full dance card and no drink." Alivia pushed herself off the rail and wiggled her eyebrows at us. "I think I need a whiskey...and maybe a mug of mead afterward. Anyone want to join me?"

"I think I shall find your father," Emma said. She wrapped her arms around me, kissing my cheek before whispering, "Happy twenty-fourth birthday, El."

"Thank you. For everything." I squeezed her shoulders, and she laughed and kissed my cheek one more time before releasing me.

"You two have fun, but not *too* much fun." With that, she winked and disappeared down the staircase.

Alivia stuck an elbow out to me, and I wound my gloved hand through it, my black silk sliding smoothly against her pink. We strolled down the empty hallway, our heels clicking on the stone, somehow louder than the party goers below.

"So, your dance card is full, hmm?" I asked while watching a particularly blissful couple sway in a small circle. They weren't particularly skilled at dancing, but they held each other in such a way, with their chests pressed together and eyes locked, that they might as well have been the only people in the room, in the world.

"Yes, per usual," she groaned. "What a ridiculous custom. To deny someone is rude, but why? Why would that be rude? I think it's rude to be forced to dance with someone who steps on my toes or smells like week-old liquor. My first one..." She lifted her wrist, squinting at the name etched on the small card. A new song started, one with a recognizable tune and coordinated steps. The sea of people parted into the dance's pattern. "Is now. Oh, lovely."

She lifted her skirt and quickly strode to the staircase, waving to the solitary man waiting for her at its base with a patient smile. As she slid her arm through his, she peeked over her shoulder at me and flashed a quick smile before she, too, disappeared into the crowd, her expert movements blending into those around her.

"Well, I certainly need a drink," I whispered under my breath as I took the rail and descended slowly.

My own dance card was sparse. While this was for my birthday, most didn't know that. This, to the outsiders, was just another royal ball at the castle—not that I minded. I was happy to attend without the expectations or pretenses. Alivia's card was full for a reason; she was *the* princess.

She was expected to dance and smile, to speak flowery, intelligent words, and appease her guests, while I got to flutter around, drink, dance with whoever I wanted, whenever I wanted, and simply *enjoy*—the best birthday gift I could have ever received.

A smile pulled at my lips as I took the final step onto the ground floor and looked around, taking in the multitude of elated faces, the sound of laughter bubbling over the lively music. From down here, the flickering light overhead cast exciting shadows over already hidden faces.

I weaved through the crowd toward the drink table, but as I neared it, Godrick stepped in my path with two small glasses in hand and a ridiculous grin. He handed me one without a word.

"To the birthday girl," he whispered and winked. Clinking his glass against mine, he nodded in encouragement, and we downed them together. The brown liquid scorched my throat, and I erupted in a coughing fit, shoving the glass back at him.

"What in the—" I managed, patting my chest, as if that would do anything.

"Fae rum," he whispered, stacking the glasses and slipping them into his jacket pocket. "I save this for special occasions, and my baby girl is turning twenty-four. Sounded like the perfect time to break it out."

My gaze softened, and I cracked a smile back at him. "Thank you, Father."

He grinned so hard, his eyes crinkled around the edges. He'd always loved when I called him Father, but I didn't do it often, although I didn't know why. Godrick was my father in every way that mattered.

"You have fun tonight, all right?" he said. "We love you, El."

"I love you too," I replied, feeling the warmth of the rum settle in my gut. "So much."

His gaze locked on someone behind me then, and without looking away, he said, "Like a moth to a flame, I must go. She's waiting and way too damned beautiful to wait even a second longer."

He patted my shoulder as he strode past me, and I turned, my gaze following him. He stopped in front of Mother and bowed at the waist ceremoniously, extending a hand up to her. She smirked before dipping into a faint curtsy and sliding her hand into his. He slipped it into the crook of his elbow and led her to the dance floor with a proud, love-struck gleam in his eyes.

A group of people walked between us, blocking my view of my parents, and the sweet scent of caramel mead drifted from them.

"Okay, drink," I whispered and spun on my heel toward the table.

A server held a glass under the pouring spout, filling it to the brim. I took it gratefully and downed a large gulp as I turned, but when I did, the hairs on the back of my neck stood on end.

I lowered the glass to glance around the room, finding nothing out of the ordinary. Everyone seemed as merry as they were moments ago.

My skin crawled, though, a heated flush rising in my cheeks. My gaze shifted slowly over the crowd, searching for...something. The dance was at its peak, women spinning under the men's hands, the music moving faster and faster.

My heart raced to match its pace.

A loud crack of lightning vibrated my bones, the brilliant light behind me casting my shadow before me. My head whipped around to the window, and for the briefest second, I saw a man standing *in* the lightning as it struck the ground. My breath caught, the glass slipping from my hand, and as it hit the floor, shattering in every direction, the lightning disappeared, as did the silhouette.

No one else seemed to care or notice anything other than the broken glass. A maid swept around me, but I couldn't bring myself to apologize. I couldn't even bring myself to look away from the window, suddenly questioning my eyesight and sanity.

Shouting at the entrance caught my attention, though, and I swiveled to see another large group of guests entering. Glancing back to the window, I waited for movement, for lightning, for anything, but there was nothing—nothing but raindrops as they slowly started to pelt the glass and roll down the panes.

I released a shaky breath, and the doors opened again,

another wave of people entering, laughing as they shook out wet hair.

Of course there were people outside. They were still arriving.

Does this mean I need more or less alcohol?

Placing a hand on the woman's shoulder as she swept the last bit of broken glass into a pile, I knelt and held the dustpan. "I'm so sorry. Here. Allow me."

She shook her head, smiling softly. "No, Elora, allow *me*. This is your night." She turned and grabbed another glass from the table. Offering it to me, she shooed me away with her free hand. "Take this and go. Leave this to me."

I took it and rose to my feet, my brows furrowed. "Are you—"

"*Go*," she ordered.

"Thank you," I whispered and took a few hesitant steps away, peeking back over my shoulder. She lifted her brows and shooed me again, with both hands this time, so I inhaled slowly and faced the rest of the party, carrying on like nothing had happened at all.

I strolled to a nearby bench, recently vacated, and took the seat before anyone else could, along with a long sip from my glass, my gaze roaming over the crowd again. How fascinating people could be when they thought no one was looking.

Truly, people-watching could be a hobby in and of itself. I chuckled at the thought and took another sip, savoring the sweet taste as my eyes bounced from one oblivious face to the next.

That was, until I found a pair of smoldering silver eyes staring back at me.

My heart bottomed out. I sat straighter, slowly placing the glass on the side table, my throat burning with the threat of tears, worse than any rum.

Standing in the corner, reclined against the wall, was a tall man with a handsome face hidden beneath a black mask and a bouquet of apple blossoms. His grin widened as he lifted the flowers to me in a toast and mouthed, "Happy birthday, sun ray."

"Wryn." The second his name left my lips, I shot to my feet and wove through the crowd. My steps slowed as I neared him, my eyes trailing over his form from head to toe. "How— What—"

He cocked a brow, clearly amused at my sudden inability to string words together, but said nothing as he handed me a folded piece of parchment.

#422

You didn't think I'd miss your birthday, did you? Do you truly think so lowly of me?

I swatted his shoulder before squeezing it, merely to further prove he wasn't an illusion or hallucination. "I sent that letter a few *hours* ago, you lunatic. How are you even here?"

He chuckled and grabbed my wrist to pull me into him, wrapping an arm around my shoulders. I sank into him and wound my arms around his waist in return, breathing in his scent—warm and masculine, reminiscent of sea storms.

"Surprisingly, I wasn't far. When you told me, I just... changed plans." He shrugged, as if that was a casual thing to do. "What kind of friend would I be if I missed your damned birthday?"

I pulled back, shaking my head, but stopped short when I noticed his ears. I reached up and grabbed his hair to pull his head down, turning it to the side to get a better look. His loud laugh encircled me like a breath of fresh air. "Your ears!" I whispered harshly. "What happened to your ears? They're..." I turned his head toward me, my eyes as wide as saucers. "*Rounded.*"

"Elora." His face was flat, but an amused spark lit behind his eyes. "I couldn't very well come to Auryna and crash their precious masquerade ball with pointed ears, now could I?"

I rolled my eyes. "*How* are they round?"

"It's called a glamour. Anyone in the realm can do it, I suppose, with the right spell."

"Like how we send letters through the fire?" I asked. He'd taught me how to do that years ago when we first started writing, but I hadn't realized more was possible.

He grinned, tapping the knuckle of his pointer finger on my chin. "Smart girl. Yes, exactly like that. Now, are you going to hold my hair all night? Because if so, I do believe people are going to whisper."

I jerked my hand back, having forgotten I was holding him in the first place, and winced at the state of his wavy, brown hair: already damp from the rain and now disheveled. I reached up to smooth the mess before taking a step back and clasping my hands behind my back. "Sorry."

His gaze dropped to my cleavage for the briefest of moments, and a wave of satisfaction washed over me. Spurred on by that simple glance, I took a step forward and closed the distance again. My chest nearly touched his, but he didn't dare move. I wasn't even sure he was breathing as I craned my neck to look up at him through my lashes.

"Could you find it in your heart to forgive me?" I whispered.

His eyes flashed, and an erratic thump in my heart nearly made me jump back.

"I could be persuaded," he whispered back, his voice huskier than it was moments ago. He stepped forward this time, only an inch, but it was enough for his chest to brush mine.

I nearly gasped at the contact, but it was when he slid an arm around my waist and grasped my folded hands in one of his, arching my back and holding me against him, that my lips parted. He didn't miss the movement—he never did. His smoldering gaze fell to my mouth before lifting back to my eyes.

Even through the silk gloves, the heat of his touch spread over my skin and settled in my cheeks...among other places. "And how might I do that?"

He didn't immediately respond. Instead, his mouth curved into a smirk as he studied every visible inch of my face, half hidden behind my black mask. He started at my neck, and I could nearly feel his gaze travel up the column of my throat, an intangible caress. My breath hitched as he found my lips, painted dark, ruby red, then the slope of my nose, following it to my eyes, lined with black above my darkened lashes, and finally, my hair, freshly curled and coated in gold shimmer.

It felt as though I was being studied by not simply a man, but an artist viewing the finest piece of artwork, truly looking and admiring every detail.

He leaned down, his lips so close to my ear that I could feel his breath along my skin. "You can beg for forgiveness later."

With that, he pulled back, body and hands leaving me at once, and I just stood there, stunned, my arms falling to my sides like a fool.

Blinking rapidly, I unintentionally asked aloud, "Beg?"

He ignored the question and grabbed my wrist, tilting it to read my dance card. He clicked his tongue. "Remind me to thank my lucky stars later."

Before I had the chance to ask what he meant, he grabbed a pencil from a nearby table and proceeded to write his name in every single blank space on the card, claiming all my dances for the night—all but one. Evander had already asked me to join him, but I found myself *deeply* regretting granting him that.

"I don't know Evander, but I don't like him," Wryn said matter-of-factly, replacing the pencil on the table. My mouth fell open, a shocked laugh escaping me, but he merely took my hand, looped it in the crook of his elbow, and led me onto the dance floor. "It just doesn't seem fair he should get to take even one dance from me when he gets to see you daily."

I rolled my eyes, a smile tugging at my lips. "It's not a competition."

"Isn't it?"

* * *

Vaelor

Evander seemed like a decent enough man. He was respectful when he approached for her next dance, dipping into a dramatic bow with a shit-eating grin.

Watching them dance was nearly unbearable, though, and not because of the rotten feeling clawing at my chest. No, it was because they were ferociously mismatched. While he clearly enjoyed his time with her, he moved like a fish out of water, while she could have been a child of the sea. Her steps were but waves on the shore, graceful and purposeful—destined, fated.

Taking a long drag from my whiskey, I swallowed with a wince. Everything about it was inferior to Fae whiskey: taste, quality, intensity. It didn't dull my senses in the way I hoped, and thus, pulling my gaze from Elora was impossible. That damned dress...

Goddess, I was hopeless, at her complete mercy.

She didn't know I was coming tonight, and yet, it felt like she wore the gown just for me. Against the blackest of silks were gold constellations, thicker at the bottom and trailing up around her waist where they dispersed into sporadic stars.

Damn it all. She is *the clear sky, the antithesis of me.*

I needed to stop comparing the two, however. It almost felt like an insult as she was infinitely more beautiful.

My eyes widened slightly, and I swallowed the rest of the whiskey in one gulp.

As Evander spun her from my sight for a fraction of a second, I jerked my eyes away before I could get ensnared in her again, making a beeline for the bar. The server handed me another whiskey, and I downed it too. If my normal whiskey burned its way down, this was merely a tickle. It wasn't enough, not when she was right there.

She—*we* were becoming too much. Six months between visits wasn't long enough to keep her at arm's length. I needed hundreds of miles and at least a dozen months it seemed, but even then, it was difficult.

She was a friend, a companion to keep the loneliness at bay, albeit a companion who knew me better than anyone else in existence. There were only three things, three significant yet simultaneously irrelevant things, I would never indulge: my name, our mate bond, and these damned feelings.

As the song came to an end, I avoided her general direction, so as to not be bewitched by her again. One look, one gaze from across a ballroom would anchor my feet here. Better yet, it would have propelled them forward to her. I would stay and dance, allowing whatever this was to amplify.

My heart raced, pressure building like a swelling storm in my rib cage. There was no doubt a storm growing outside to match.

She *should* be just a friend.

She should be, but she wasn't, was she?

Friends didn't lust after each other. They certainly didn't dream of depraved nights, or imagine the feel of the other's mouth, or long for a taste.

They didn't feel this type of warmth at their smile, and they sure as hell didn't feel this type of fear at the idea of them.

Fuck.

When the server reached across the table to hand another guest a small glass filled with clear liquid, I snatched it, much to their dismay. An angry huff sounded beside me, and I muttered, "Sorry," before swallowing it with diminishing hope that it would do anything.

Fuck.

Lightning cracked outside, and there was a collective gasp among the guests standing near the windows. Rain pelted the glass as another wave of lightning bounced across the clouds.

I didn't care enough to dispel it. Rain was rain, regardless of who created it.

Before I realized what I was doing, I weaved through the crowd, but not toward Elora. No, I headed for the door. Despite the guilt, the regret, the growing urge to turn around and find her, I moved faster, and people stepped out of my path before I pushed through them.

"Wryn," Elora shouted, her voice laced with easy laughter, and I clenched my jaw. I could nearly hear her smile. I made it three more steps, within mere feet of the exit, when a small, gloved hand grabbed my forearm. My feet froze, my chest rising and falling quickly.

"Hey." She tugged my arm.

I turned begrudgingly, my mouth still pressed into a tight line, but I didn't meet her gaze. Instead, I looked past her, at her birthday ball, filled to the brim with people as happy as she was. She deserved that, not the fear and reservation I offered.

Her fingers wrapped around my jaw, her sweet scent filling my senses as she pulled my face down. I resisted looking upon her face, I really did, but the second my eyes grazed over her shimmering hair and down to her eyes, those Goddess-forsaken eyes, I was lost. And those lips. Damn it all, those lips, full and red and tilted up in an intoxicating smirk.

Who needs liquor when I can stare at her? *My own drug, specially curated for my damned soul.*

Her fingers gripped my chin as she pulled me an inch closer, her eyes flitting to my mouth and back up.

Fuck.

I was hers—if only for tonight.

"Don't tell me you were planning on leaving without saying goodbye," she whispered, cocking her head to the side. My jaw clenched, and she paused. The smirk fell from her lips, and I could nearly see her processing my lack of response. She dropped her hand and stumbled back a half step. "You...were?"

She wore every emotion plainly on her face, and this one in particular sank beneath my skin in the most infuriating way. With her wide eyes, parted lips, furrowed brows, and a flush seeping into her cheeks, it was hurt, clear as fucking day.

"Damn it all," I muttered, grabbing her hand. She tried to pull it back, but I wound my fingers through hers and led her to the closest set of double doors. Once through, I glanced down the dimly lit hallway, flickering with candlelight. *Empty.*

I released her to close the doors behind us and leaned forward, pressing my palms into the wood, my head hanging low. "Elora, I just... I need..."

"What, Wryn?" The quiver in her voice struck me in the chest. "What do you need *so* badly that you were going to leave without even saying—"

I could've sworn I *heard* the snap of my self-restraint a second before I swiveled on her. Her lips fell open in an O, but she didn't have a moment to say anything else. Hell, she didn't have a moment to breathe before I was on her, one hand wrapping around her pale throat, the other gripping her waist. Her back hit the wall as my lips met hers in a kiss that had been long, *long* overdue.

She panted as I broke the kiss, but I offered her no space. I couldn't even if I wanted to. "I needed this," I rasped.

I needed to bask in her, her uneven breaths, her touch, her lips. I needed her scent to fill my lungs. Goddess, I needed mine to fill hers too.

My lips skimmed along hers as I smirked and whispered, "I needed to taste you, and that's not very....friendly of me."

She arched into me with a soft moan as my hand moved along her waist, my mouth devouring her like a starved man—because I fucking *was*. I had been starving for this, for her, and Goddess, she tasted *good*. I didn't think I could ever be completely satiated; I could lick and kiss her skin for months, years, decades, and it would never be enough.

But I'd be damned if I didn't try.

"Y-you're..." I grinned at her lack of words as I kissed down her jaw, her neck, her collarbone. Her breath hitched as I pressed my lips to the swell of her breast. Her hands found my hair again and wound into it. Somehow, I knew they would, and I slid mine through hers too, cupping the back of her head. "You're still my friend."

I chuckled against her skin, wrapping the long strands around my fist before I wrenched her head back as I stood, forcing her to meet my gaze. "Am I your friend, dear, sweet Elora?"

She bit her lip, nodding. My thumb circled her nipple over the fabric of her dress, and a muffled moan escaped her. "Then I must be the very best friend you have, hmm?"

She nodded again, and I smirked, sliding my hand lower, lower, lower until I bunched her skirts up and slipped my hand underneath. She jumped as my fingertips met the bare skin of her thigh.

"Then as your 'very best friend,' I want to *know* you better than anyone else." My hand trailed to the inside of her thigh, her skin prickling with goosebumps. Her breath hitched as my hand moved up, but she widened her stance ever so slightly to grant me access. I bit back a groan of approval and slid my knee between her legs, nudging them farther apart. "Tell me, has anyone tasted you before?"

Her brows furrowed at my question, and I paused my perusal. "Answer me."

"No," she panted, her cheeks flaming. I cocked a brow, and she added, "No one has...*tasted* me."

I did groan then, my grin growing devilish. We couldn't last forever, I knew that. I couldn't be her last, but I could damn well be her first. I wanted to *burn* the feel of me into her mind so that she'd be as haunted by me as I was by her. I wanted her so lost in euphoria that no one else would ever satisfy her, not in the way she would *know* I could.

My hands trailed down her form as I sank to my knees, her wide eyes tracking my movement with anticipation. With shimmering hair, cheeks as flushed as her parted lips, pupils blown and skin cast golden under the flickering candlelight, she looked every bit the temptation she embodied—a true goddess.

I didn't pull my gaze from hers as I lifted her skirts higher. They bunched around her waist to reveal her black undergarments, and her breath hitched when I ran a finger along the lace's edge, biting back at a groan at how *soaked* they were.

"Did you expect to be touched tonight, sun ray?"

With furrowed brows, she shook her head.

"Then why would you wear such..." My finger hooked into them and pulled. She hissed as the band bit into her skin before stitches popped, and the fabric ripped. I cocked a grin as I lifted them to show her like she hadn't put them on herself. "Enticing undergarments?"

"You—Why—" she sputtered, her eyes flashing between me and the torn lace.

I clicked my tongue and slid them into my pocket before skimming my fingertips along her calf, her skin smooth and hot. She watched intently, her breasts heaving with heavy breaths as I moved to the back of her knee and pressed my lips to the inside. Goosebumps spread over her skin in my wake, and I continued my way up her inner thigh, kiss after teasing kiss.

She panted, her hands braced on the wall behind her, fingers splayed. I moved slowly, excruciatingly so; I wanted her on edge, so wanton there wasn't a single thought left in her pretty head, so lust-driven that no other person existed beyond me, much like there was no one but her for me.

I wanted to reduce her entire world to this room, to my touch, to this feeling, to *me*.

As I moved closer to her sweet little cunt, the smell of her desire broke through the fog of Iaso's tonic. I closed my eyes when I felt the lightning crackle within my irises, a deep ache settling between my thighs as my cock strained against my trousers.

Her scent was one I wanted to drown in, and Goddess be damned, I *would* if it wouldn't lead to me taking her here and now, claiming her in every imaginable way: with my cock, my teeth, my mark, on the wall, the floor, the stairs, in the damned ballroom.

Her scent and sounds, every mewl and moan, were intoxicating, but *nothing* could have prepared me for how exquisite she'd taste.

A vicious wave of hunger consumed me when I ran my tongue over her cunt, her echoing moan music to my ears. My tongue circled her clit, and her hands slid into my hair as she bowed off the wall.

"Sweet, *sweet* Elora," I groaned, my hands sliding up the backs of thighs. I hooked one of her legs over my shoulder, exposing her bare cunt to me. With one hand gripping her hip and the other splayed across her lower back, I thrust my tongue into her. She cried out so I did it again and again.

She writhed in my grip, but I held firm. She would not escape my mouth, escape *me* until she exploded—until I tasted her as she came, heard it, saw it, experienced it. It would be such a beautiful shattering.

As she grew more desperate, her leg over my shoulder pulled me ever closer, using me as leverage to grind her hips in motion with the thrusts of my tongue, her cunt growing wet enough that she dripped down my chin. My hand trailed from her lower back to the apex of her thighs, so my thumb could circle her clit.

She trembled, a broken sound leaving her, somewhere between a sob and a moan.

Fucking perfect. The way she unabashedly rode my mouth, chasing her own pleasure, was nearly enough to make me come in my trousers.

I wanted to praise her. She deserved to hear how good she was doing, how delicious she tasted, how I had never in all my years wanted anything or anyone more than I did her in this moment—but my mouth was much too occupied. My mouth, among other things, was at her complete disposal, hers to use and ride and fuck. Hell, if she wanted to suffocate me in her cunt, then I would die the happiest man in existence and thank her from other side of the veil.

I wanted her delirious because of me, breathless and spent, legs too weak to hold even her own weight.

But then, the tonic stifling the mate bond wavered, and I felt *everything*. Unfettered lust knocked the air from my chest, and I wanted nothing more than to fill my lungs with the scent of *her,* sear it into my body until that was all I would smell for the rest of my days.

I jerked my face back, resisting the urge cover my mouth and nose, while I slid a finger in and out of her. She gasped when I added a second, but I didn't stop.

Goddess, I want it. Her. Her moans. Her cunt. Her screams.

"Are you all right?" Her words were laced with pants, her body still rocking on my hand.

A deep groan reverberated through my chest. "No."

Her eyes snapped to my face, but I didn't pull my focus from her cunt. I added a third digit, and she slapped a hand over her mouth to stifle a moan, her head falling back on the wall.

I needed to hear that again, louder, against my skin, my mouth. I needed to swallow it while I plunged into her. I needed to slide my hand from her and suck the taste of her from my fingers—or better yet, use it to wet my cock before I buried it in her.

Damn it all.

I needed so many things, every single part of her. Everything. All of it. Now.

My skin burned, my jaw clenched so tight, I feared my teeth might crack. I hadn't even known I held such restraint, but I fought it, sitting back on my heels. It took every damned muscle in my body not to lurch forward.

I was on borrowed time, but when the tonic settled over me again, fainter than it should be but enough, I sucked in a cautious breath, not daring to move until I was sure I had regained a bit of clarity.

The scent of a mate's arousal was supposed to be the strongest drug, an irresistible temptation, and I would not subject myself to such torture. I would not take her like that, driven by the bond.

No, when I took her—and I would—I wanted it to be *me*.

When I was sure I was clearheaded enough, I dove in mercilessly. She needed to come, and she needed to come *now*. My fingers curled, hitting the spot that set her trembling and writhing again. My tongue swirled over her clit until her cunt pulsed around my fingers.

Nothing was gentle or slow, but she seemed to like that as her slick ran down my hand, her hands nearly ripping my hair from the root. When her entire body tensed, her back arched and mouth hanging open in a silent scream, I picked up the pace, dragging her orgasm out until she went lax.

I pulled my fingers from her, licking my lips as I stood, basking in her post-orgasm glow. Her skin shone with a sheen of sweat, face flushed as her gown fell back around her legs.

She had never been more beautiful.

With a deep sigh, she opened her eyes, smiling faintly, her head still reclined on the wall.

Much to my surprise, the little nymph cupped either side of my face and pulled me down while standing on her toes to crash my lips to hers, tasting herself. My cock strained against my trousers, and I groaned into her mouth as my fingers wound through her hair.

I slid my tongue along the seam of her lips, and she gasped, parting them long enough for me to slip in. She tasted of mead, caramel, and herself—a delicious concoction.

When she finally broke the kiss, her chest heaved breathlessly, her lips swollen and glistening.

Her palm found my cheek with a certain gentleness that felt too close to affection, her head tilted to the side. "I think...I think I'm in love with you, Wryn."

Warmth bloomed in my chest, mingling with that of whiskey and the aftermath of *her*. "I—"

The blood drained from my face when the weight of her words hit me.

I almost said it back. I almost told her I...loved her.

Fear, stark and vivid, knotted in my gut.

Everyone. Dies.

Flashes of her cold and still, her skin wrinkled beneath my touch, bombarded me, and my chest tightened.

She didn't love me. I didn't love her.

We couldn't.

When a beam of silvery moonlight fell over her face, I glanced at the nearby window, framing the setting moon and revealing how late it was, and I did what cowards do best.

I ran.

"I have to go, Elora. I'm..." I started to take a step back but paused. Confusion flashed across her features, and she opened her mouth to say something, but I quickly silenced her. My lips brushed against hers before I kissed her how she deserved, how she should be kissed every day for the rest of her life.

But not by me.

It could never be me, because I would never survive her. I just hoped my touch was scorched into her memory like her taste was in mine.

"I have to go, Elora. It's...late." I glanced to the window again, shamefully looking to my excuse once more, but I winced and forced myself to meet her gaze. I could do that much. My thumb found her lower lip and ran along it once, twice. "I'm sorry."

With that, I slipped back into the ballroom and strode toward the exit.

This time, there was no dainty hand stopping me, no teasing voice calling my name.

I walked away, and she let me go.

* * *

#423

Wryn,

Did I do something wrong? It looked like you ran away from me, but that can't be right, can it?

If me telling you how I felt made you uncomfortable, I'm sorry for that, but just so you know, I didn't expect you to say it back. I simply wanted you to know. I just...wanted to say the words. I made myself a promise a long time ago that I would always follow my heart and never stifle it.

Life is too short to hide such important things, don't you think?

For what it's worth, it's all right if you don't feel the same way. It's all right if you needed space or air.

I can be a lot, I know that, but I won't apologize for it.

Love is meant to be shared, and I'll never stop doing just that.

Please at least let me know you're all right. Just a quick "I'm alive" will suffice.

> See you in 5 months and 30 days,
> Elora

* * *

#424

Wryn,

It's been two months with no reply. I've waited and worried, but I think I've done enough of that.

I'd say I've paid my debt by now, hmm? A letter for every apple.

I've certainly written infinitely more letters than apples stolen, so this will be my last.

Goodbye.

With all my love,
Elora

9

YESTERDAY

#425

Elora,

Meet me tomorrow at noon.

I'll explain everything.

Sincerely,
Wryn

10

Vaelor

A tight knot had taken root in my gut and refused to release me all morning. Even as I sat at the table piled high with food, my appetite was nonexistent, my foot tapping on the floor.

"Are you nervous?" Ewan asked. "You look nervous."

Iaso elbowed him with a glare, the morning sun glinting off her golden armband. "Why would you say that?"

"Well, he does." Ewan shrugged, his brows lifted as he sipped from his mug.

"That doesn't mean you need to point it out," she sighed and turned to me. "You shouldn't be nervous."

"Ah, yeah, no, don't be nervous." Ewan waved a hand through the air. "It's just the woman you lied to for two years, fell madly in love with, and—"

"I *did not* fall in love," I bit out, my pulse hitching. Growing tension wound through my body and would burst a blood vessel soon.

He merely sighed and continued. "*And then* disappeared on."

I closed my eyes, my hands balling into fists on the table. "I'm not a liar." My shoulders slumped when I released a slow breath and raked a hand through my hair. "I've never been a liar."

"We know that," Iaso whispered.

"And she will, too," Ewan added. "She'll understand, Vaelor."

"Will she?" I asked. For some reason, I didn't think she would. "We've been friends for two years, and for two years, through hundreds of letters, I never once mentioned my name. My damned name. Doesn't that feel...substantial?"

"A name is just that—a name," Iaso said. "It's not your person or your character. It's not *who* you are, especially not now that your name is attached first and foremost to the crown. The King of Ravaryn would've been her first impression."

"She would've kept her distance," Ewan said. "Will she be angry that you lied? Maybe, but will she understand eventually? She has to. If everything you've told us about her is true, she will."

"Let's say she doesn't care about the name. What of the last six months? We...danced, and then I left and ignored her letters." The question wasn't directed at them as much as it was my thoughts slipping past my lips, and they didn't answer. These same few words had cycled through my mind since we received the notice that a second daughter of sorts was to be present at the meeting, repeating incessantly, spurred on by the panic that settled in my chest the moment I read it.

Elora was attending, and she'd see who I was—*what* I was. She'd see the web of lies I'd spun and have nothing to base her truth upon, which was why I'd asked her to meet me today before the meeting. She hadn't responded to my letter, not that I deserved it, but she would be there, if for nothing but the truth.

I turned my gaze to the window overlooking the apple orchard. The number 424 scribbled at the top of her last letter haunted me still, despite that it'd been folded and on my person for over four months. I had always been the evens, she the odds. That had been our way for over two years, and she broke that, because I was a coward.

But that was nothing compared to her words: *"I'd say I've paid my debt by now, hmm?"*

Two years of friendship reduced to a debt. That was what it was, wasn't it?

Repayment.

"I'll see her at the meeting, regardless of whether she forgives me." I sighed, turning back to Iaso. "She hasn't told Godrick of me, nor his daughter. Well, she hadn't when we spoke six months ago."

"I doubt she has now," Iaso said. "If she hadn't in the years you two were friends, she wouldn't now that you're..."

"Not," I finished for her.

"You don't know that yet," she said.

"No, not yet." *But I will in a few hours.*

"What are you going to do if she does forgive you?" Ewan asked.

I opened my mouth to answer, but the words died on my tongue. I hadn't thought that far ahead because that scenario felt too easy, too good to be true.

"I don't know." I brought my mug to my lips and stifled a groan after taking a sip—cinnamon apple tea. I glared at Iaso's innocent expression, placing it back down on the table.

To be utterly honest with myself, I wasn't sure I wanted her forgiveness. That would reopen the door I had slammed shut six months prior and everything would come rushing back: soft smiles and letters and whispers and exciting secrecy. If that door did reopen, I wasn't sure I'd have the strength to close it again.

Fuck.

Today would decidedly be the last time I ever saw her. I

would deny Godrick's request to bring her next time. Regardless of the fallout or the lengths I would have to go, I would never see her again.

A deep pain rooted in my chest, but I ignored it. I couldn't let myself feel this. I couldn't let myself want her—Goddess forbid, love her.

It wasn't fair to her. She said she thought she loved me.

I winced, my grip tightening on the handle of the mug.

This had gone too far, much farther than I ever intended.

Today, I would say goodbye.

Today, our friendship would die in that orchard, along with any love she thought she held for me.

Today, I would crack my heart in hopes of preventing its shattering.

* * *

OUR COTTAGE WASN'T FAR from the orchard, so I had left only minutes before noon, and they beat me here.

Yes, *they*.

I saw her first, and my heart stopped. She was dressed in... apple blossoms, her long hair curled softly and swaying around her waist.

She was stunning—an orchard nymph—but she wasn't barefoot, and that didn't feel right.

Then, I saw who trailed behind her: Godrick, right on her heels with a hopeful smile on his face.

My brows furrowed in confusion until I saw *him*.

My heart thundered, and the skies shortly followed. Somewhere off in the distance, lightning cracked across surging clouds.

Evander stood in *my* orchard, holding *my* flowers, waiting for *my* mate.

Pounding in my ears drowned out any sounds of nature. I was too far away to hear their conversation, but I didn't need to hear what the bastard was saying. I could see it plainly from where I stood as he pulled something small from his pocket.

My vision tunneled on what he held, the clouds overhead growing denser, blotting out the sun and sending them into thicker shadows beneath the trees.

I had never been a jealous person, nor an angry one. I didn't crave violence.

But when he knelt on one knee before her, I was no longer myself.

Suddenly, I was wrath incarnate. I wanted to spill his blood directly onto my palette—the perfect red to paint Elora's teasing, ruby lips. I wanted to use his bleached bones to build a throne for her to sit on at my side and feed his soul to the creature of night roaming the Cursed Wood so he couldn't even meet her in the afterworld.

When she held her hand out, he slid the gold band onto her finger, and I lost all rationale.

Rain released from the clouds, pouring so hard, I could barely see them any longer, but I didn't look away. Not as Godrick turned his face to the sky, shielding his eyes and glancing around like he knew I was near. Not as Evander shucked his coat off and placed it over Elora. Not as Elora smiled at him in thanks.

Smiled.

My smile.

My mate.

My Elora.

Tense muscles strained against my too-tight skin, sparks licking at my fingertips. White energy crackled over my forearms as I balled my fists, but I let it. It sizzled and seethed against the falling rain.

I stalked back to the cottage, soaked to the bone and filled with so much rage that when I finally slammed the door open, Iaso and Ewan jumped up from their seats in the foyer with matching looks of shock, followed by concern. Water pooled around my feet onto the floor as I met their gazes, one after the other.

The room, dark without the sun to brighten it, was lit with pale light, the lightning in my irises brilliant, burning, *angry*. Iaso stepped forward, her gold dulled by my silver.

"The plans have changed."

11

Elora

My hands trembled harder with each passing hour since the metal band had been slipped around my finger.

Were we sure it was merely a ring? It felt like a chain—the smallest of shackles with the heaviest weight.

My entire left side felt heavier as Alivia and I followed behind Godrick to the meeting, my eyes unfocused but hovering on the bottom of his flowing black cape trimmed in gold.

We were mere minutes from the room that held the King of Ravaryn and his council, but I couldn't be bothered to feel excitement or nervousness or anything at all. No, I felt...nothing, as though my heart were protecting me from the inevitable breakdown, but not here, not now. Tonight. Tonight, I could fall apart and shatter into pieces on the floor. Tonight, I could flood my room with tears until there were none left to be shed.

But for now, I was grateful for the shield of numbing hollowness.

Even my breaths felt forced, like if I didn't remind myself, I would simply stop breathing. My heart didn't race any longer, but each thump nearly made me wince. Perhaps my rib cage was bruised from the force of my heart pounding against it just hours ago, because I had never felt an ache in my chest like this.

My feet had walked along on their own accord as my mind wandered—or rather, didn't think at all—and stopped when Godrick's did. We stood by as one guard knocked twice and another announced what I assumed was our arrival on the other side of the closed double doors; I could hardly hear anything over the ringing in my ears, or maybe it was cotton, or maybe my ears simply refused to listen to anything else. Not after today, not after the words I had forced them to endure in the orchard. I might as well have had my head underwater.

Two men pulled the doors open, revealing those inside, but my gaze stayed on Godrick's cloak, billowing behind him as he strode forward. Alivia slid an arm into mine, hooking our elbows, and led me to the side of the room, where we stood with other higher-ranking officials.

As Godrick moved away, my gaze fell to a beam of silvery-white washing over the black-tiled floor from the window. The two panes of glass were propped open, allowing the soft sound of falling rain to fill the silence as people waited for one of the two kings to begin.

It was almost comforting, the silence. All I wanted to do was stare until I no longer saw anything around me and sink further into the world confined in my skull. I didn't want to listen or look or exist. I wanted silence, isolation, and a hefty glass of wine, a bottle, even. I wanted my scream to be the only thing I heard. I wanted—

"I want to renegotiate," a distinctly familiar voice said.

My entire being froze, *listening*. Ice poured through my veins. My lower lip trembled, but I forced my face to lift toward the voice, knowing what—*who* I would find.

Two silver eyes looked back at me.

Silver. Eyes.

Silver.

Silver.

Silver.

Why? Why would Wryn be here? Why was he standing next to...

Every memory flashed behind my eyes so fast, my head spun, and I tightened my grip on Alivia's arm to keep from swaying.

"Wryn?" I breathed.

"Wryn*wood*," Alivia corrected. "Vaelor Wrynwood."

I'm going to collapse. Tingling replaced the numbness in my extremities, my chest rising and falling too quickly. I tried to take a slow breath, but he *looked* at me.

He looked at *me.*

Across the room, despite every watchful eye. A dozen people stood among us, and he looked at me.

Wryn, with a blue, velvet cloak and a silver crown on his head, looked at me.

Why is he looking at me?

My attention snapped to Godrick, his expression as confused as I felt, eyes wide and brows furrowed. He slowly followed Wryn's gaze to me, and we locked eyes. I shook my head faintly, not knowing what else to do before his gaze returned to Wryn.

"There's been peace between Auryna and Ravaryn for over a hundred and fifty years, peace *you* established with my great grandfather," Godrick said. "Why would we need to renegotiate?"

Against every screaming instinct, I faced Wryn to find his gaze still firmly locked on me, as silver and blazing as ever. It remained, unwavering, as he spoke his next words to Godrick. "If you want to keep that peace, I want her."

The blood drained from my face, and the engagement ring suddenly felt like it weighed a thousand pounds. I don't know why, but my other hand found it and spun the gold band around my finger. Wryn didn't miss the movement. I knew he wouldn't because he *never* did. A muscle ticked in his jaw, and the room grew tense, a few men whispering and discreetly stepping away from Wryn as thunder rumbled in the distance, the sky darkening. When his gaze lifted from my hands, it crawled up my body so languidly that an uncomfortable amount of time passed. I shifted on my feet, my cheeks burning furiously.

"Elora? You want...Elora?" Godrick asked, shaking his head. "She's engaged—as of this morning, actually."

Wryn's head snapped to him with a ferocity I had never seen in him before, and I jumped at the abruptness, but time slowed as he stepped closer to Godrick and looked down at him, standing at least a foot taller, a silver light illuminating Godrick's face. "If you want to keep the peace, I. Want. Her."

Godrick didn't shrink away. Instead, he met Wryn's gaze with the fierceness of not just a king but a father. "She's my daughter," he whispered, his hands clenched into fists at his sides.

Wryn's face softened slightly. "I know, and I will treat her with nothing but respect."

"Why?" Godrick's brows furrowed, his eyes imploring. "Why do you want her? You don't know her. She will not—"

"My reasons are mine and mine alone."

"I cannot..." He shook his head before tipping it back to the ceiling with closed eyes. He inhaled slowly before meeting Wryn's gaze again. "I *will not* force her to go. If she goes, that's her decision."

Panic clawed at my tightening throat when they both turned to me. I clutched Alivia's arm for dear life, glancing up at her, only to find she was already staring at me in bewilderment, her eyes bulging and mouth hanging open in a slight smile. She nodded faintly, giving my arm a quick squeeze.

The weight of every gaze in the room was too much. My ears rang. My throat went dry—so dry and tight, I didn't even know if I could utter the word yes...or no. I wanted to run out of the room, out of the estate, out of Wryn's reach. I wanted to crawl out of my damned skin.

But I didn't because I *was* Godrick's daughter.

I took a slow, deep breath, my heart thundering as I pulled my trembling arm from Alivia's and shifted my attention to Wryn. He stood tall, his shoulders back and chin high, the crown atop his head glittering with blue stones, the metal shaped into bolts of lighting that wound through his dark hair. I tried to find the Wryn I knew—the gentle artist, the friend who wrote me again and again, then surprised me at the ball with flowers and a grin, the man who pushed me against the wall and devoured me, the coward who ran from me when I admitted my feelings.

At least if I saw the coward, I could feel sympathy for him.

But he wasn't here. This man was not my Wryn.

This man was a...king.

My stomach bottomed out as it suddenly dawned on me, as if it hadn't fully hit me minutes ago, and I quickly locked my knees before my legs gave way, weak and trembling beneath the pink chiffon. I glanced down and cringed at the multitude of apple blossoms, swallowing *hard* against the rising knot in my throat.

This damned dress wrenched the dagger of lies in my gut. I wanted to rip that dagger from my insides and cut the dress from my body. Fuck being naked in front of everyone. I didn't even think I would truly care in this moment. I would let my heart bleed out onto the floor to not be clothed in Wryn's flowers before him.

Wryn was a king.

Wryn was *the* King.

Wryn was Vaelor Wrynwood. The Kind King. The Unmarried. The Storm Bringer.

My eyes darted to the window for a split second, the rain pelting the glass, the storm that had interrupted our engagement, before turning back to Wryn, the man who stood in the lightning six months ago.

Wryn was a *liar*.

I couldn't stop the scowl twisting my expression, a bitterness filling my mouth, my hands balling into fists at my sides. Dismissing Wryn entirely, I said to Godrick, "I'll do it. I'll go."

Godrick strode toward me to grab my hands, his head tilted, the crease between his brows furrowing deeper. "Elora, are you sure?"

I closed my eyes in search of some semblance of solitude. *No.* "Yes."

After my agreement, I was whisked away, and everything happened in a blur. A woman named Iaso entered my chambers at some point, and my world was thrown on its axis yet again.

With deep brown skin kissed with gold and amber eyes, I recognized her immediately. Despite my silence, she was kind and warm. She spoke freely, speaking to me like a friend, and brought another dress for me to change into. I didn't know how I knew, but I did. I knew in my bones this was at Wryn's request. He didn't want me to ruin this sweet apple blossom gown.

"Are we riding back to Ravaryn?" I asked.

"Yes," Iaso replied as she pulled two dresses from her bag and held them up, glancing between the two. "We thought maybe you could wear a more comfortable dress, one less...special."

"No, I'll wear this. Thank you, though."

She lifted a brow. "Are you sure? I don't mind letting you borrow one of mine. It's a long journey, several days of travel."

"I'm sure," I said with a nod. If Wryn wanted to protect this dress, then I wanted to destroy it, cover it in mud and muck, tear the hems, fray the ends. I wanted the pink to turn black.

I wanted to upset Wryn as he did me. It was petty and childish, I knew it was, but I couldn't help it—or maybe I could. Maybe I could try to make the best out of an inevitable situation, but I didn't want to. Not yet.

It wasn't Wryn who gave me this gown, though, and I needed to see the woman who did. I needed her and my sister, but I had a sneaking suspicion the moment they entered, the numbness would dissipate and I would burst into tears. I probably needed that, a good cry with my people before I sealed this emotion off —something I didn't do often.

I cleared my throat. "Do you know where my...mother is? She hasn't come to say goodbye yet."

Iaso tilted her head to the side, a sympathetic smile curving her lips. "They'll be by soon."

Not long after that, she was gone, and there was another knock on the door. Alivia and Emma entered, Alivia with a phony smile, but Emma...

"Oh, Mother," I managed through my burning throat, my eyes brimming with tears. My hand flew to my mouth when a choked sound broke free. I didn't call her Mother often, but she was. She was my mother, and I was leaving her, leaving them all.

Her eyes were red and swollen, her bottom lip still trembling like she was barely holding herself together, but the moment "Mother" left my mouth, she broke too. She ran to me and threw her arms around my shoulders in the tightest hug she'd ever given me. I couldn't breathe, but I didn't need air. I needed her. I needed Alivia. I needed my family.

My tears fell faster than the steady rain pelting my window, and I sobbed into her shoulder with Alivia's hand on my back for what could have been hours. When I finally looked up, a deep wave of exhaustion threatened to take me under.

"You should know, they decided it would be best to keep your departure with him a secret, for now at least," Emma said.

My brows furrowed, and Alivia and I asked simultaneously, "Why?"

Emma shook her head. "Safety, I suppose? I wish I knew specifics. Godrick merely said that Vaelor requested secrecy. No one outside of your father's circle is to know."

"That's..." My voice trailed off when I realized I was spinning the engagement ring around my finger again. I looked down at it before pulling it off slowly and handing it to Alivia, closing her fingers around it. "Don't tell Evander why I left or where I went. Tell him...Tell him I left to travel. Tell him I got cold feet, but that I do love him, as a friend. Tell him he deserves better and that I'm sorry. So, so sorry."

My heart broke for him, the kind, goofy man I'd known nearly my entire life. He did deserve better than this, and while I didn't want to hurt him, I was marginally relieved I didn't have to marry him—but this was worse. This was taking me from my family.

My poor heart broke for both of us, no longer protected by numbness. No, now it was distinctly painful, breath-stealing, demanding to be felt.

Alivia nodded and slipped the ring into her pocket with one hand but held onto mine with her other, refusing to release me, her face strained.

"You'll have to go soon," Emma said.

I clutched both of their hands, closing my eyes and committing the feel of them to memory. "I know."

"You'll be okay," Alivia said, her voice deathly serious. I opened my eyes to her, and my head jerked back a few inches at her expression, burning with intensity. "I'm serious, Elora. You *will* be okay. More than that, you'll thrive. You'll reside with King Vaelor in Draig Hearth, and you will live. Do you hear me? You live, Elora. *Live.* Bake and read and explore and smile and laugh. Do you understand me? You do not let this dull you, because you've always been bright, far too bright for this world, and if you weren't in it, then...who knows? We may all be plunged into darkness."

I didn't know how or what to say. She had never spoken like that, but Goddess... "I love you, Liv."

"I love you, too, El." Her voice cracked on that last syllable, but she cleared her throat, lifted her chin, and any emotion slid from her face, carefully hidden behind her mask of royalty, just as she had always been taught to do.

"You will bring him to his knees," Emma said quietly. We both swiveled to her, shocked. "Such is the power of a woman. You can bring any man to his knees, and this time, it will be the King of Ravaryn. You do not break, Elora. You bend, but never the knee. You never surrender. Not to any man. Ever."

They didn't know the King of Ravaryn had already knelt before me for entirely different reasons, but chills spread over my skin regardless, a renewed strength rushing through my veins. I nodded once and squeezed their hands. "I will not surrender."

"No, you will not," Alivia whispered.

With that, she kissed the back of my hand and released me. Emma did the same, and then, with one last sympathetic glance, I was alone.

Utterly alone.

I glanced around the room, the one I'd stayed in every year for as long as I could remember, every inch tainted with memories and love, especially after Wryn had come into the picture. He'd become associated with these peace treaty meetings, long before I knew of his actual association. He'd become the reason for my excitement, and now...

The walls were closing in, the memories suffocating. I was drowning in nostalgia, my lungs filling with regret before I had even left the estate.

I sucked in a deep breath, snatched my bag off the bed, and walked out the door without another look back.

When I made it to the courtyard, horses were already prepared, Iaso and her male friend already atop theirs. Godrick's face was tight, his hand motioning through the air as he spoke with Wryn who stood by with two sets of reins in hand.

A subtle wave of relief washed over me. At least I would have my own horse.

Wryn spotted me first, his head swiveling in my direction. I averted my gaze to Godrick who stopped everything and strode toward me with a sad smile and that deep furrow between his brows. My feet stilled where I was, and I dropped my bag when he neared me with open arms. As he threw them around me, my breath hitched, and tears threatened to fall again. I slowly wrapped my arms around his waist when my body was wracked with a held-back sob.

"You are so brave," he whispered.

I shook my head against his chest, fighting to not start crying again. "I learned from the best."

He released a breathy chuckle and tightened his hug. "We love you."

"I love you all too."

With that, I steeled my nerves, stood tall, and gave him one last smile. He returned it with one as false as they came; the corners of his watery eyes didn't wrinkle. I would miss that sight.

Peeking around him, I found Wryn atop his horse with averted eyes.

"I'll see you later." I refused to say a final goodbye. I *would* see him later. My hand landed on his arm to give a quick pat as I walked around him, taking a slow breath.

"See you later," he mumbled behind me.

My horse, a dappled gray, remained still and steady as I grabbed the horn of the saddle, slid my foot into the stirrup, and hauled myself up. I didn't so much as look at Wryn when he clicked his horse forward. I merely stared ahead, looking much farther than my eyes could see.

I looked to the apple orchard, to the border mountains and Ravaryn, to the crashing sea and Draig Hearth.

I looked to the future, because it was inevitable and rushing toward me faster than I ever could've imagined.

12

Elora

The morning was quiet, the world still among the soft waves of fog drifting over the forest floor. While it was beautiful with beams of sunlight cutting through the foliage overhead, it'd been impossibly cold last night and the ground too hard, leaving my joints stiff.

I had hardly slept a wink, and that left me...irritated. The others surely wouldn't have coffee. Perhaps tea, but that didn't feel strong enough.

I wanted to bathe in a steaming bath of coffee, or better yet, stand beneath a hot waterfall with my mouth open until my body—namely my eyelids—didn't feel as if it was weighed down by stone.

At the sound of footsteps, I bit back an audible groan of frustration.

"You'll have to talk to me eventually."

"No, Wr—" My grip on my bag tightened, a deep sigh leaving my lungs. "No, I don't."

Exhaustion had long since swept through me. My muscles

screamed, my body and mind tired, and my patience had worn thin. We'd been traveling for an entire day, and while I had ridden horses my entire life, I'd never done so continuously and certainly not in a damned gown. I should have taken the clothes Iaso offered, but I let my foolish pettiness decide against it. I'd been silently kicking myself since the moment we left.

He braced a hand on the tree trunk over my head when I stood and slung the bag over my shoulder. His body caged me against the tree, but I kept my eyes firmly locked on my boots, dangerously close to his large, black leather ones. Rolling my eyes, I swallowed hard and tried to focus on the foliage peeking up around our feet—anything but him.

"Elora," he whispered, "you can't ignore my existence forever."

My head tilted to the side, my brows raised. *I could.*

I didn't bother disagreeing, though. I'd be playing right into his hand; he *wanted* me to react, if only to engage with him, angry or not.

I'd been avoiding him in every way since we'd left, not even daring to look upon his face for fear we'd accidentally lock eyes. I didn't want to see anything in his expression that would soften me. If I looked into his devastating eyes and saw he was hurting too, I would cave. I always did. My heart bled for others, and I wasn't ready for that. I was allowed to be angry and upset, and it wasn't fair of him to expect anything else.

"What did you expect me to do?" I shook my head. "Did you think I'd be happy? Did you think I'd smile and pretend you're just Wryn, the apple orchard owner?"

He didn't immediately respond. My eyes darted around our feet, landing on his before following them upward to his trousers, but I forced myself to stop before I reached his knees.

His finger touched the underside of my chin, and I tensed, my breath hitching. My grip tightened on my bag, and as he lifted my chin slowly, I averted my gaze to the forest surrounding us. The others had left already, conveniently leaving us alone.

"Sun ray," he whispered, "look at me."

I closed my eyes and bit my lower lip, but stopped abruptly when his thumb ran across my lip gently.

"Please." That one word held so much weight, my chest nearly caved in.

"I... I don't..." I didn't know what to say, but none of this felt fair. I shouldn't be forced to look at him. I shouldn't be forced to speak with him. "I shouldn't *be* here." The words spilled from my mouth, a thought escaping.

The air stilled between us, and I bit back an apology threatening to escape, because I didn't owe one. I didn't say anything untrue or unwarranted. This may not have been a kidnapping, but it was undoubtedly coercion. *He* owed *me* one.

He dropped his finger, and my breath left me like I'd been holding it, my shoulders slumping. He took a step back, followed by another.

"You're right," he said. "You shouldn't be, and..." I winced and clenched my jaw, even though he agreed with me. "I'm sorry, Elora."

Leaves crunched underfoot as he walked away, and I lifted my gaze to watch him go. He ran a hand through his hair, his abdomen heaving in a deep sigh. For a moment, I wanted to run after him and turn him to face me, to see the silver eyes I'd avoided for the last twenty-four hours, because I knew they'd be brimming with emotion, whether that be anger or regret or hurt or...

I shook my head, adjusting my bag on my shoulder, and followed after him toward the horses and the rest of the group.

I didn't know what I'd find on his face, but I didn't think it'd be an explanation for *why* he did this.

He hadn't given a reason to Godrick or to me, and that was

what I needed most. If I was to be ripped from my family and home, it'd better be for a damned good reason, and right now, I couldn't think of a single one worthy of *this*.

When I laid eyes on the group, however, my heart sank.

"Where...Where is mine?" I asked, suddenly feeling frantic. My eyes darted around the small clearing, searching the trees for any sign of the dapple-gray horse but finding none.

"It seems the knot came loose in the night," Iaso said.

I stared at her, mouth open, heat seeping into my cheeks. "We had stable boys in Auryna. I didn't... I do know how to tie knots, just not leather ones, it seems."

"They're a bit more difficult," Ewan said with a shrug. He stood close to Iaso, and his eyes followed her as she strolled toward me, like he needed her nearness in any way he could have it. "It's different than tying rope."

"I didn't realize," I sighed.

"We tried searching for him," Ewan said, "but we haven't seen him anywhere yet. He'll find us eventually, though. He always does."

"We should've checked the knot, considering he tends to run when he can, but until he shows back up, you can ride with me." Iaso tugged her bag around her shoulder and yanked out another dress. She chuckled as she handed it out to me, her mouth tilting up in a small smile. "But you will change. I'm not riding pressed up against all that tulle."

I eyed the dress and couldn't stop the cringe that pulled at my lips moments before a laugh bubbled in my throat. I covered my mouth as my sanity started to slip. She lifted a brow at me, and I laughed harder into my hand.

"I'm sorry," I said, shaking my head.

First, the engagement, then Wryn, then this damned dress and travel and poor sleep. Now *this*? My damned horse was gone due to my own careless mistake.

My body shook as the laugh slowly turned into sobs, the choking sound stifled by my hand pressing over my mouth, harder and harder. My eyes brimmed with tears, burning until one slipped past my lashes.

"I'm sorry," I managed, shaking my head. "I'm—"

Large arms wrapped around me and spun me into a solid chest. The scent of sea and storms enveloped me, and I broke. My hand moved from my face to clutch at the shirt I was pressed into. His hand cupped the back of my head, his other wrapped around my shoulders, but he said nothing.

No one did, not for a long while.

"You can ride with me," Wryn finally said. "The others have gone ahead."

I stayed pressed into his chest, my arms wrapped around his waist. "Can I borrow some trousers?"

He paused, his chest rising and falling before he released a small chuckle. "Of course. Although, they may be a tad bit big."

My own laugh left me then, hoarse and broken. "Do you have a belt?"

"Yes, I have a belt. Do you want a shirt as well?"

Unwinding my arms from around his waist, I stepped back and dropped my eyes as I wiped my cheeks. "Yes, please."

He pulled an outfit from his bag and handed it to me in silence before striding back to his horse to pull a brush from the saddle bag. With soothing whispers, he brushed the coat down its neck, and it leaned into him, shifting on its feet to move an inch closer.

Quickly, I dropped my bag and pulled the long shirt over-head before I reached around to unlace the corset. I strained to reach the knot, my shoulders burning, and barely managed to grab the string and yank. It loosened slightly, but not enough. I suppressed a groan and a scream of frustration. With a deep breath, I reached again but couldn't feel it at all this time, and I was going to tear a muscle if I contorted any farther.

"Damn," I muttered under my breath and dropped my arms, letting them hang limply at my sides. Tilting my head back, I took a deep breath before glancing at Wryn, still standing with his back to me. "Can you help me?"

I waited for his reply, but he said nothing, his footsteps growing closer my only answer. I swiped the hair over my shoulder and turned as he neared me. Slowly, so slowly, he lifted the shirt to reveal the corset strings. He held it up with one hand as his other loosened the strings bit by bit, and I had to cup the front of the dress to keep it from falling to the ground.

"Thank you," I whispered, my heart in my throat.

Still, he didn't reply. I started to step away, but he slid a finger over my shoulder blade. I tensed, my spine arching as I sucked in a breath. My heart thrummed against my rib cage, chills spreading from his touch.

"You have freckles down your back, too," he whispered.

I furrowed my brows. "I...know."

His finger trailed to my spine and down the center line. "Constellations."

I barely heard the word, but my breath stopped in response, my eyes frozen on whatever placeholder filled my line of sight while I imagined him staring down at me from behind, seeing even my freckles through the eyes of an artist.

"Wryn..." I took a step forward to cut off his touch, and he released the shirt suddenly, jerking his hand back like I'd burned him.

"Sorry," he bit out, followed by receding footsteps.

My heart ached again, for many reasons—more reasons than I cared to ponder—as I removed the dress and pulled the trousers on, tucking the shirt in the waistband. Even after tightening the belt as much as it would go and rolling the pant legs up a few times, the trousers were entirely too big. I knew I looked a tad ridiculous, drowning in his clothes, but it was still better than chafing thighs.

With a deep sigh, I returned to Wryn's side. There was no teasing or humor, no words at all, as I mounted his horse. Once I settled in the saddle, he reached in front of me to grab the horn and pulled himself up behind me. I tensed when his chest pressed into my back and his legs lined mine. I attempted to inch forward to no avail, heat burning in my cheeks.

I hadn't ridden with someone since I was a young child, and this was very different. Two grown people on one horse forced us so close that no part of me was free of him, not even my lungs. His scent threatened to choke me as his arms wrapped around my frame and grabbed the reins.

Clicking his tongue, he tapped the horse with his heels, and we started forward, catching up with the others in a matter of minutes.

Then, we rode, not another word spoken between us.

13

Vaelor

G oddess above, at least Elora had some sense, because I had clearly lost all of mine.

She, the one who'd never been shy in telling me exactly how she felt, was now the one holding *me* at arm's length, and her doing so made me realize just how much of a mistake this was—a tortuous mistake.

Because she *was* showing me exactly how she felt. Why should she have to say anything at all when her lack of words told me everything I needed to know? She was hurt and angry, rightfully so. She possibly hated me—although, I didn't quite believe that, even though she should. It would be understandable, albeit fucking awful.

Still, Elora was near. She was *with* me, traveling across my kingdom with the knowledge of who I was, what I was. Everything my soul had yearned for but my mind had fervently denied. Yet, it was all wrong and entirely my fault.

What was I thinking, taking her? I had been ready to end it all to avoid this exact situation. I had wanted her as far away as possible so we could live separate lives the way it was supposed to be, and now, she was as close as she could possibly be—asleep and slumped into me.

My chest ached. I wanted to move her, needed to. I wanted to jump down from this horse and lead him with her atop it just so I didn't have to touch her, smell her. Her cinnamon vanilla was going to smother me, especially if Iaso ran out of her tea. I was barely hanging on as it was, even after she doubled the dose.

I want to take her back.

Damn it all, even as I thought it, I knew that wasn't exactly true. I didn't want her with me, but I sure as hell didn't want her there. I was selfish, purely and cowardly selfish.

I couldn't give her what she deserved, and I couldn't allow her to find what she deserved in someone else.

Fuck. She didn't exactly look happy when Evander proposed, her smile forced and movements stiff, but she could've had a happy enough life with him. She wouldn't have been hurt, not like I had hurt her.

She stirred and nestled farther into me, releasing a small whimper.

The ache in my chest deepened and burrowed, tightening my ribs like a wrench around my lungs. My heart started to hammer against its shrinking cage, and I sucked in a deep breath to dispel it, but it did nothing. My hands gripped the reins so tightly, they started to shake, and I forced myself to remain as still as possible to not wake her.

Fuck, this was such a mistake.

I released my grip on the reigns and hooked them over the horn to lift a hand to my chest, running it over my sternum repeatedly.

A painful, damning mistake.

Mistake.

The word screamed in my head over and over, refusing to let

me forget, even for a moment. I glanced around at the surrounding forest and listened for steadiness, my breaths coming quicker.

The repetitive sound of hooves on soft ground caught my attention, and I swiveled my head to watch Ewan's horse walk beside us, one hoof at a time.

One. Two. Three. Four.

Again and again and again.

I didn't know how long I stared, counting each step and listening to each sound before Ewan noticed me.

"What's the plan when we get to Nautia?" he asked, rescuing me from my thoughts. "You going to visit Fauna?"

I gritted my teeth before forcing my gaze up to meet his. "Yes, I told her I'd come by for a while and help out where I could."

"How are things going over there?" Iaso asked from the other side of Ewan.

"Good from what I've heard. They gained another resident recently, but they've been able to keep up. With the new supplier, they've had more than enough food, and the extra funds allowed her to hire a new hand to help."

Iaso nodded. "Born or found? The new resident, I mean."

"Born." A smile pulled at my lips. "The first creature of night born in over fifty years—that we know of. Another female."

"Amazing," Ewan breathed.

"*Very* amazing," Iaso said, her voice dripping with awe. "That's a good sign."

Legend said the birth of a creature of night was an omen of greatness to come. Something or someone would arise to be as light as they are dark—something that would save as many lives as the creature would take.

"We should be able to release them soon, raising the total of creatures in the Cursed Wood to four." I turned to face the path again, lifting the reins. "The mother and baby seem to be doing well."

"That's exciting," Iaso said. "I'd like to come as well, if that's all right. I would love to see them."

I glanced over at her, biting back a wince as I said, "I was hoping you could take Elora to the shops to get what she needs or maybe show her around. I'll pay for whatever you two find or get into. Whatever you need."

"Are you saying the day's on you, then? Because if so, I may just take her to the modiste and..." Her words trailed off as she looked over and took in my expression. Her head tilted as her eyes filled with pity, and she nodded. "Of course. I'm sure she could use a hot meal and maybe even a bed for a few hours. I don't think she's used to sleeping on the ground—understandably so. She could probably use a stiff drink, too. Perhaps we'll just go to the Sopping Sailor, then the inn."

"I'm sorry, I just..." I shook my head, letting my gaze fall to the dirt path ahead, echoed on both sides by emerald-green foliage. "I need time."

I needed to breathe air that didn't smell like cinnamon and think with a clear head. I needed space away from the woman I'd forced to my side.

Damn it all. I'm much more selfish than I realized. Guilt pricked my gut, and I shifted uncomfortably in the saddle, causing her to stir again. *Damn. It. All.*

"I understand, Vaelor," Iaso said. "No need for apologies. I have a feeling we'll see more creatures of night in the near future anyway."

"Thank you," I replied with a quick glance in her direction. She nodded, her golden eyes glowing faintly before she winked and turned away. A familiar warmth spread out from my chest, the painful tension easing, and I took a slow, deep breath. I whipped my head back to her to find her knowing smile in her profile.

"Thank you," I whispered again, and her grin widened farther.

* * *

ELORA HAD AWOKEN by the time we reached Nautia, and I had hopped off to allow her to ride alone and avoid rumors. I'd also placed a glamour over her ears so she'd blend in.

Warm spring air greeted us like an old friend as we ambled into the village. People lined the walking paths, chatting, laughing, and occasionally waving our way when they recognized me.

When we arrived at the Sopping Sailor, the others hopped down and tied their horses to the posts as I tied ours.

Iaso slipped her arm through Elora's. "I bet you're hungry, hmm?"

"Goddess, yes," Elora groaned without so much as questioning Iaso's proximity or touching. Rather, she relaxed her hand on her forearm and strolled forward like she'd known her for years rather than days, and the sight sent a pang through me I didn't have the will to explore.

I smiled faintly as they entered through the swinging doors before turning to Ewan. "I'll see you later, all right?"

He eyed me curiously but nodded in response. "All right."

With that, he strolled around me to enter the tavern, and I continued down the street toward Fauna's Oasis. That was what she had named it—her oasis—because the animals residing there needed a peaceful place to rest and recover.

She'd housed many injured animals over the decades, nursing them back to health to release them again, but her biggest project at the moment was raising the creature of night population. At one point in our long history, Fae had seen them as evil, vicious creatures, and thus, they were hunted to near extinction. When I was crowned, Fauna was one of the many people to come forth with issues and complaints, and now, here we were, with an entire animal rescue facility.

The walk was long but beautiful. All of Nautia was beautiful, but this trail along the shoreline had always been my favorite. It followed the peninsula around the town with the ocean on one side and rows of houses on the other, all painted varying shades of white, green, or blue and lined with vegetation: flowers, ferns, grasses, tall trees that swayed slightly in the breeze. Some even had small, overflowing gardens. Spying a particularly full fruit tree, I glanced left and right before sneaking over to pluck an orange. I quickly returned to the trail, peeling and tossing the rinds to the birds as I walked.

There's nothing more beautiful in this realm than Nautia.

I forced myself to not correct that when her face popped into my mind, and I stumbled over my own feet, nearly dropping the orange. Pausing, I closed my eyes and took a deep breath.

I needed to truly and fully distance myself from Elora. I couldn't send her back, fine, but I didn't have to be near her. We didn't have to be friends or speak. She could live a full and happy life separate from me in Draig Hearth. It was certainly big enough.

Perhaps she could even open a bakery in the nearby village. I could see her now, baking her days away, her cheeks flushed and covered in flour, hair piled atop her head with wild strands breaking free, and her smile... It would be just as wild and genuine as the rest of her. I wondered if she'd ever considered that before, owning her own shop and sharing her passion with the world.

When the Oasis finally came into view, I groaned in relief and shoved Elora from my mind, stifling the feeling in my chest.

I could not be Elora's friend. I could not be Elora's anything.

No matter how wrong it felt or how much regret or guilt grated my nerves, I would avoid her. I would let her live.

This was such a mistake. The thought hadn't left my mind since the second she was whisked out of the meeting so we could hash out the details, but I was committed—extremely regretful but committed. Meetings and demands such as that left no room for indecision or vacillation. Once those words left my mouth, it might as well have been set in stone.

I knew that when I said them, but I had let that damned engagement cloud my judgment. I knew it had, and I still pummeled forward in a fit of jealous rage regardless, which had never happened before. It was exactly those kinds of foolish actions and thoughts that led to instability in a realm, and I jeopardized my kingdom to prevent a wedding.

I wagered *lives* to prevent someone I didn't even plan to marry from marrying another.

My stomach rolled, and my feet stopped. I tossed the rest of the orange and braced a hand on a nearby tree, breathing slowly. It wasn't the first time I had come to that realization, but I never felt less sick. Each time, I nearly retched at the atrocity.

It was selfish and dangerous. *She* made me selfish and dangerous, through no fault of her own, and those were two qualities unfit for the crown, which was exactly why I was done —done attempting to be her friend, or anything, for that matter.

My people deserved better than the man I was becoming.

I might not be able to put hundreds of physical miles between us, but I could build an impenetrable wall. Elora was a loyal friend, but even she would eventually turn away from cold-ness, and I would be the coldest person she'd ever met.

My gut twisted again, and this time, I did retch, expelling everything in my stomach, along with every ugly, unwanted, suffocating emotion. Slowly, I stood, rolling my shoulders back, and took a deep breath.

Steel yourself.

14

Elora

My chest clenched as Wryn came into view, weaving through the maze of tables and waving at the bartender. I quickly dropped my gaze to the mug in my hand when my heart leapt into my throat, and the world threatened to spin around me.

Was this really only my second cup? It very well could've been my sixth with the way my head felt, but my stomach was full, as was my soul, if only for the moment.

Footsteps approached, a shadow falling over the table.

"Holy hell," Iaso said. "You smell awful."

I stifled a smile, my hand covering my mouth as I snickered into it with scrunched eyes, but then the scent hit me, and I had to physically hold back a gag. "Oh, my Goddess."

"Well, I told Fauna I'd help," he said, his voice so warm and soothing, I wanted to curl up in it and sleep. Why did it have to be his voice that sounded like that? *I wish he sounded like...trolls and crying babies.* I laughed harder into my hand. "And I was lucky enough to stop in on stall-mucking day, so that's what I did."

My laughing ceased immediately. My face whipped to him, and for the first time in days, I *saw* him. Stubble had grown in around his jaw, framing that perfect mouth, but smudges of brown smeared across his cheek and neck, and I cringed. I could only imagine what that was. My gaze continued upward until I found his eyes already on me.

My head jerked back an inch, heat creeping into my cheeks. For some foolish reason, I hadn't expected him to be staring in return. "You...mucked stalls?"

"I helped wherever I could," he replied.

It was as if no one else existed. Maybe they didn't. Maybe it was just us two in this room. Maybe his two silver eyes were the only things that existed at all. It sure felt that way.

"That's...nice." It was all I could conjure at the moment because it *was* nice—too nice for a king, but not for Wryn. No, Wryn would absolutely do that.

His mouth tipped up in a smile before it fell just as fast, dragging my drunken heart down with it. He cleared his throat and glanced over his shoulder at the bar. "I'm going to get a drink, then head for a swim before turning in for the night."

A swim? I glanced to the window, but it was too dark to see anything other than the moon. The thought of being in that black sea, freezing and breath-stealing, tightened my throat. I swallowed another large gulp of mead.

I knew exactly what that icy water would feel like, so cold the heart forgot to beat before it raced painfully, so cold the lungs gasped like they were drowning until the skin went numb and everything burned.

I blinked rapidly and forced my eyes from the window to find Wryn taking a step back, then another.

He dipped his head toward Iaso. "Please show Elora to her room for me."

My mouth fell open. I would have retorted *something*, but I was a little stunned, maybe offended he thought I needed an escort, and my mind was swimming in mead. It didn't matter, though, because Iaso nodded, and Wryn just...walked away without a second glance. No goodbye or farewell or wave or words at all. Nothing.

"Iaso, do you have that cure by chance? I have a feeling I may need some." I lifted the mug to my lips, my gaze following Wryn's back as he walked across the room. "This is much stronger than what I'm used to."

She chuckled softly. "Of course."

At her confirmation, I downed the rest before flagging down the barmaid walking by our table. She nodded once when I ordered another, and Iaso lifted a brow at me. I merely shrugged my shoulders.

My eyes narrowed onto Wryn, though, his back wide and large. Anger pulsed through me again, and my leg bounced under the table.

I knew where my room was. I knew that. He knew that. Iaso knew that. We all fucking knew that. I didn't need an escort just because I was me, and if I did, why couldn't it be him?

Scratch that. I don't want it to be him, because he kidnapped me. That was what this was, right? A kidnapping?

"He should go to prison," I mumbled under my breath, too low for anyone else to hear.

My heart thundered as I watched him take a shot, then another. His throat bobbed as he swallowed the brown liquid, but there was no other reaction from him, like he'd done it a thousand times.

I waited for him to turn around. My thoughts screamed for him to turn around, peek over his shoulder, glance in our direction. I wanted to see *something*—remorse, guilt, regret, longing, lust, warmth, love.

But nothing.

He pushed the door open, exited, and it closed softly behind him. Chatter continued, the small band continued, everything continued, like he'd never been here at all, which was beyond baffling to me. The fact that others' eyes didn't track him through the room, that his scent didn't threaten to consume them, that his voice didn't carry over every other baffled me.

I blinked, and the room swayed slightly. It wasn't until my hip hit the table that I realized I'd jerked to my feet.

Fuck.

One enraged step after another, I followed after him, my gaze locked on that damn wooden door. It didn't open. It didn't move at all, only growing larger as I neared it.

If the others called after me, I didn't hear it. I heard nothing over my pounding heart as I shoved the door open and stepped into the chilled air.

I glanced left and right but saw nothing. My fists clenched at my sides. Heat flushed my skin as I released a scoff.

"How does he get to drag me here then disappear?" I mumbled, shaking my head.

I spun back to the door and swayed as the world kept spinning, even when my feet stopped. I inhaled slowly, my hand on the handle, but I was so damned angry. I didn't want to go in there and sit back down. I didn't want to roll over and do as he expected of me, of everyone.

He can't order me around.

I turned away from the door.

He's not my king.

Clenching my jaw, I lifted my skirts and jogged toward the sounds of crashing waves. When I stepped onto the sand, snapping my head left and right, my chest heaved from running *and* anger.

If he was going to force me to his side, then he was going to hear what I had to say.

Down the beach a ways, Wryn stood with his shirt off and pants rolled above his ankles. He stood at the water's edge, letting the cold water lap at his feet, and my sights narrowed to it.

Cold.

Cold water.

Cold skin.

When fear started to slither up my spine, I jerked my eyes up to his face and stared daggers at his profile. If he felt my gaze on him, he didn't show it. He remained with his hands in his pockets, staring at the water.

Why does he get a moment of peace when I've been ripped from my home? When he shoved me against a wall and licked and kissed me in a way no one else ever had, then left me? Ignored me for six months?

I'd finally come to terms with the end of our friendship— mostly—when he'd sent me that damned letter, and as pathetic as it was, I was going to meet him. I was going to show up, so he could inspect the damage he'd done. I assumed he'd simply crush the rest of my heart under his boot, but I hoped, in the very dark, very hidden depths of my heart, that he would apologize.

I wanted to hear an apology, and still, he hadn't given one. No, worse. He hurt me, and then stole me from the ones who actually cared about me.

My cheeks flamed; my eyes burned. When my throat tightened, I swallowed against it. He simply stared out over the sea while my heart beat against the confines of its cage, faster and faster like whatever cracks I'd healed over those long six months were trying to shatter all over again.

I lifted my skirts again and strode toward him. My feet moved quickly—quicker than I would've thought possible considering the way the ground kept trying to sway from under my feet. The sand dipped and moved, tripping me when I gained speed.

"Fuck, stop moving," I whispered at the ground.

But when I looked back to Wryn, he was closer than I'd thought, and now those eyes, those damned silver eyes that had moments ago been watching the waves, watched me.

His brows furrowed in confusion before his features fell flat. "I'm not moving."

I rolled my eyes. "I wasn't talking to you, asshole."

His eyes flashed, and he closed the distance between us in two large strides. I stumbled back a step when his closeness, and thus his scent, bombarded me.

I started to take another step away, but my foot caught on my other or the sand or the damned ground reached up and snagged my ankle, determined to see me fall into its clutches.

Wryn caught my wrists and wrenched me forward.

I shrieked and collided with his front, my palms finding his chest, bare and warm and hard.

My mind stuttered when I looked up to find his eyes hard and his expression tight.

What the fuck does he have to be angry about?

I tilted my chin up, my jaw clenched as I narrowed my eyes at him. "I don't need protection just because I'm a human. I've been doing quite well on my own, thank you."

He quirked a brow, and my cheeks burned.

"I don't need Iaso to walk me back to my room."

His chest heaved with a sigh, alerting me to the fact that I was still pressed into him. I jerked my hands away from his skin and stepped back, but he didn't release his grip. Rather, he pulled me back into him, and I squirmed against his hold. I jerked and jerked, which only made the world threaten to spin again.

"I didn't ask her to do that because you're human, Elora."

I stilled, tense as I slid my gaze back up to meet his. He lowered his face ever so slightly, and I inched backward, feeling my pulse in my throat.

"I asked her to do that because you're *my* human."

My breathing stopped. My heart stopped. I feared the realm might have stopped. Or maybe it ceased to exist.

He tended to do that—eclipse the rest of the world until he was all I could see.

He released me then and dove into the water. I stood on the sandy beach, more confused than ever as I stared at my wrists. They suddenly felt cold at the absence of his warmth, and I wanted to scrub his touch away.

I stared at them, stared and stared until I started to doubt he was ever here, until I had started to convince myself he didn't touch my skin and light me on fire from the inside. Maybe I'd imagined the entire thing and he didn't call me his human.

Why would he say that? I wasn't his human. I wasn't anyone's human.

But I could still feel him, could still smell him, could still hear his voice echoing in my ears.

He did touch me, but he'd touched me before, so I couldn't understand why this moment felt different.

I didn't know how long I stood there, but he never returned. It could've been seconds, minutes, hours, a day, a year, a lifetime.

My heart had calmed some, but I could feel the deathly, hollowing, terrifying feeling awakening within its chambers again, replacing the blood in my veins bit by bit.

After six long months of shoving it all down and telling

myself over and over again that whatever we had was done, it was coming back—*hope.*

I didn't know if I wanted to cry or laugh or both.

* * *

AFTER WRYN LEFT, I didn't see him again for the rest of the night, but I did imagine him and run through every event for the first time since I'd left. The bed at the inn was comfortable, and I'd propped the window open to hear waves crashing on the shore. The breeze blew through, billowing the linen curtains and bringing with it the scent of brine and blooming flowers.

It was an impeccable lullaby, yet here I lay.

Because no lullaby, no matter how sweet, could drown out my racing thoughts. I wouldn't be surprised if those in nearby rooms could hear them too, because they were screaming in my skull. My eyes kept falling to the door like it was only a matter of time before someone came to bang on my door and complain about the noise.

When a beam of moonlight landed on the bed, turning my skin a soft silver, my memory flashed back to the conversation I'd had with Alivia mere days ago. My heart physically ached from how much I missed her, and tears slid down the sides of my face to soak the pillow, but I couldn't help the laugh that bubbled up. It was a broken sound, sadder than it was humorous, but it grew until my belly burned, just as it had so many times with her.

"Perhaps he was sent as a gift—a gift to bless our eyes and feed our midnight activities," I'd said. How ironic, truly, because he had fueled my 'midnight activities.' Many times, in fact.

Just without the crown or title.

Tonight, my midnight activities consisted of wallowing in

drunken self-pity, and my thoughts certainly kept circling back to him, but not for the reasons I'd implied.

Stupid, foolish reasons.

Another sob broke free, and I rubbed my already swollen eyes, tired and burning. I didn't know how long I'd been lying there, but the moon had already peaked and begun its descent, so a few hours, at least.

"Ugh." I slapped my hands down on the mattress and threw the covers back to crawl out of bed, pausing for a moment when the room swayed around me. When my head stopped spinning, I downed the second vial of cure from Iaso and stumbled to the open window. It framed a perfect view—clear black skies, speckled with stars and a bright full moon, its reflection bouncing off the even darker waves below. The sea was beautiful from afar, soothing, even. I'd always thought it was, as long as it didn't lick at my skin.

I grabbed a nearby chair with both hands, not flinching in the slightest when I started to drag it and an obnoxious scraping pierced the silence. I merely moved faster and hoped the sound was confined to the room.

With it facing the window, I plopped down and pulled my legs up to cross them beneath me. The chair was large enough to sink into and lean my head back, even comfier than the bed, cozy in a way that swallowed me. Sitting up, I reached over the back of the chair to grab the blanket from the bed, then snuggled in, tucking my hands beneath my cheek as I leaned my head on the armrest.

* * *

PALE SUNSHINE BATHED my face in a welcomed warmth.

I yawned, my joints cracking as my arms stretched up, and the blanket fell to my lap to expose my skin. When a crisp breeze drifted in through the open window, I gasped and my eyes flew open before squinting against the bright light. I pulled the blanket back up around my shoulders and greeted the morning with a growing smile. Clear blue skies and a deep blue ocean beneath it stared back at me, waves lapping softly at the shore.

Even after a few measly hours of sleep, I felt refreshed—truly and thoroughly invigorated. Sometimes, a person needed the emotional release of a good cry to be able to breathe again, and now, as I sucked in a slow, deep breath, I was comforted by the feel of cool air filling my lungs, tinted by that same salty scent and nothing else—not worry or sadness or hurt. For now, it felt good. *I* felt good.

The sun had only just risen, barely peeking its head over the horizon, so I didn't think anyone else would be awake, but my stomach growled and gnawed at my hollow insides.

Bracing myself, I threw the blanket off and darted for my clothing to pull on my new blouse and trousers. Iaso had bought them for me yesterday, or rather, Wryn did, and they fit like a glove. I wasn't used to wearing pants, and I still preferred dresses, but I found riding in them to be much more comfortable.

I tucked the shirt in and slid the belt on before facing the mirror, wincing at my reflection. I may have felt refreshed, but my hair was wildly knotted, and dark circles had settled under my eyes.

Sitting at the base of mirror, I crossed my legs and began the strenuous task of braiding this much hair. The longer it got, the longer it took me to braid, but I loved its length; it made me feel feminine, so I didn't mind the burning in my arms much. It was a necessary price to be paid—one all women shared and understood.

A smile tugged at my lips. I liked any connection to the

women around and before me. It felt special, like I knew a piece of them, and they knew a piece of me.

Once I was finished, I stood and gave myself a once over before my stomach growled again.

"All right," I whispered as I twisted the doorknob and peeked into the hallway, glancing up and down. It was silent, all the doors closed.

I wasn't a captive, so why did I feel like one as I stepped out and pulled my door shut?

I briefly studied each door as I passed, like they would somehow tell me who slept inside. They were old and wooden, each one showing signs of age and care. The doorknobs were brass, clearly polished as they hadn't tarnished. Lifting my eyes, I found naught a cobweb or speck of dust along the walls, and the floors were equally as kempt.

Whoever owned the inn must have loved it dearly.

At the end of the hallway, I descended the staircase wearily, unsure who or what I'd find, but none of my sneaking could have hidden the loud grumble from my stomach when the smell of baking bread reached my nose.

I paused, my foot mid-step and hand on the rail, to inhale deeply. A hint of something sweet undercut the scent, and I could've moaned—blueberry bread. Opening my eyes, I darted down the stairs and around the corner.

Off the side of the main entrance, a curtain wall had been pulled back and tied open to reveal a breakfast room with a long table, topped with an assortment of food—fruits, rolls, nuts, even eggs and a few fresh vegetables I didn't recognize.

Good Goddess, how many patrons did they have here? There had to be enough to feed a small army.

A short, elderly woman with graying hair stepped into view then, carrying a silver tray of those blueberry muffins I'd been smelling.

I smiled and strolled forward. "Good morning."

She gasped and swiveled, the tray wobbling in her hands. I jerked forward and caught her elbow with one hand and the bottom of the tray with the other. One muffin managed to roll onto the nearby table with a soft thump, and we both looked at it before chuckling.

"Thank you, deary," she said and turned to slide the tray onto the table.

"Don't thank me. I nearly made you drop the entire tray." I picked up the fallen pastry, inspecting it for damage or dirt. It seemed fine enough, so I blew it off and took a bite. My eyes widened with a dramatic moan as I chewed slowly. "And what a travesty that would have been. My Goddess, these are phenomenal."

When she peeked over her shoulder, her eyes were unnervingly green—shining like they were lit with a stray beam of sunlight. "*That* is why I thanked you."

My brows furrowed, my mouth opening to say something, although I didn't know what, when a voice behind me spoke first.

"Good morning."

I swiveled to find a tall man with long white hair, braided back just as mine was, and tan, wrinkled skin, smile lines deepening around his eyes as he grinned at me.

"Long red hair and a face full of freckles..." He tapped his forefinger on his chin. "Elora?"

My head tilted to the side, and I studied him in return. His eyes were so...silver, metallic but warm all the same. They weren't the only features he shared with his son, but I already knew that based on Wryn's sketches—frighteningly accurate, it seemed.

A smirk curved my lips, and I cocked an eyebrow. "Alden?"

"That'd be me." He laughed and stepped closer to stick a

hand out to me. I smiled and slid mine into his, giving his hand a quick shake. "It's nice to finally meet you."

It occurred to me then: Alden, Wryn's father, recognized me on description alone, which meant Wryn *told* him of me—perhaps even showed him a sketch too.

My cheeks burned, and I swallowed hard, pulling my hand back and turning to the multitude of food.

No one in my family would have recognized Wryn had they seen him one random morning.

My heart sank.

That wasn't true. They most definitely would have. They all would have recognized him as the King of Ravaryn. If I had told them, told anyone of my mysterious Fae friend, of his silver eyes and towering height, then maybe I would have been warned. Maybe none of this would have happened.

Heat deepened in my cheeks at how foolish I'd been. I had wanted to keep Wryn all to myself, my sweet secret, and he knew that. He had to have known if I told anyone of him, he'd have been exposed.

Had he wanted me to tell someone? Or did he know I wouldn't? What *did* he want?

Alden had taken his food outside to eat on the beach, and the baker had disappeared moments after Alden, so I was left to my own thoughts for the rest of breakfast, allowing those questions, so simple and seemingly trivial, to consume every minute.

Why had he done any of this?

15

Vaelor

Why had I done this? Any of it?

I asked myself this exact question repeatedly, all day, every day as if this time might provide answers. I was beginning to wonder if I'd broken my own mind, if those were the only words it could conjure anymore.

This was a special kind of torture.

I'd thought she was inescapable before, because her letters could find me anywhere, because she invaded my thoughts more consistently than anything else, but the distance made it possible to forget for a few moments here and there.

As it turned out, *that* was easy.

But this? Having her find me, touch me, speak to me, invade me at every turn was torture at its finest. She was truly and thoroughly inescapable now, and I had done this to myself.

Maybe I'm a masochist after all.

Last night, when I turned to see her stumbling toward me, so dainty and inebriated and fucking *angry,* I couldn't have walked away if I wanted to. I had to hear what she had to say. I had to know what filled her with such fiery passion that she followed me from the tavern, but I hadn't expected her to be angry about my simple request.

That was illogical, and I wanted to chalk it up to the Fae alcohol wreaking havoc on her human body, but I knew better. I knew *her* better than that, and she was only scratching the surface of the real issue.

She was angry at me in every regard, and she had a right to be, but that was the simplest issue, the easiest fight.

And I couldn't handle more either, so I let it be—albeit in the worst possible way.

Why the fuck did I tell her she was my human?

That wasn't even true. I didn't own her...

I closed my eyes, inhaling deeply.

I *wanted* to own her.

I wanted to do a great many things to simmer her anger and defuse that damned attitude. When she'd called me an asshole, I wanted to do incorrigible things to that mouth, those lips, full and red and spewing a voice that snaked under my skin in the most maddening ways.

I jumped in the freezing ocean simply to douse the flames consuming me inch by inch.

In layman's terms, I ran away from her. I, the six-foot-four Fae king, ran from her, the five-foot-nothing human woman.

And then, of course, she was there first thing this morning when I entered the breakfast room. Perhaps she did have magic somehow, some special, unheard of magic that allowed her to be everywhere all at once, because she fucking was—infuriatingly so.

Her eyes were in the clear blue skies, and for some unfathomable reason, I couldn't bring myself to cover them in my clouds. I wanted to, needed to, just for a single moment so I could breathe, but I *couldn't.* Her scent found me in every street, drifting from the bakeries, her hair in every orange and red flower, every flickering flame, her freckles among the stars. Her memory was everywhere, in every place I'd ever received a letter and read them in her voice, laughing and imagining and falling into a friendship I hadn't realized my soul needed.

Until it became too much. That friendship became something else, sneaky and growing and deepening until it pulled its mask off at that damned ball and revealed it wasn't friendship at all—or rather, it was and so much more.

It was dangerous, lethal and intangible.

It threatened to steal my focus from my people, and that could never happen. I would never allow it to.

So, I left. I steeled myself and bit my tongue like I wanted to sever it and choke on my own blood, so I wouldn't have to choke on the feeling tightening my throat. I ignored her. I darkened the sky every day, allowing only enough sunshine for the vegetation to survive. I avoided the stars and Iaso's flowers and the flames in every fireplace. All I did for those six long months was work. I worked and worked until my very bones were tired, and I could sleep a dark, dreamless sleep.

It was my cycle—distraction, sleep, distraction, sleep—and it worked.

Until it didn't.

It wasn't even her who shattered my perfectly curated routine. It was Evander. *Fucking Evander and his damned ring.*

But then she'd said yes. *Her.* The woman in the orchard. Elora Stirling. Sun ray. The one full of laughter and sugar and warmth and unabashed bravery when it came to her feelings. She remained true to herself; she always had, yet I'd seen the look on her face. She was losing herself in that moment.

No, not losing.

Sacrificing.

For what, I didn't know, but that wasn't even why I took her.

As much as I wished it was—because then at least I could tell myself I wasn't a self-serving *asshole,* as Elora had so eloquently put it—it simply wasn't.

I took her because I *was* selfish. Because in that moment, I'd rather have had her angry with me than happy with him.

I should've let her marry him. Hell, I essentially pushed her into his arms, then had the inconceivable audacity to steal her. I kidnapped Elora Stirling like a fucking thief in the night, a villain, like a selfish, merciless, bloodthirsty king who saw nothing beyond his own wants.

That was the one and only time I'd done something for no other reason than myself, because I wanted to.

And it was foolish.

Now, I was facing the consequences: *her.*

When I'd spotted her this morning, seated at a table in the breakfast room and staring off through the window, seemingly lost in her thoughts, I turned on my heel and exited the inn to grab breakfast elsewhere.

A thought occurred to me as I left, and my chest ached as it always did when I was reminded of her. It'd been decades since her passing, but that pain never left. It dulled, sure, became more of a hollowing ache, but at least it wasn't the sharp, piercing pain that stole my breath and flooded me with devastation.

They say time heals all wounds, but I knew that wasn't true. Some wounds were meant to stay, if only to remind the living world of their existence—a permanent memorial and warning.

Stepping into a local shop, I grabbed two pastries and a few stems of woman's revenge: a simple white flower that resembled daffodils. However, their sap, when carefully removed, was a poison commonly used by women in the olden days, hence the name. It had to be ingested to kill the intended, but women were sly and men were foolish.

Like this, however, unless someone pulled the stamen out and licked it, they were harmless—harmless and beautiful.

And they were her favorite.

The walk to the cemetery was quick, too quick for my liking, as the hurt in my chest grew with each step closer. When the ancient metal gate came into view, I had to pause to take a deep breath, clutching the paper sac and flower bundle in my hands.

Her gravestone was visible from here, a simple white stone, polished and shining in the morning sun.

My hands shook, but I continued forward, hurrying through the gate and down the path, afraid that if I slowed even a fraction, I would turn around.

It wasn't until I reached her that I finally halted. I'd carved her face into the stone over two hundred years ago, and it still looked exactly how I remembered her—warm and caring, with a dusting of freckles. Her long hair no longer held the soft yellow pigment, but her eyes, one green and one blue, were still faintly colored, just enough to distinguish them.

I swallowed hard, my appetite gone, but sat where I was and pulled the pastries from the bag. I couldn't come to visit her and not eat; I could practically hear her threatening to whip me from the other side of the veil for merely considering it.

My eyes burned as I laughed to myself. I knew she would be nearby, sensing my presence. "Good morning, Mama."

I took a large bite of the cinnamon roll while laying the other one at the base of her headstone alongside the flowers. These specific flowers being her favorite had always been a running joke between her and Father.

"I'm just waiting for the day she decides she's tired of me," he'd say with a grin, echoed by her laughter.

She would inevitably reply with, *"If that day were to come, I think I'd end you in a more spectacular way than simple poisoning. Don't you think you'd like to go out in a show?"*

He'd wrap his arms around her and kiss the top of her head. *"I believe I'd like anything dealt at your hands, sweet Ara."*

I'd seen that exact scenario dozens of times, and it flashed through my mind every time I came to visit. I couldn't escape their happiness, no matter how many years passed, and it somehow made the lack of it so much more painful, so much more glaringly obvious.

A child, even grown, never expected their parents to die. Of course, everyone died at some point, but not parents, not in the mind of their own child. No, they were supposed to be invincible.

"Everyone dies," she'd said in an attempt to soothe me, chuckling as she did so, which only set off another round of coughing, another spray of blood into her napkin.

I had heard that same statement too many times to count over my long life, but hearing that and understanding it were two entirely different things. Then, watching the significant other of said parent grieve the loss of their love... That was something *no one* prepared me for.

It was like watching his soul wither and die while his body refused to follow. The pain in his soul was so utterly deep and visceral that it changed him in every aspect—mind, body, *and* soul. He became a shell of a person, alive but not, tethered to this realm by the sheer determination of his beating heart. Merely breathing, barely eating or moving, and never smiling.

Watching my father grieve my mother was the hardest thing I had ever experienced, worse even than her death itself. That had been long and drawn out, but when it was over, it was over, and she was gone. We could bury her and mourn and eventually, begin to live again, even if her death left a hole where she should have been.

But his? His temporary death had been excruciating. The way he roared for her still rang in my ears sometimes. Mother had embedded herself in his soul, and when she died, she ripped part of him out with her, leaving him wounded and bleeding where no healer could ever dream of reaching.

He changed that day, that year, that decade, but in time, he mended in a way that allowed him to breathe. The stitches were crude and weak at best, disintegrating at the mere mention of her, but at least, he was alive again...mostly. At least he could leave his bed, change his clothes, eat and drink, even smile occasionally.

He was managing in any way he could.

He changed, and so did I.

Approaching footsteps sounded behind me, and I turned to see Father holding a sack of his own. His eyes darted to the cinnamon roll on the ground before meeting mine, a soft laugh drifting from him.

"Morning, you two. Seems Vaelor beat me to breakfast today." He lifted the pastry bag, giving it a light shake, before taking a seat beside me. "That sketch of Elora was spot on."

My head whipped to him. "What?"

"I met her this morning at breakfast," he mumbled through a bite of cinnamon roll and lifted his hand to gesture around his head. "With all that red hair, I recognized her immediately. Although, she's shorter than I thought she'd be."

I stared at him, an uncomfortable knot forming in my gut. "Ah."

"Ah?" He quirked a brow at me, swallowing his food. "That's all you have to say? 'Ah?'"

I averted my gaze to Mother's face, still smiling like she always had, as she always would be. "What else do you want me to say?"

"Perhaps why she's here, Vaelor, in Nautia, in *Ravaryn*."

I closed my eyes. A warm ray of sun fell over us, and I exhaled slowly, reminded of Elora's touch once again.

Glancing to Father, I cleared my throat and told him everything from start to finish. His face gave away nothing, no reaction, which was unusual for him and made the uneasiness grow
in my chest.

"And you intend on avoiding her," he repeated back to me.

It wasn't a question, but I answered regardless. "Yes."

He stared flatly for a split second before smacking the back
of my head. "That one was for your mother. This one"—*smack*—
"was for Elora. What is wrong with you?"

I gawked at him. "I know. Trust me, I know. She's...changing
me, though. I can't." I shook my head. "I risked the welfare of my
kingdom for this. It was reckless and foolish. Dangerous."
Clouds rolled on the horizon, swelling and darkening, but I
looked at Mother as I spoke, because I wanted to say these
words to her. I wanted her to hear them and hear her voice in
return. I wanted to feel her arms wrap around me in a hug only
a mother could give and tell me exactly what I needed to hear. "*I*
became dangerous because of her, and it will *not* happen again."

Father was quiet for some time before I finally looked at
him, his expression unreadable, but his eyes, as silver as mine,
were...sad. For the briefest of moments, I wondered if they were
merely a reflection of my own.

He didn't touch on anything I'd said. Instead, his gaze turned
to his mate's, meeting her stone eyes, as he whispered, "I want to
talk to her too."

With that, his gaze went distant, reminiscent of his grieving
days, and I had to look away, the sight unbearable, digging up
unwanted memories of my own.

Clouds filled the sky, a drizzle falling over Nautia, the air
chilled as raindrops fell like tiny pricks of ice. I stared upwards,
letting them hit my face for a few minutes, wishing they could
wash away the tightness in my chest before sending it away. The
storm dissipated as I rose to my feet.

Rays of sunshine cascaded over the freshly soaked graveyard, making the greens greener and the browns darker. Nature became more vibrant, despite the soft waves of steam rising from the ground as the sun warmed it all.

"I'll see you later," I muttered, placing my palm on Father's shoulder. He didn't respond; I knew he wouldn't. He never did when he fell into his past.

Today was our last day in Nautia before we left for Draig Hearth tomorrow, and I wanted to stop by the Oasis one last time to check in, so I turned in that direction—the opposite way of the inn.

The streets were full to the brim with people strolling and laughing, the shops' bells constantly ringing with customers coming and going. A few waved or stopped to speak with me, but I couldn't focus on any of them, which made the knot of guilt grow and twist.

These were the people I risked for Elora, innocent lives turned into a bargaining chip. My gut rolled again, and I swallowed hard, continuing toward the Oasis.

Fauna's white hair glinted near the containers of feed when I entered through the front gate and rolled my sleeves up. Humidity clung to the town after the rainfall, and within her wooden gate, the lack of airflow left it feeling thick and stagnant in the sun's heat.

"Well, hey there." She beamed when her head popped up, her green eyes bright and hair nearly glowing, in stark contrast to her brown skin, rich and dark from years on the coast.

I released a silent sigh. "Put me to work, boss."

A laugh bubbled from her, and she wiped her forehead with the back of her hand as she stood, rising to meet my eyes at a solid six-feet tall. "You sure you wanna work? Wouldn't wanna callous those soft, artisanal hands of yours."

I narrowed my eyes at her, but my thumbs felt along my

palms; they were not soft. Lifting a brow, I hooked a thumb at the door behind me and took a half step toward it. "Would you prefer I go?"

"No, no," she said, waving a hand through the air. "We have a new volunteer today, and she might need guidance, or at least company. She seemed excited, though. I put her with the horses, just to feed and brush them out for now."

A sinking feeling in my chest told me I knew exactly who was here, but I didn't want to believe it. *Why? Why would she be here? Can't I have one place to escape?* I stifled a groan of frustration, feeling the pricks of guilt again. She wouldn't even be in this kingdom if it weren't for me.

"You sure you don't need help with something else? I can muck more stalls or—"

"Muck *more* stalls? How many do you think we have, V?" She chuckled, shaking her head as she lifted the two feed buckets and strode past me, the scent of decay wafting from them. I held back a gag, and she laughed louder with a shrug. "Creatures of night eat too."

"Any other animals to feed?" Desperation bled into my voice, but she didn't seem to notice as she walked away with a bucket in each hand and her back to me.

"Nope! Just the horses. Go," she shouted over her shoulder.

That was one thing I greatly appreciated about Fauna: she didn't treat me like a royal. When I was at the Oasis, I was just another volunteer for her to put to work. She respected me as much as she did any other person, and I respected her more for it.

I turned my face to the sky, clear and blue—as blue as the eyes I would soon greet.

Fauna kept a dozen horses, split into two pastures. Perhaps I could slip into whichever field she wasn't in and miss her entirely. I let that foolish hope guide me down the path toward the fields, one half closed off by a dense forest, the other half meeting the ocean. The gate was loosely tied, easily pushed open by a curious snout, and I let out a long groan.

Definitely Elora.

Several buckets of feed were lined up outside the gate, but the horses were nowhere to be seen. Usually, they'd be lined up at the fence, attempting to push their heads through the gaps in the wood to get a taste of the grain just outside.

My brows furrowed as I held a hand up over my eyes to block the sun and glance out over the fields. Out in the middle were a group of at least six horses, some grazing the green grass, some lying down, but I saw no Elora.

I unlooped the crudely-tied knot and swung the gate open, the hinges groaning. With a quick glance back at the horses, I turned to the hinges, finding them partly rusted, and made a mental note to return with vinegar and sand.

I closed the gate and tied a proper knot before striding toward the group. Her soft voice reached me long before I saw her.

"And with his long sword, the brave knight swung down, slicing the rope. The basket of apples fell to the ground, rolling across the grass."

She paused, as did I, my feet frozen and eyes wide.

"Would you like that, Patchy? An apple or two?" She laughed. "Or ten? Should I return with some?"

Patchy?

"The girl joined the knight then, giggling as they plopped down, surrounded by mares, and together, they all feasted until the sinking sun cast them in glowing embers, the day long and..."

I didn't catch what she said next as my eyes fell on her, and my ears stopped listening, ringing instead. My hands itched for paint, a pencil, charcoal, any medium to mark this image on paper.

Patchy was a paint horse, splotches of brown and white scattering over his large body, lying flat over the thick grass, his head rested in Elora's lap, her legs folded beneath her. Another horse had settled down beside them, sitting up but seemingly listening, the rest standing and grazing around her.

She ran a hand down Patchy's neck, smoothing his coat, while her other hand held the small children's book she read from.

I turned on my heel and strode away. I couldn't do this. I couldn't. I wouldn't.

I made it ten measly steps before I heard, "Wryn?"

I didn't stop.

"Are you avoiding me now?" Her words were barely audible, but they reached me, carried on the breeze. They wound around my heart and threatened to snatch me back.

I paused and looked over my shoulder at her without meeting those devastating eyes. Bitterness filled my mouth as I replied, "Yes."

I vaguely saw her sit up straighter, the book falling to the ground beside her, but I turned and strode toward the fence with a burning chest. By the time I unlatched the gate and shut it behind me, my lungs were on fire.

Any air that entered burned up in the flames of panic, utterly useless. I braced a hand on the metal bar, my knuckles turning white from the force, my eyes darting around.

Calm.

A darkness on the horizon threatened to swirl again, and I fought it off too, refusing to let the growing storm reveal my inner torment.

Calmer, I corrected. *Anything calmer.*

Closing my eyes, I listened.

Birds chirped somewhere.

A slight breeze whistled through nearby trees.

Waves crashed—constant, steady, rhythmic.

My eyes opened to watch them, counting each small roll of water against the sand. Relief found me slowly, loosening panic's grip on my rib cage, and I sucked in a slow breath, reclining on the gate.

We had to leave today. I needed to get away from her and fall into a routine again. I needed duty and obligation to numb this feeling. I needed distraction.

At least at Draig Hearth, I could stay away from her. I knew the rooms and passageways like the back of my hand and wouldn't accidentally run into her every time I turned a corner.

With renewed determination, I stalked back to town, bought another horse, as the escaped one had not returned, and alerted the others.

Father wanted to stay behind and visit a while longer, but the rest of us were leaving.

Soon.

16

Elora

The departure for Draig Hearth had been sudden, a day earlier than I'd expected, and the journey uncomfortably quiet, Iaso and Ewan the only ones to speak.

They would occasionally say a few words to Wryn or me, but we mostly shrugged and nodded, both content with the silence.

Well, content was a strong word.

He was avoiding me. He told me as much, and his words had stung. He regretted taking me as much as I regretted being taken.

Something about knowing the feeling was mutual hurt more than it should have. I couldn't blame him, though, I supposed. I'd avoided him too during our travels to Nautia. I deserved the same.

Or that was what I told myself—until I realized I didn't.

He took *me*, not the other way around. If he hadn't wanted to speak to me, then he should have left me in Auryna like any sane person would.

Who even was this person? I didn't know him. He wasn't the

same kind artist who had filled my head with laughs and dreams. He was not the man who wrote me all those letters, and he certainly wasn't the man who shoved me against the wall.

This man didn't move with the same ease. He didn't smile and tease.

He didn't call me sun ray. He didn't even call me Elora. He didn't call me anything, because he didn't speak to me.

"Yes," was the last word he'd said to me.

Yes, I'm a coward.

Yes, I'm an asshole.

Yes, I deserve a huge kick in the ass.

Any of those would have been much more adequate.

I had stewed over this thought for the past full day while we rode, allowing the hurt to fester into anger. He had no right to avoid me.

It didn't matter that he was a king or a coward. *He* was the reason I wasn't home. He was the reason I was forced to his side. He didn't get to drag me away, then ignore me like I was some nuisance.

By the time Draig Hearth came into view, my grip was tight on the reins, my knuckles white and jaw clenched. Under normal circumstances, I was sure I would have been enamored by the grandeur of it all, but at this moment, all I saw while looking at this giant fucking castle was the lack of my own home.

When Wryn led us into the bailey, a few grooms came to assist with the horses, and I jumped down and handed the reins off without hesitation. I didn't want to speak to Wryn in front of the others, so I hadn't breathed a word about anything, and holding it all in had been difficult.

That anger, every damned word he *would* hear, had grown and grown until my skin felt tight, like if I didn't say them, or at the very least scream at the top of my lungs, I was going to explode.

Iaso strolled over, a smile on her face, and stuck an elbow out. "Ready to see your room?"

"Yes." I turned to Wryn, and he caught my gaze. He started to walk away but stopped dead in his tracks when I said, "But I would like Wryn to escort me."

His chest rose and fell, his spine rod straight and muscles tense. He turned back to us stiffly, seemingly resisting whatever invisible force pulled him in my direction.

Iaso glanced to him, and he nodded once.

"Well, all right, then." She chuckled and stuck out her other elbow. "Ewan, escort me to mine?"

He grinned. "Of course."

They left, arm in arm, as Wryn waited for me to join his side. He didn't offer an arm or even a word in response, and I didn't push. I waited, biding my time while he led me inside.

My feet slowed, my eyes following the grand staircase upwards to find ancient wood carved with dragons, flames, and skies, all flickering with candlelight.

He continued up the stairs, and I sighed, shuffling after him. We took a left and followed the hallway down to an inconspicuous door. He opened it before stepping to the side and motioning forward, but a dark spiral staircase was all that was inside.

I slowly shifted my gaze to him, my eyes narrow. "No."

"Yes."

"No," I bit out again.

He finally looked at me, his silver eyes blazing. "*Yes.*"

"Who are you?" I hissed, rage bubbling out of me in the form of tears.

My eyes and throat burned, and his expression somehow simultaneously softened and hardened—maybe one after the other, but it happened so quickly, I couldn't distinguish them. Shaking my head, I clutched my skirts in a huff and began the climb. His footsteps echoed behind mine as we ascended, and I had the sudden urge to turn and push him back down them.

My thighs burned when I reached the top, my breathing labored. The door at the top was already propped open to reveal a simple room with a bed, two chairs, and a fireplace.

"This is a keep," I breathed. He might as well have punched me in the gut. I swiveled to him, a tear sliding down my cheek, a scowl twisting my mouth. "This is a keep!"

His jaw clenched, his gaze tracking the tear as it slid down my face until it fell to the floor. "You are not a prisoner, Elora. You can come and go as you please."

Another tear fell, and he didn't miss it either. "Who are you?" I asked again, barely above a whisper, and staggered back until the backs of my thighs hit the bed, shaking my head. "You are a lie. *Wryn* is a lie."

His fists clenched at his sides, the pitter-patter of rain filling the tense silence between us.

"I..." He started but stopped, the unfinished thought followed by the sound of footsteps. "Feel free to explore, as this is your home now too."

My eyes snapped to him as he stepped over the threshold to the staircase, his back to me. He should have apologized. I should have said everything I wanted to for the last day. There was so much to be said, from both sides, yet *nothing* was being said.

We had never had a problem communicating before, but something had shifted between us. Long gone were the days of easy friendship I had come to adore, but I couldn't understand how *so much* had changed.

What happened?

So much to be said, yet all I did was snatch the closest pillow and throw it as hard as I could. "*Not* my home."

His next step landed hard as he stumbled when the pillow struck him in the back of the head, but he didn't turn. He merely looked to where the small cushion lay on the step beside him and continued down without another word.

He ignored me *again*. He was *still* actively ignoring me, and not only did it enrage me, it hurt me.

My chest hurt in every way: aching, slicing, tightening. I didn't know what I wanted or expected him to do, but not that. I wanted him to show some kind of emotion, even if it was irritation.

Why—*how* did he feel nothing at all, after years of friendship? He knew me so well, better than anyone, and even though he may have lied about his name and title, I felt like I knew him too.

We were friends, true friends, before he left me high and dry for six long months. He surprised me for my birthday, touched and kissed and licked me in ways no one else ever had, then disappeared for six months, only to pull this?

It made no sense at all. It was as if he couldn't decide what he...

And then, like a lightning bolt of realization, it hit me. Wryn, sweet Wryn, had called me brave because I wore my heart on my sleeve.

Why else would he call me that if not for the fact that he didn't—couldn't?

Did he feel nothing, or did he feel...everything?

I heard step after step as he descended, each one fraying my nerves further and further until I couldn't take it any longer. Before I could think better of it, I jumped up and ran to the door.

"Wryn," I shouted.

His steps paused.

"We *were* friends once, right?"

I waited and waited for a response, starting to doubt he was even in the staircase any longer. Perhaps his steps ceased because he exited. Perhaps—

"Yes," he replied so quietly, it sounded as if only the echo of it against the stone walls reached me.

My heart lurched, my eyes darting around aimlessly. "Then, why did you take me? Why are you doing this?"

No more steps had been taken. "What is it that I'm doing, Elora?"

Heat flushed my neck and face. "What are you doing?" I repeated back at him, my eyes bulging. "What are you doing?"

I descended the staircase quickly, my heart thumping so hard, I could feel it in my throat. I nearly ran down the stairs until I saw him, eyes closed and reclining against the stone. My feet slowed before coming to a halt.

"What am I doing?" he said again, like his thoughts were merely escaping him.

"I don't think you know what you're doing," I whispered. He opened his eyes, tilting his face to me. "For some unfathomable reason I don't think I'll ever truly know, and maybe you don't either, you took me, and now, you have no idea what to actually *do* with me. Talk to me, then avoid me. Lead me to the keep, then tell me I'm not a prisoner. You have no idea what you're doing, do you?"

His gaze, for the first time in days, roamed over my face and drank me in the way he used to. He savored every line and curve, every freckle, and it deepened the blush in my cheeks, but I didn't look away. I couldn't as I waited on bated breath for his next words.

"I haven't a damned clue, sun ray."

My jaw fell slack, my breath leaving me in a whoosh. He

pushed off the wall to descend the last few steps, and I let
him go.

For now.

*I'm here, because he wants me here, whether he admits that to
anyone, namely himself, or not.*

A subtle smile curved my lips.

* * *

I HAD DECIDED if this was to be my home, I would make myself at
home.

After a quick nap, of course.

The sun was still high when I woke, so I strolled down the
stairs and through the halls. I supposed I should be scared or at
least timid, but I felt neither. Surprisingly, I felt...welcomed.

The staff seemed utterly uninterested in me, not bothering
with a second glance in my direction as I passed by, but the
castle itself felt warm and homey, the floor lined with colorful
rugs and candles lighting each hallway and room.

I explored the library but didn't spend too much time there.
Books weren't my preferred form of distraction.

When I passed a dining room—large with a wall of windows
overlooking the sea and a long, oak table in the center—I knew I
must be getting close to what I truly sought.

I hurried to the door right past it and knocked, leaning my
ear to the wood to listen. Hearing no response, I pushed the
door open slowly. A wide grin spread across my face, and giddy
excitement bubbled up my throat in the form of uncontrollable
giggles.

The kitchen.

I stepped in and shut the door behind me, leaning on the
door as I covered my mouth and studied the room. It was much
more than I expected, even larger than the one Mother and I

baked in, but what caught my immediate attention was the odd-looking box in the corner. My fingertips trailed along the wooden counter top as I strolled over and lifted the lid, gasping when a wave of icy air hit me.

Ice?

The inner walls of the box were frozen, the bottom packed full of ingredients: milk, eggs, fruits, vegetables, all kept fresh.

"Genius," I mumbled under my breath. This had to be one of my favorite uses of magic I'd ever seen.

After closing it gently, I turned to the nearby cabinets and found bag after bag of flour and sugar alongside several jars of honey.

I lifted one of the jars and held it to the sunlight beaming through the window. It flooded the room with a yellow glow, and my excitement dissipated. So much honey and sugar—Godrick's dream.

The jar clinked faintly as I set it back on the wooden shelf before closing the cabinet and turning to recline on the counter with a deep breath.

Roughly a week had passed, so they would be back home by now. Normally, we'd be having our annual night of cards, wine, and pastries. We always did when we arrived home from travel; it was our tradition. I wondered if they still played. I hoped so.

My heart ached the more I thought about them until my gaze fell to the unlit fireplace. An idea struck me, and my grin returned tenfold.

I darted out the door and straight to the library.

Parchment and quills were spread along the center of one table. I quietly pulled a chair out and took a seat to write letter after letter. I wrote one for each of them, three total, with at least a dozen discarded papers crumbled and tossed in the bin.

When I was satisfied, I smiled, feeling a flutter of nerves in my chest as I folded the letters one at a time. Standing, I searched for the closest fireplace and found one already lit.

I walked over, said the necessary words, and tossed them in, where they disappeared in a puff of black smoke.

They wouldn't know how to write back, but at least I could talk to them when I wanted. A one way conversation was better than nothing at all. I wanted them to know I was okay and safe, that they could live without worry for me. They needed to know I loved them, regardless of how much time or mileage was between us. They were my family then, and they still were now.

Filled with a new lightness, I took a deep breath, turned, and headed back toward the kitchen, but halted when I spotted Iaso leaving her chambers with an empty bag in tow.

Biting my lip, I clasped my hands behind my back and strolled over. "Where ya going?"

She gasped and jumped, chuckling with a hand over her chest. "Good Goddess, you scared me. I'm heading for the village."

My eyes widened, and I lifted a brow, suppressing my growing grin. I didn't know what had gotten into me today, but after my realization with Wryn and a nap, I felt...good. More than that, I felt hopeful, and that was the best of feelings, like being washed in warm sunshine.

She eyed me knowingly. "Care to join me?"

"I thought you'd never ask," I replied and slid my arm into hers.

She glanced down at it before a grin slowly spread across her face, her golden eyes twinkling as they met mine again. "I think we'll be fast friends."

"The fastest." I nodded.

The hallways echoed our laughter as we left—a welcomed reminder of the way the hallways overflowed with it at home, but instead of nostalgia sweeping through me, a sense of belonging settled in my chest.

17

Vaelor

I set my empty glass on the bar, the clank barely audible over the bustling tavern. The bone chandeliers overhead were lit, the flickering growing stronger as the sun sank on the horizon, shifting the room from glowing orange to soft shadows.

Orrys met my gaze, his snakes stationary along his neck and arms as he grinned and gave a quick wave. His partner, Correnyk, was also behind the bar, passing out drinks at lightning speed, his laugh loud and rambunctious—an interesting sight, considering he was a warrior, both tall and muscular.

Orrys strolled over and swiped a bottle from under the counter before tipping it upside down to pour the brown liquid in my glass. He filled it much more than was customary, but I was thankful.

"What number is this now? Three? Four?" He lifted a dark brow, his one-sided smile growing curious.

"Six," I replied flatly, and both of his brows shot up.

"What's got you in knots today?" He set the bottle down and

reached under the bar to pull out a glass of his own which he filled and sipped from.

"Not a what." I took a long drag and relished the burn as the whiskey slid down my throat. "A who."

"Interesting," Orrys said. "I've never known you to be bothered by anything, much less any*one*."

"I know," I replied.

Problems only existed to be solved, and I understood that, which allowed me the ability to step back and look at it from every angle. Every problem had a solution.

But this? *She* wasn't a problem. She was the solution, and *I* was the problem. How could I even begin to solve a problem that resided in my own deep-rooted faults? How could I view that objectively and with a level head? I wasn't even sure I wanted to be solved or fixed or whatever the fuck I needed.

Damn it all.

I took another long drink from the glass, swallowing once, twice, three times, and then, it was empty.

Orrys whistled and wiped the bar with his rag. "Whoever tied those knots must be an expert," he whispered with a laugh, "because you're inexplicably bound."

I glared at him, but he merely laughed again before joining Correnyk's side to tend to the rest of their many patrons.

The more I thought about his words, however, the more a laugh bubbled in my chest until I couldn't contain it any longer. I dropped my forehead to my palm, my elbow rested on the bar as my chest shook with silent laughter.

She was so far from an expert in tying knots that she couldn't even tie a horse to a tree, but he was right. She sure had me thoroughly bound. My hands were nearly tied behind my back at this point, and perhaps it was the alcohol swimming in my veins, but I almost wanted to cave. It *almost* felt like I was fighting a losing battle.

We'd been here less than a day, and she'd already managed to see straight through my feeble attempts. In that stairwell, I'd wanted to crawl under a rock when she *looked* at me, like she'd seen through my skull and into to my mind, freely reading my thoughts like they were hers for the taking.

I didn't know what or how or when, but *something* clicked for her in that damned keep. I watched the shift in her expression when it registered for her, and I knew she knew something about me that maybe I didn't even understand.

I didn't like it. I didn't like being read like an open book by this small, fragile human—this delicate, kind, loving human woman. But of course, she could read me, because she *saw* people. She saw souls, not strangers or the potential for hurt or doubt.

She saw each and every person in the best possible light, because she lived for now. She lived to love and be loved. She'd told me that once.

"Nothing is certain, so why be afraid? Someone could love you as deeply as they could hurt you, and I choose to be loved. The rest can go to hell, because I won't accept it, and neither should you."

Like the epitome of naivety, I had chosen to reply with: *"I derive my expectations from experience, Elora. I envy your hope, although I fear it may be based in your own innocence."*

Where was my so-called experience now when I needed it most? I felt a twinge of embarrassment even recalling the letter, because she so clearly outmatched me in this situation.

Here I was, running away from her with my tail tucked between my legs, all because I was *scared*.

She could live with her heart while I had to live with my brain...but I hadn't when I was Wryn, not with her. I had allowed her optimism to bleed into me during our yearly meetings. I smiled with her and shoved the fear from my heart so her laughter and bravery could fill it, if only for those few hours

—*because* it was only a few hours. I could pretend to be something, someone I wasn't.

When I was Wryn, I was an artist. I was free.

My heart ached deeply to be that fearless person. I wanted to be free. I wanted to travel with her and paint every landscape we passed through. I wanted to sketch her expression over and over, a different version for every emotion. I wanted to see the light in her sky-blue eyes when she saw the infinite stars, when she saw the Silver Hollow and the Marsh for the first time. I wanted to see her awe when she walked through Canyon and ran her fingers over every trinket laid out on the tables.

I wanted to be free, but I couldn't be. This was my sacrifice. I was an artistic soul shoved into the role of a king, and I had changed everything about myself to be the best possible ruler.

Where I was carefree, I became rules and safety.

Where I was impulsive, I became steady.

Where I was Wryn, I became Vaelor.

I became the man Ravaryn needed, because I had to. Because they deserved it. These people had been through enough after the War of Brothers, and I wanted—needed to offer them peace. *I* wanted peace.

So, that was what I did: poured myself into my kingdom until there was nothing left. I might have lost bits and pieces of myself along the way, but I'd always accepted that, because they were given to my people.

But she made me want to be selfish.

I was being rational, logical, in an attempt to correct the mistake I'd made. My people were thousands, and I was only one. One life sacrificed for a kingdom. It was a sacrifice I had agreed to hundreds of years ago and one I would not falter in, even now.

If I could be nothing but a king, then I couldn't also be hers.

I couldn't be selfish.

But damn it all, I almost wanted to be.

What then, though? If I were to give in, I'd only be subjecting myself to inevitable pain. That deep, aching reminder had been etched into my chest over two hundred years ago—unyielding, unending, unfading.

I was bound to my fear the way she was bound to her love. Two sides of the same coin, destined to be near but never touching, never one, never whole.

We were destined for *almost.*

Releasing a deep sigh, I lifted my head from my palm, only to take another long draw of whiskey, because when I truly thought about it, I would be selfish no matter what choice I made. I could be selfish and love her, or I could be selfish and not love her. No matter which way I looked at it, *someone* would be left with a little less of me.

Loud, familiar giggling reached my ears then, snapping me from my inebriated thoughts, and my heart sank so low, I thought it might have hit my stomach. I knew before I turned who I'd find, but what I didn't expect was quite literally everything else.

Time slowed around me, and my sight narrowed to her, my shining beacon.

Arm in arm with Iaso, she was no longer in trousers, or even one of her gowns from Auryna. No, this dress was undeniably Fae. Made of soft, flowing emerald silk and free of any kind of corset, it looked to be tied around her waist before two strips reached up over her breasts and tied at the back of her neck, while many more strips fell down to sway around her legs.

It revealed more of her skin than I'd ever seen, her shoulders and chest bare to unveil cascading freckles, and I knew if she turned, I'd be able to follow those same freckles down her bare spine.

Her hair—Goddess, her damned hair—was long and loose,

caressing her waist with soft waves. Her pale cheeks were tinted pink like she'd been in the sun just a minute too long.

But it was her smile that enraptured me most—wide and genuine. I wished it was directed at me like it had been so many times before.

Breathtaking. Literally, as I sucked in a deep gulp of air like I'd forgotten to breathe the moment I laid eyes on her. Time resumed, the chatter of people and beginning of the next song fading back into existence.

Who would've thought a human could fall so into place in a Fae tavern?

Although, fall into place wasn't exactly the right terminology, because she didn't blend in in the slightest. I didn't know if Elora had ever been able to blend in anywhere.

I highly doubted it.

Minutes passed, hours, perhaps days, and my eyes hadn't left her. I'd reclined back on the bar, glass of whiskey in hand, mouth tilted up in a smirk.

Two mugs of caramel mead, and Elora was a goner. Her skin was flushed as she danced with Iaso and a few other women, swaying her hips to the beat of the music, moving more sensually than I'd ever seen.

While one hand took a shot glass from Iaso, her other slid along her hips, her waist, her chest. A sheen of sweat had formed along her spine, bare to me from her Fae dress, and I found myself wanting to lick a trail up to her neck.

I took a large gulp of whiskey and adjusted myself.

Then, she glanced over her shoulder, looking directly at me as she downed her shot and fucking *winked.*

The little nymph knew I was watching her.

I slid off the stool and disappeared into the crowd around her. I kept my eyes on her and caught her expression when she realized I'd moved.

She looked around for a moment before turning back to Iaso with a shrug and a smile. Closing her eyes, she tilted her head back, her hands sliding into her hair as her hips resumed their infernal swaying again.

Fucking spellbinding is what it is—what she is.

I might have had more whiskey than blood running through my veins tonight, because it was making my every decision with no regard for tomorrow. The moment Iaso walked away, I stepped into Elora from behind. She gasped as my hands slipped around her waist, one trailing upward between her breasts, my thumb grazing her nipple.

Her chest rose and fell quickly, but when she realized it was me, she relaxed and moved her hips again, against mine, purposefully, slowly, teasing.

I ran a thumb along her bottom lip before slipping it into her mouth. She squeaked, and I opened her mouth wider, enjoying the sight as blood rushed into her already flushed cheeks.

Goddess, I want to do so many things to this damned mouth.

"Dear, sweet Elora, if you wanted to put on a show, all you had to was ask." Her breath hitched, and I bit back a groan as I slipped my thumb from her lips to wrap my hand around her throat and pull her flush with my chest. "You'd put on such a pretty show, wouldn't you?"

Her skin was hot beneath my touch, and I nipped her throat before releasing her and stepping off to the side. She didn't spin around or look for me. Instead, she merely stood there, dazed, eyes wide and lips parted, until Iaso returned with another round of shots for them. Elora took both, one after the other.

Iaso's laugh reached my ears, and I grinned to myself as I made my way back to the bar.

Before I even had the chance to order another drink, a letter materialized in my fist. I closed my eyes, exhaling slowly before glancing left and right and unfolding it.

One woman. Two children.

Blackburn, south of Main. Small house, black
door.

Drunk and unconscious. Wielder of large flames.

I crushed the letter in my fist as a pulse of energy sizzled down my forearm to consume the evidence. The parchment immediately caught fire, and I dropped it to the stone floor to stomp out the flames under my boot, leaving an indistinguishable blackened smudge.

As I strode around the bar to the back exit, I pulled a vial from my pocket and downed Iaso's cure to clear my senses as much as it could, even knowing the alcohol would burn out of my system the second lightning took my form.

With one last long glance at Elora, I watched as she held her hand up so Iaso could spin beneath it to the quickening music, despite that Iaso was over six inches taller and had to duck each time with Elora standing on her tiptoes to reach as high as she could.

Their faces were so painfully happy and content, my heart ached when I had to pull my gaze away.

I stepped out behind the tavern, and the door slammed shut behind me, cutting off the sounds from inside. A storm brewed unnaturally quickly overhead, black and heavy against the already darkening sky. Lightning raced across the horizon, and I knew without a doubt, it'd be seen in the skies above Blackburn—my calling card to let them know help was coming.

When the lightning came close, I stuck my hand into the air and disappeared into it with my destination in mind.

It didn't take long to find the house after I was dropped in Blackburn. The mother clutched her children, covering them both with a large coat as they stood outside under the overhang of their cottage to avoid the rain.

When she heard my approach, her face snapped in my direction before crumbling in relief. A sob broke from her lips, and she tightened her hold on her children, her legs wobbling until she fell to her knees and buried her face in their chests.

I sprinted over and placed a hand on her shoulder. She lifted her gaze to me, igniting a newfound rage in my chest. Rain pounded against the wooden roof, the dull roar loud enough to drown out the relentless rumbling thunder.

The same wind whistling through the nearby trees whipped her hair around her, but the dim light from inside illuminated her face enough for me to see why I'd been summoned. She was bruised, swollen, and bleeding in some places.

My eyes flitted to her children: two girls, no older than six, with their hair crudely cut to the scalp. Their eyes, while not bruised like their mother's, were red and blood-shot like they'd been sobbing.

My heart broke, shattered, and burned for them.

I dropped to one knee and tilted my head to the side as one girl peeked around her mother's arm—which I now noticed bore a blackened handprint on her bare forearm, blistered and bubbled.

For such a young child, her warm brown eyes looked tired.

I offered her a gentle smile and extended a hand slowly. "What do you say we get you three out of here, hmm?"

She eyed it cautiously, edging backwards, but her mom held her in place before moving her hands to their cheeks.

With one palm on each of them, her eyes flitted back and forth between their tear-stained faces, a tear of her own falling to drip onto her tattered dress as she forced a shaky smile. "He'll take us to safety, baby. All of us."

"All of us?" the one with brown eyes asked and peeked at her shy sister.

The smaller one's blue eyes rounded, her lip beginning to tremble again. "I-I don't want us all to come. Just us three, Mama. Not him. Not Daddy. H-he can stay and sleep."

"No," I interjected, my throat tight and burning. "Not Daddy. Just you three, and I'm going to take you somewhere beautiful, where you can frolic in the flowers and eat pastries and play and swim all day."

A choked sound left their mother, a hand flying to cover her mouth as she met my gaze. She nodded fiercely, her one and only word barely audible but desperate. "Please."

"Hold onto them." She wrapped an arm around each of their shoulders and pulled them into her embrace. They both wrapped their tiny arms around her waist tightly as I stepped in front of them to wrap mine around them as well. I grabbed their mother's wrists on either side to enforce the hold. "Don't let go, no matter what happens or how you feel. Keep contact with me. No matter what. Do you understand?"

She nodded with the determination of a mother—fierce and protective.

"This is not going to feel good. They'll probably fall unconscious when we drop, but it's normal, all right? It happens every time with children this small."

She nodded again, swallowing hard.

"I *will* get you to safety, and he will never touch you again."

Then, it all happened within seconds.

Lightning struck me in the back, and I strained, holding onto them as tightly as I could to pull them with me. Energy consumed our forms within the same second that I urged another bolt to strike the thatch roof of the house. Flames burst to life and raced down the main beams. The bastard would be dead in minutes. Wielder of flames or not, no one was impervious to smoke inhalation, and he was too inebriated to get himself out.

Not three seconds later, we dropped at the estate outside Rainsmyre, all soaked to the bone and trembling. The girls fell limp to the ground, their mother gasping as she caved to her knees. She gently checked each of their faces and laid her head on their chests one at a time to listen for heartbeats before swiveling to the right and retching.

I staggered on my feet, the world spinning. For a moment, grass became sky, the sky falling below me, and I staggered before my hands and knees hit the ground with a thud.

Black crept into my vision, my skin growing cold, but a hand gripped my chin to tilt my head back and held a vial to my lips. I swallowed its contents gratefully, knowing it would be Iaso's tonic to refill my magic's well as much as possible.

"Thank you...Drak," I mumbled breathlessly as I rolled onto my back and laid flat on the cool grass with my arms out to the side. I took slow, even breaths to steady the world around me.

"Thank *you,* Vaelor. I'll bring you another soon," he replied, but his sights had already turned to his new residents. He extended a hand to the woman, who took it cautiously, and pulled her to her feet. "Welcome to the Sanctuary."

Another form came into view, sprinting around the estate. He halted before us and braced his hands on his hips, his bare chest heaving with each ragged breath. "Need any help?"

"May we carry your girls to your room?" Drak asked gently, slouching at the shoulders to appear less threatening, but it didn't do much; it never did. He towered over men, his red-black wings massive. "They may not wake for some time."

She worried her bottom lip, her forehead creasing, but she nodded. Drak slid his hand beneath the neck and knees of the older girl while the young man did the same for the smaller one.

His back was revealed to me, the two vertical scars between his shoulder blades reflecting silver under the moonlight.

"You're safe now," one of the men whispered, but ringing in my ears made it impossible to distinguish which.

When they stepped away, I shifted my gaze to the dark expanse above, dreaming of blue skies and cinnamon and apples. Thousands of stars twinkled before multiplying and fading into nothingness as I slipped further under.

When it was impossible to keep them open any longer, I closed my eyes, vaguely hearing the others along with the sound of a door clicking open.

"My name is Drakyth."

"And my name is Adon."

The door shut, and the world went black.

18

Elora

The hallways were surprisingly empty, open windows casting the stone in a silver haze.

It'd rained day and night, shifting between pounding and drizzling repeatedly until everything was drenched and gray.

I hadn't seen Wryn since he'd surprised me in the tavern and disappeared for the rest of the night, but I wasn't exactly looking either. He'd clearly been drunk off his ass that night; otherwise, he never would have done what he did. Still, I couldn't deny that I liked it. Liquid courage or not, Wryn's hands on me again felt *damn* good.

At this point, I wasn't sure what I wanted to say when I saw him, or what I wanted him to say, but I knew one thing for certain—I needed him to say *something*. I could hardly hold anything in, and there he was, holding *everything* in.

What would he do if I bumped into him at this very moment? Would he miraculously speak to me? Or would he turn on his heel and stride away?

I couldn't promise I wouldn't throw the closest thing within reach if he did the latter. His avoidance of me got so under my skin, I couldn't think rationally.

Wryn, though, he thought and considered. He mulled over his actions and traced every possible path like another one of his paintings, each varying outcome another line marked onto parchment for him to study and explore.

That was only one of the many things that made him a great king.

I started and gasped when lightning cracked over the ocean and flashed through the closest window. My heart pounding, I strolled over to rest my elbows on the windowsill and watch, wondering if these were Wryn's storms—I hoped not. I didn't know how his magic worked, but something in my gut told me rain wasn't a good sign. Perhaps he was sad or angry or upset. Maybe all three.

How could rain mean any other emotion? Certainly not happy, in any case.

"Vaelor Wrynwood," I whispered and winced slightly. "Wryn." A loud laugh bubbled in my throat. "Wryn, the ruler of the apple orchard and many other things, it seems."

He'd told me that once, that his name meant little ruler. When I'd had asked him what he ruled, he carefully evaded the truth—ever the careful one. The cautious one. The one who looked at every situation from every angle while I... Goddess above, I'd been oblivious.

What had he thought of me in those moments? Had he considered me naive?

The laugh died, heat creeping up my cheeks. I had been, but he hadn't given me any reason to doubt him—not one that I knew of at the time, anyway. Trust had always been my first instinct, a foolish trait, but mine nonetheless. I didn't want it to have to be earned when my heart told me to give it freely.

I *chose* to be optimistic. Everything in life was uncertain, and nothing was guaranteed—my blood parents were proof of that —so why bother with fear? The future was inevitable, our fate inked into the fabric of our souls, so why bother worrying about what was unavoidable?

Fear shrunk the vast world down to one familiar yet exhausting cage. Yes, those metal bars locked in place around a distrustful heart might prevent pain, but they also prevented excitement and love and freedom. They prevented *life.*

Heavy wind whipped the hair away from my face, sending a shiver down my spine, and I sucked in a breath, rubbing my hands along my arms as goosebumps pricked.

The ocean below thrashed, foaming and angry. Poking my head out farther, I glanced down to watch the waves crash on the cliff face, but instead found a ledge and...

I squinted, standing on my tip toes to push farther through the window. With my top half out, arms gripping the windowsill, and toes dangling, I tilted my head to see a massive opening in the castle wall one floor below me. Ancient columns carved of shining, black stone were the only barriers between the outside world and whatever room lay within.

My mind traced a path through the castle that would lead to that mysterious room when lightning cracked again, striking that very ledge and electrifying the air. My hair tickled and stood on end like the air itself might shock me, but it was over as fast as it began.

I jolted with a shriek, and like my worst fucking nightmare, my hands slipped. My ribs hit the stone, knocking the air from my lungs, and I gasped painfully before my entire body tipped forward. It seemed to happen in slow motion, my stomach, my hips, my legs, even my feet, and then, I was falling into open air.

Stone. Not water.

My hands covered my face, my scream ripping from my throat.

Hit the stone. Hit the ledge.

Anything but cold water.

But I hit neither.

Instead, I landed in strong arms.

I wheezed. The arms, while softer than stone, still knocked whatever breath remained from my lungs. *I'm going to faint.*

"Open your eyes, sun ray," a warm and soothing voice said.

I hadn't realized my eyes were scrunched until they flung open at his words to meet two blazing silver irises—more than blazing. Glowing?

Crackling, like lightning.

In fact, with each pulse of his irises, another bolt lit the stormy sea.

"I don't even want to ask how that just happened," he muttered, turning to walk inside. "Goddess, you could have killed yourself." His feet stopped as he looked down at me, eyes wide. "You...weren't, were you?"

"No, it was an accident," I replied, my voice as breathless it felt. "That was you—the lightning, right? Where did you come fro..." The questions died on my tongue when he strode inside, and I took in the chamber. It was massive, the ceiling carved with hundreds of dragons and a towering fireplace in the corner made of the same black stone as the columns I'd seen from the floor above.

My jaw slack, I patted him on the chest and squirmed to be put down, but he did the opposite. His grip tightened around me, and my heart lurched into my throat when the scruff along his chin tickled my neck.

"What are you doing?" I squealed and shoved at his chest. "Put me down."

"You smell..." His eyes were closed as he inhaled deeply,

sending a wave of chills over my skin and uncomfortable flutters through my belly. "Fuck, you smell *good.*"

His eyes snapped open, the heat in them nearly searing me on the spot. I gasped and jerked my head back before leaning forward again.

"What is wrong with you?" I whispered, studying his eyes as they crackled. I had never seen them do this before; he never once allowed them to shine when he was just Wryn, but they were...beautiful, mesmerizing even.

As if he realized what he was doing, he dropped me like I'd burned him. I landed on my feet, jerking a hand out to grab his arm before I fell on my ass.

"Go, Elora. Go before I—" He shook his head. "*Go.*"

My feet didn't move an inch as I crossed my arms over my chest and cocked a brow. "Before you what?"

His gaze crawled up to meet mine again, blazing a trail along my skin. "You're playing a dangerous game."

My heart fluttered, instantly intrigued.

So it seemed I *did* want to push, but only because he looked to be on the edge. Of what, I wasn't sure, but I was going to find out.

A smile curved my lips. "I like games."

That wasn't a lie. I did like a challenge, and right now, Wryn's waning restraint was the most irresistible challenge I'd ever encountered. I wanted to crack it and see what poured from him. Would it be words? Fears? An explanation? Lust? His hands on my skin—or rather, his tongue?

I wasn't sure what we were on the cusp of, but I desperately wanted to find out.

His jaw clenched along with his fists. His entire body was laced with restraint, muscles tense, his gaze averted. He took a step back, but I matched it with one of my own.

"Elora," he warned. "Steel yourself."

Did he...Did he really just say that?

Something rushed through my veins, straightening my spine. Anger? Shock? The need to push harder?

I stepped toward him with my hands clasped behind my back until we were close enough that his warm scent invaded my lungs—leather and sea storms.

Stifling a laugh, I knocked on the center of his chest. "Is that what you call this? Steel?"

He still didn't look at me, his body so taut, so utterly still, I wondered if he was holding his breath.

"Why should I *steel* myself?" I flattened my hand on his chest, feeling his racing pulse beneath my palm. "Perhaps you should melt instead."

A muscle ticked in his jaw—the first crack in that impenetrable exterior.

Walking around him, I lightly trailed my fingertip across his chest and over his shoulder to his back before standing on my toes to whisper, "Don't tell me the mighty king of Ravaryn is afraid of losing to a measly human woman?"

A pained groan reverberated through his chest before he whirled around so quickly, I stumbled back a step, liquid heat pouring through my veins and pooling in my core.

He matched my step, his entire demeanor changed, no longer the tightly leashed man. No, I'd shattered his restraint, if only temporarily, and that shot a satisfying thrill through me.

His head tilted to the side as he inhaled deeply once again. "I have never in my life smelled something so delectable as your cunt dripping for me."

All that satisfaction drained from me in an instant, and he had me on my metaphorical back foot. My cheeks flushed furiously. Hell, it felt like my entire body flushed.

He couldn't...smell me, could he? *How* could he smell me?

My brows furrowed. "You can't..."

"Oh, I can," he purred, slinking ever closer.

"How?" I took another step back. "That's not a Fae thing, and you're not a shifter."

My heart raced when he didn't reply, and we continued this tense dance. I would take a step back for him to match, but I could feel the wind from the storm on my back, my hair whipping. A faint mist fell over us, tiny droplets clinging to his hair and skin.

We were approaching the ledge.

"*How?*" I asked again, the excitement from before replaced with urgency. This wasn't right. It wasn't normal, and the sinking in my gut told me the answer would change things—or at least me. Maybe even us.

His mouth curved into a knowing smirk. "Don't tell me the measly human woman is afraid now."

This wasn't Wryn, not as I knew him. I clenched my jaw and tilted my chin up, my spine rod straight.

"Aw, don't steel yourself now, dear, sweet Elora. Don't you think it's a bit too late for that?"

My heart pounded painfully, something akin to fear urging it on. Although, fear didn't feel quite right. Not as my body heated under his gaze, the mist coating my skin the only thing keeping me from bursting into flames.

I had wanted to provoke him for this exact reaction—to reveal every dark desire he kept so carefully guarded. I wanted to see what he was hiding. I wanted the man who shoved me against the wall and devoured me like he was starved and I was his favorite meal.

My fingers laced around my throat absentmindedly, replacing where his hand had been all those months ago. His eyes darkened when they fell to my neck like he could see straight into my mind.

I wanted him to do a great many things with that devilish

mouth, those hands, those fingers. My eyes slid down to his arms, his soaked sleeves rolled to his elbows to reveal the veins pulsing over muscle. My eyes locked on his hands when he clenched and unclenched his fists, and my mouth went dry.

His dark chuckle was all I heard as I took one last step back. Rain pelted my skin when my heel met with nothing. I tipped back, but he lurched forward to grab my hand and snatched me forward. I hit his chest, and he quickly wrapped an arm around my waist. When I didn't immediately pull away, he took the opportunity and slid a finger under my chin to tilt my face to his.

Our eyes met, his so silver and bright and beautiful, and suddenly, I was tumbling through storms, rain licking my skin while wind kissed my cheeks, clouds caressing and lightning searing.

His hand slid from my chin along my jaw and wound into my hair to cup the back of my head. A light moan threatened to slip past my lips at the simple touch.

His smirk deepened into a grin because he knew.

The bastard knew my fight was gone, and I was... What was I? All I knew was I no longer cared why he could smell my desire, only that he could, because I was *burning,* and I needed his rain to douse the flames.

"I need..." I started, blinking the raindrops from my lashes. My long hair was soaked along with the thin Fae dress, both clinging to my form.

"Sweet sun ray." He combed his fingers through my strands, his other hand sweeping along my waist. "Trust me when I say I know *exactly* what you need."

He lowered his mouth to skim it over the column of my throat, and a moan did fall past my lips then, my eyes falling closed. He was everywhere, touching, tasting, exploring.

"More," I breathed. "I need more."

"More?" His smile was nearly audible. "What more could you want, sun ray?"

I gasped when he nipped at my earlobe and a hand cupped the nape of my neck, forcing my head to fall back and grant him more access.

The rain had stopped, leaving humidity and thick air to cling to our skin instead, steam rising from the ledge when a few beams of sunlight washed over us.

He kissed my neck, my jaw, my chin, my cheek. "Do you want my mouth?"

I nodded breathlessly.

He kissed my lips, and I whimpered into his mouth, earning an approving groan from him. He broke the kiss long enough to ask, "My hands?"

I nodded again, but none of that was enough. I wanted all of him, every single stiffening inch that nudged against my stomach when I arched into him.

He *wanted* me. That simple fact alone skyrocketed my confidence—and my pulse, thumping wildly. My hands found his waist and explored the hard muscle beneath his sopping shirt. I slid my fingers beneath the open buttons above his chest, and he shivered when my fingers brushed his skin.

"Your cock," I whispered into his mouth.

His hands tightened, his fist knotting in my hair to rip my head back, the one on my waist gripping hard enough to bruise.

I hoped it did. I wanted his mark on my skin—proof of his shattered self-control.

His eyes blazed, angry and lacking *any* restraint. Excitement thrummed in my lower belly, and I squirmed, my thighs pressing together when the burn in my core worsened.

"I will *not* take you because of the bond," he grated. "When I fuck you, and I will, it will be *me*. Nothing else. When I finally sink my cock in you, sun ray, I want to *savor* the sweet little cunt I've craved for four long years."

My heart stopped. I went limp in his hold, my hands falling away from him, my head pulling back an inch. "Bond?" My eyes bulged. "Four years?"

I staggered back, my balance swaying and arms flinging out to the side when I met the ledge again. He attempted to steady me, but I jerked my arm away from him.

"Did you say...*four years?*" I wasn't sure what emotion swirled in my chest. Anger? Not quite. Shock? Absolutely.

My cheeks heated. We'd never explicitly talked about this; he still didn't know I saw him the year before we met. The twinge of embarrassment at watching him for hours but never revealing myself had always prevented me from telling him.

But if he was saying four... "You saw me there before, didn't you?"

I didn't have to clarify or elaborate. His answering smile told me he understood exactly what I meant.

He tilted his head and stepped closer to twirl his fingers through my soaked tresses. "I wanted to touch your hair so badly, to see if it'd burn my skin like the flames it resembled."

My chest fluttered, and I swallowed hard. "Does it?"

His eyes flashed to mine. "Yes."

My lips parted, my breath leaving me in a whoosh, only to be replaced by his scent once again.

"Yes, I've been burning in your fire for so very long."

My tongue swiped along my lips, and he didn't miss the movement. He watched intently as I pulled my lower lip between my teeth. With a sigh, I released it to say, "Three years ago, I saw you in the orchard."

His fingers stilled in my hair. "Three years ago?"

"Yes. I saw you waiting for someone, and I just..." I dropped my gaze to his chest, unable to look him in the eyes. "I watched you."

His hand gripped my chin and forced me to look at him.

"You...watched *me*?" I couldn't read his expression, what emotion lay behind it, but he didn't react with disgust or even disapproval like I'd thought he might.

"It looked like you were waiting for someone, and I let curiosity get the better of me. I wanted to see who you were waiting on, but then..." Dear Goddess, I wanted to bury my face in my hands, but he held firm.

"Then she never showed," he whispered.

Unwarranted jealousy twisted in my gut, and my lips pressed into a flat line. *So it was a she.* "No, she never showed."

He stared incredulously for an uncomfortably long time. My eyes flitted around us, to everything but his intense stare.

Then he *laughed.*

The sound grated my nerves. I yanked my jaw from his hand and moved to stalk around him, but he caught me by the waist and swiveled me back to him before I could take another breath, leaving us chest to chest as he clicked his tongue.

"Don't pull away from me just yet, sun ray."

"Don't laugh at me," I gritted out, narrowing my eyes at him.

He shook his head, another faint laugh leaving him.

"So help me, Wryn, if you don't stop laughing, I'm going to throw you off this damned cliff." I jerked my hand out and pointed a finger to the edge, merely a few feet away.

When I looked to him, though, truly *looked,* my anger simmered and dissipated. I hadn't seen his smile so simple and genuine since he was just Wryn, since that night of the ball. I hadn't realized how much I'd missed seeing it until now.

I wanted to go back so badly, back to the easy friendship and laughs and lack of expectations. The letters and yearly meetings allowed him to open up for some reason like the miles between us dampened his fear.

I hadn't realized how much I missed him—*this* him, the one who wasn't fighting like my presence was the root cause of all his problems.

His hand found my cheek again, his touch gentle and warm. I leaned into it and closed my eyes as my soul screamed for my friend. I missed him so damned badly, and he hadn't been that person in so long. Not in six long months.

"I was waiting for *you*," he whispered.

My eyes snapped open. "What?"

"I'd seen you there the year before, four years ago now. I went back to see you." His laugh started again, bubbling and growing. "I was waiting for you, and you watched me from across the orchard."

My hand flew to my mouth when my laugh joined his, but my eyes burned, my throat tight. "*What?*"

Both of his palms rested on my cheeks as we laughed together, hot tears rolling down. He wiped them away with his thumbs and pressed a light kiss to my lips—tender in a way he'd never been.

"I miss you," I mumbled against his mouth, more tears falling. I slowly crumbled in his hold, and he wrapped a sturdy arm around my waist when my knees trembled.

"I miss you, too," he replied.

I couldn't stop the next words as they poured from the crack in my heart. "If you don't *want* me, then at least be my friend again. You were my best friend once, and I miss that person. The ignoring and avoiding and lying and—"

"Stop." His smile faltered, his chest heaving with a deep exhale. His touch fell away when he took a step back.

Please. I lifted a hand toward him. *Please don't run again.*

But I didn't want him to stay because I wanted him to. I

wanted him to stay because he couldn't bear to leave, and this was clearly not that, so I dropped my arm, letting it hang limply at my side.

Clouds thickened again, blotting out whatever sunlight had managed to break through. Rain drizzled, but I didn't move. This was the closest I would get to him—his soft touch of rain, even if it was in his own sadness.

"I'll always be your friend, Elora, but I *do* want you, and that's the problem."

He strode through the open chamber with his back to me, and I let him go, but not before shouting over the rain, "If you ever decide to be brave...be brave with me."

He stumbled a step and paused, his fists clenching and unclenching at his sides, but he didn't turn.

I didn't think he would.

His storms were all that remained when he left me alone on the ledge, but we'd made progress, and that was all I could let myself focus on.

He does want me. I'd known that, and I assumed he knew too, regardless of his endless denial, but now it was out there. He'd said it.

I inhaled slowly and forced a smile on my face, despite the ache in my chest and burning eyes.

One day, I would watch him walk away for the last time. I just desperately hoped that when that day came, it was because he chose to stay and not because he never returned.

19

Vaelor

I had admitted I wanted her seven days ago. Seven painfully long days ago, I watched her brilliant blue eyes shift from excitement to disappointment.

Then, I'd left her again, and the disgusting pit in my gut was torturous, reforming each and every time I thought of her and that night.

The damned tonic I used to keep the mate bond in check had burned off when I traveled through the lightning. I should have anticipated that, although it didn't truly matter. I couldn't have let her fall to her death. I had to catch her, regardless of the tonic.

And damn it all, if she didn't pick up on the change right away. She *wanted* to push. She wanted me to snap, and I nearly had. I had nearly given her everything she wanted.

And for some unfathomable reason, what she wanted was...me.

Fuck.

I dropped my head to my hand, the midday sunshine bright

overhead and bouncing off the waves. Sea mist sprayed over us, cool against my heated skin.

"Hey, you all right?" Ewan shouted.

I immediately dropped my hand to adjust the back stay traveler. The doublehanders required two people to steer, no more and no less, hence why Ewan and I had favored them for centuries—our favorite getaway.

We pulled and leaned, shifting the sails in the direction of the island.

When the boat slid onto the sand, we grabbed our bags, hopped off, and dragged it onto shore before finding the hidden staircase in the cliff face. Already tired and sweating, we moved slower than usual but eventually made it to the top.

The grassy plateau was utterly beautiful, an ocean of green, pastel flowers rippling in the breeze like waves. The sparring circle held the only patch of dirt with no vegetation, surrounded by boulders, created by my father all those years ago.

We dropped our bags onto the ground, and Ewan's clanked with metal on metal. I swiveled around to gawk at it before meeting his gaze and lifting a brow. With one sword strapped to my hip, I thought I'd already been outnumbered by the two strapped to his.

He shrugged. "I didn't know what we'd want to practice with today."

"So, what? You brought it all?"

He laughed and plopped down on a stone to pull out a canteen. "Pretty much."

After he took a swig, he tossed it to me, and I swiped it out of the air. I lifted it to my lips and took a long pull before choking on the burning liquid. "What the—"

Ewan stifled a laugh. "Oh, did you think that was water?"

"What is it?" It wasn't the Fae rum we normally drank, that was certain.

"Some combination of tea and whiskey." He shuffled through his bag and pulled out a fucking mace, the ball of it tipped with shinning spikes. He spun his wrist to swing it in a circle before facing me with a growing smile. "I honestly couldn't tell ya."

My eyes widened; I wasn't sure they'd ever been wider. "What do you mean you couldn't tell me?"

He shrugged again and said, "Iaso," as if that was answer enough.

I didn't have the chance to question further or choke him like I wanted to, because he swung at me. I rolled to the side, noticing another handle sticking out of his massive bag. I should've realized what he brought based on size alone.

I snatched the weapon and pulled out a... "Machete? Really?"

"We always practice swords." When he swung this time, I blocked, my blade cutting into the wooden shaft of his weapon. We were mere inches from each other, and he wiggled his brows. "This is infinitely more exciting."

I cracked a smile. He wasn't wrong.

* * *

SWEAT ROLLED DOWN MY FOREHEAD, and I wiped it away with the back of my hand, taking another swig of the mysterious concoction from Iaso. After tasting it a few times, I'd come to the conclusion that the tea mixed in was the tonic she used to prevent the aftereffects of alcohol, which was...genius, to say the least.

I handed the canteen back to Ewan. "I'm leaving for Rainsmyre this evening." A decision I hadn't made until this past hour.

He cocked a brow at me. "To see Drakyth?"

I nodded. Ewan didn't know of the Sanctuary, and neither did Iaso. I'd kept my mouth sealed, and while Iaso made the multitude of tonics for Drak to keep on hand, she didn't know why. She'd stopped asking questions when she realized I wasn't going to answer them.

I didn't want them involved in any way. It was dangerous—for the people who stayed there and my small family—so Drakyth and I had decided long ago that it would stay between the two of us. Even he was reluctant to be involved until I brought Adon home.

I still remembered that day like it was yesterday.

It'd been raining, the streets of Rainsmyre muddy, the stench of decaying fish and filth thick in the humid air. Iaso, Ewan, and I had been there to follow through with our "happy plan," as Iaso had named it.

During our visit months prior, she'd grown uneasy, covering her mouth and nose as we walked through the town, but not because of the fishing village stench we all abhorred. No, she'd said she smelled misery, the heavy scent of depression clinging to the people. After that, it didn't take us long to concoct our "happy plan." We were going to bring music and *good* food to the town—good being the operative word. We couldn't change their careers or how laborious it was, but we could offer them this much.

It took a few months of hashing out details with the taverns, inns, and housing owners, but eventually, we came to an agreement, and that was why we'd been there that day: to set up free housing for all musicians and kick start the cook-off, in the hopes that Rainsmyre would find the best of the best and become a music hot spot. The top three winners of the cook-off would be guaranteed a well-paying job at the most frequented taverns, and a stipend had been established to pay for housing for a full year—for both chefs and musicians—so they could get settled.

The people needed a touch of happiness; they needed something, anything, to offset the hard labor and lift their spirits.

After countless meetings and several handshakes, I'd left to meet with Drakyth, excusing myself for a walk while Ewan and Iaso went to supper. I headed toward Drak's estate and took the path that followed the sea, which coincidentally went right by the piers.

I stopped dead in my tracks when I spotted a group of children hiding under one of the taller boardwalks. They sat in the sand, faint giggling coming from the younger ones while the older ones rolled marbles or dice. A few chewed on the parts of fish that fishermen disposed of, but all of the kids were skin and bone, their clothing tattered and dirty.

Orphans, either by death or abandonment.

One, no older than thirteen, met my gaze, his eyes a reddish brown and hair black. His expression turned from confusion to shock, and he dropped the fish bones in his hands to bolt. For some reason I didn't quite understand, I sprinted after him. He ran straight for the most crowded street, weaving through people and behind carts, like he knew it all like the back of his hand.

He glanced over his shoulder as he knocked over a bucket of apples. They rolled onto the ground and into the street, echoed by the shouts of a few people falling to their asses.

I merely jumped over them, narrowly avoiding hitting the cart owner as I pulled a large gold coin from my pocket and tossed it to him. "Sorry!"

He caught it gratefully and shot me a toothless smile, waving it in the air as he turned to his companions. They grumbled, vocalizing their wish that it'd been their carts to overturn, but their voices faded out as I followed the kid into a damned alleyway, spotting him halfway up the far wall. I sprinted faster, but the stones were slick with algae and runoff, and I nearly slipped more than once.

He hooked his arm over the top of the wall and flashed me a smile when he pulled himself up.

"Who are you?" I shouted. Only a few more feet. "Damn it all, why are you running?"

"Why are you chasing, *Vaelor*?" he replied as he swung a leg over, emphasizing my name.

He knew who I was. That gave me pause, and I nearly lost my footing, but not quite. As he went to throw himself over, I grabbed his ankle and jerked.

He yelled as he flipped off the wall, but I caught him before he hit the ground, breathing heavily. My legs burned, my heart racing.

"Goddess, I need to train more," I mumbled under my breath. I held onto him by his skinny bicep as he jerked and thrashed, his eyes growing wilder with each passing second. "I'll let you go if you promise not to run again."

His mouth twisted into a scowl. "I won't promise that. You are *not* taking me to him or anywhere."

And then, he spit.

I flinched when it hit my cheek, utterly surprised he would do that knowing who I was. I wiped it off with my sleeve and laughed. "Boy, you're lucky I'm not the malicious type."

He didn't say anything. Instead, he held his chin high and mouth pressed into a flat line.

I shook my head and released him. He paused, glanced at my hand, and bolted for the wall again. I laughed and grabbed the back of his shirt to jerk him back down. "I'm not taking you anywhere."

"Then why did you chase me?" he asked, ripping his shirt

from my grasp. He didn't take off, though, and that felt like progress.

"Why did you run?"

His eyes flashed to mine, something akin to confusion behind them as his brows furrowed. "No reason."

I tilted my head. He had to be twelve or thirteen, but it was hard to tell with how starved he was, his cheeks and eyes sunken in, his black hair mussed and filthy. But his eyes... They were a muddy red, like dried blood encapsulated in his irises.

My heart raced again for a different reason, my mind trying to count back years. "How old are you, boy?"

He took a half step back, cautious once again. "Why?"

I grabbed his arm, and he jerked against it, baring his teeth at me. "How old?"

"Thirteen!" he shouted.

My breath left me, my hand falling away. He took another step back and rubbed at his arm, but still eyed me wearily.

"Come with me," I whispered, a newfound urgency winding through me.

"No." His spine stiffened as he shook his head. His gaze darted around the empty alleyway like he was looking for another escape route. "No, you said you wouldn't take me anywhere."

"How would you like a real meal?" I cocked a brow. His eyes flashed back to mine, and I knew I had him. "Cake, even?"

He licked his cracked lips and paused for a moment before dropping his eyes. His fight left him in one long exhale, his shoulders slouching and arms hanging limply. "Are you..." He met my gaze again. "Are you going to hurt me?"

My heart sank. Those were merely the words of a kid who'd been fighting for entirely too long.

I dropped to one knee so I wasn't towering over him when I promised, "*No one* will hurt you."

He looked like he wanted to believe me, a faint hopefulness sparking in his tired eyes, but distrust won out. Even so, he nodded and followed me to Drakyth's house.

When Drak exited his front door, wings on full display, the kid gasped and sprinted in the opposite direction.

I remained where I was and hooked a thumb over my shoulder at him when Drak's eyes flitted to me. "That's your grandson."

Drakyth went completely still. "Adrastus' son?"

I nodded. "He's thirteen."

His eyes bulged and darted to the kid still sprinting toward the tree line, and he shot into the air with a thrust of his wings. He didn't have to go far, though. When Drak dropped in front of him, the kid snapped to the side in an attempt to dodge him to no avail.

Drakyth grabbed both of his shoulders to hold him at arm's length and studied his face before pulling him into a hug, Drak's massive form swallowing him whole. The boy froze, his arms hanging at his sides.

"Stop fighting, kid. You're home," Drak whispered. He tightened his hold. "You're home."

The kid, slowly and hesitantly, wrapped one arm around Drak, followed by the other. "My name is Adon."

"I've waited a very long time to meet you, Adon. My name is Drakyth, but you can call me whatever you want: Drak, bastard, old man...Grandpa."

That was the day Drakyth became the makeshift dad to twelve kids, and thus, the Sanctuary was born. Soon, his estate became the safe haven for all Fae who needed it—namely women and children, but the occasional male too, although we'd found men were less willing to accept help.

It was Ravaryn's best kept secret, safe guarded by a seemingly ferocious Draig, hidden deep within the forest, and funded by the crown.

Ewan shoved my shoulder. "Still in there, V?"

I blinked rapidly and turned to find him offering me the canteen once again. "Yep, still here."

"Why are you really going to Rainsmyre? For some reason, I don't find Drakyth to be one who enjoys visitors."

To get out of here. To be as far away from Elora as possible. To distract myself with work. "To check in on the musicians. They seem to be settling in well enough, though, their numbers growing daily. We're currently paying for fifteen different apartments, and from what I've been told, music plays somewhere every night."

When his grin grew, mine matched.

He nodded slowly. "Iaso's brilliant plan is working, then."

"It would seem so."

"And you need to go check on them?" He lifted a brow.

My smile faltered, and I took the canteen from him to drink a large gulp, wincing at the taste.

"No other reason?" he asked.

I narrowed my eyes at him. "No other reason."

He held his hands up in front of him, his answering laugh grating my nerves. "Right, right. Okay, sure. If that's what you want to go with."

I smacked the back of his head, and his face whipped to me a second before he tackled me off the back of the stone we sat upon.

20

Elora

The wooden chair creaked under my weight as I joined Iaso at her table, overlooking the greenhouse and the sunrise behind it.

A multitude of tiny vials lined her table, each filled with a green liquid. They looked similar to the tonic she'd given me in Auryna, but smelled very different, more bitter and much stronger.

"Did you know who I was at the tavern that night?" I asked, filling another vial and sliding the cork in.

She smiled and glanced up from her mortar. "Yes."

"How? Or better yet, why? Did you know he was going to do what he did the next day?"

She dropped her eyes back to her mixture, grinding it with the pestle. "Surprisingly, no." She took a deep breath and set the bowl on the table. "Can I be truthful with you?"

I eyed her, trepidation settling in my gut. I wasn't sure if I wanted to hear her next words, but I couldn't have said anything but "Yes," if I wanted to.

She worried her lip like she was considering whether she should say anything at all.

"Well, go on. Spit it out," I urged with a nervous chuckle.

"Vaelor was going to tell you everything, because he knew you'd be at the meeting, and then... Then, he was going to say goodbye. Permanently."

The vial slipped from my hands and shattered on the floor, but I didn't pull my gaze from hers. I didn't move, and neither did she.

"He knew you would see him in the meeting, as Godrick had alerted him he was bringing another daughter this year, and Vaelor didn't want you to find out by seeing him in the meeting. That's why he asked you to meet him."

Was my heart still beating? Or was there a storm in my chest, crackling and pounding and relentless?

"I can't breathe," I whispered under my breath.

I had been angry with him for not telling me, for taking me, for so many things, but to know he planned to end our friendship once and for all hurt infinitely more.

Never seeing his face again.

Never hearing his laugh.

Never seeing him lost in his artwork.

Never smelling his scent, the one that comforted my soul in a way nothing else ever had.

Never...

My eyes fell to the table, my hand to my chest. "Never?"

Iaso stood and walked around the table before kneeling carefully to avoid the glass and placing her hands on my knees. Warmth flowed from her palms, and I gasped, shoving the chair back.

I didn't want comfort. I didn't want air. I didn't want Wryn to *leave me.*

Had I been pursuing someone who hadn't truly wanted me? Or was his want merely lust?

Mine wasn't. I didn't just want his body. I wanted his soul, his mind, his heart. I wanted his artistic eyes to gaze at me for eternity. I wanted to bake for him until he was soft under my touch, so we could laugh and joke about the days when he was all muscle. I wanted to be at his side until our skin wrinkled and the sun set over the world and—

Whatever air remained in my lungs left, and I was gasping, hyperventilating.

My skin would wrinkle much sooner than his.

I would be dust among the stars by the time he ever wrinkled at all. I hadn't thought of that before, because I was *foolish* —hopelessly, foolishly optimistic. Naive. But surely he had.

Of course, Wryn was afraid. If he let himself love me, he *would* lose me.

"*I envy your hope, although I fear it may be based in your own innocence.*"

He was right. He was always right, and this whole thing had been a lapse in judgment on his part. I had taken that lapse for something it wasn't, for something it could never be.

He did want me, and that was the problem. He'd said that, and I thought I had understood, but now... Now, I truly understood the depth of his fear and hesitation.

"Breathe," Iaso whispered.

"I...cannot." My ribs were tight, my lungs empty. I sucked in breath after strangled breath, but no air came.

I had been pushing him to inevitable heartbreak, and he knew that but had never told me. Maybe he thought I knew, because what sane person wouldn't realize that? I was setting him up for devastation.

I will not do that to him. I cannot. "I cannot. I cannot. I cannot."

"Calm, child. Calm." Iaso's palms grew hot, and I jerked to my feet.

"No." I waved my hand through the air. "No, I cannot be calm right now."

I turned to stride out of the room, only to find Alden standing in the doorway. His skin was wrinkled.

"How old are you?" I asked out of desperation, feeling my world await his answer.

"771," he replied.

My world crumbled. My knees buckled and cracked on the stone floor as I fell to them, the blood draining from my face.

Hundreds of years.

He would live hundreds of years without me, even if I lived to be the oldest human in existence.

His expression turned soft, rich with an empathy I didn't want when he stepped forward, his gray robes swishing around his feet. There was no way he could know why I'd asked, but he looked at me like he read my thoughts.

When his forehead wrinkled with his furrowed brows, I suddenly felt nothing at all, my eyes unfocused, looking but no longer seeing as they sank to the stone floor.

I wondered if Wryn's skin would wrinkle that way when he reached such an old age. Would he grow his hair long? Would it turn white? Would he wear ridiculous robes like an old maestor?

Would he remember me after he'd lived such a long and full life? I hoped his life was full—full of love and bravery and laughter. I hoped he learned to let down his walls for someone. I hoped *someone* would teach him it was okay to be afraid as long as he didn't let it win.

Fear could never win. He needed to know that, even if it wasn't me who convinced him.

"What does the bond mean?" The words left me of their own volition, my mouth moving faster than my brain or any other part of my body—all except my heart, which still pounded painfully against its tightening cage.

I'd been waiting for Wryn to explain it. I didn't *want* to hear it from anyone else, but for some unfathomable reason, my soul needed to know here and now.

Iaso's hands landed on my shoulders, warm once again. "The bond?"

"Wryn can smell me because of some bond. Why?"

They were both silent for too long, but I couldn't be bothered to lift my eyes. It didn't truly matter, I supposed, because I would only last a small fraction of Wryn's life.

"That's not our place to say," Alden whispered.

"Iaso," I pleaded, resting my hand on top of hers. "I need to know. Please."

"The mate bond," she said in a rush.

A tear slid down my cheek, and I swore I heard a crack emanate from my heart. The lack of air and my unwillingness to search for it caught up with me, stars sparking in my vision.

The mate bond?

"I didn't know humans could even have mates," I whispered, too low for them to hear. "I don't feel it. I don't feel anything."

The fire flared in the fireplace then, and we all gasped. A letter floated gently from the flames, drifting as if on a breeze until it landed in front of me. A strangled laugh left me—I certainly did not feel entirely safe right now.

What would have happened had I felt so unsafe that the letter couldn't find me? Would it have gone to my chambers? My home in Auryna? To Wryn himself, the one who had always made me feel the safest?

No, I thought, *it wouldn't go to him.*

My hands trembled when I leaned forward to lift it. It was small, the edges burned like the spell had been a little butchered but said well enough to still work.

I unfolded it and recognized the handwriting immediately. A choked sob broke from me, tears welling in my eyes thick enough to blur the words into unreadable scribbles, so I clutched the letter to my chest and sat back on my heels.

Alden sat on the floor in front of me and crossed his legs —an almost goofy sight, as he was every bit as tall as Wryn, and his knees stuck high in the air. A smile curved my lips when I glanced up at him, my cheeks soaked with rolling tears.

His eyes were warm, albeit concerned. "Who is it from?"

Another cry slipped from my lips, still curved into a growing grin.

"Child, spit it out before we assume the worst." Iaso joined Alden on the floor in front of me.

I wiped my eyes with my palms and looked down at the letter once again.

"My sister." I took a slow breath to calm my frayed nerves. "It's from my sister, Alivia."

Dear El,

Vaelor found me in the Capitol and taught me the spell. He told me we could communicate this way, so I really, really hope it works. He made me practice a few times, and I think I accidentally burned through an entire book of parchment before it went anywhere, but you know the old language isn't my strong suit. I also asked if this made me a witch, but he only laughed and brushed it off, so... if you could answer that in your next letter, that'd be great.

All I have to say today is I miss you. I

miss you so much, it hurts, but I think about what you may be doing or seeing or experiencing and... Well, don't come back, El. Live. Be happy and explore this new world and take this opportunity and make it <u>yours</u>.

Remember this above all else: you are the light in a very dark world, and I know that you brighten the land wherever you go. Never lose that. Never dim. Never dull.

Shine, and live.

I love you with every bone in my damned body. Write me back <u>soon</u>.

Love,
Alivia, the poor girl you left behind

P.S. Out of pure curiosity, have you and Vaelor... touched, if you know what I mean? (This is the part where I wink and nudge you with my elbow, and you swat me away, but I <u>have</u> to know. You must tell me.) At the very least, is he less boring when he's so infatuated with you?

"Wryn taught her to send letters through the flames?" I asked aloud, more out of confusion than anything. My head snapped up. "He's not here?"

Iaso and Alden glanced to each other, a soft smile gracing Iaso's full lips before she turned to me. "No, he left for Rains-myre last night. Although, it would appear he made a detour."

I should be thankful he did. I *was* thankful, but I couldn't stop the hurt that wound through my chest. He left without even a goodbye. "How long will he be gone for?"

"He didn't say," Alden answered.

I swallowed hard. Perhaps this was just the beginning of our slow estrangement. It should be. I should take this time to heal and grow apart from him. I should let him live because any time with me would just be...pointless. Perhaps he knew that. Perhaps that was why he left.

"This may be a strange request, but does your family have any cottages anywhere? We used to have a small house to get away to, and I frequented it often." *When I needed to be alone, to think and weep and mourn without others seeing or worrying.*

The last time I'd visited our own cottage, it'd been on the twenty-first anniversary of my parents' death.

Wait. My blood chilled, the parchment in my hand crumpling in my shaking fist. *What day is it?*

Dates flew threw my head, over and over, checking and rechecking. That trip had been on their anniversary a year ago... last week. Five days ago, to be exact.

I'd forgotten their anniversary. An entire day, twenty-four hours, one thousand, four hundred, and forty minutes, the few *seconds* it took for our carriage to go from rolling down the road to crushed and sinking, passed by without a single thought.

Two lives. Two deaths. Two parents.

My parents, forgotten.

Shame slithered through me so viciously, I thought I might expel breakfast right here on Iaso's floor. I braced a hand on my stomach, not letting it show on my face.

I tried not to think of them often, because their loss threatened to pull me under that river again, icy and suffocating and biting. I could still feel the lick of freezing water on my bare skin if I fell too far into the past.

But once a year, I went to our family's cottage alone and

allowed myself to feel every ounce of longing, every ounce of pain and hurt. I let myself grieve the memories that would never be, the hugs I would never feel, the words I would never hear. I mourned the day I would walk down the aisle without them, the day my first child was born and neither of them would hold him or her. I cried for the day my future child asked about their grandparents, and I would finally have to tell the story. They wouldn't be here for their first smile or first laugh or first steps. They would never be here, just like they hadn't been for the last twenty-two years.

Yes, I need to go. I need solitude and the freedom to shatter.

My bottom lip quivered, my throat tight, but I forced a smile on my face so they wouldn't see it. I didn't fear crying or showing emotion in front of others—I never had—but this pain, these tears, were mine. They were raw and deep and sharp, and I wouldn't dare inflict it on anyone else.

Now, at least, I could grieve my parents and Wryn at the same time. On this trip, I could let him go, and then, next year, when I visited the cottage again, it would hurt a little less. Each year would hurt less, I knew that, and eventually, he would join my parents as nothing more than an ache in my chest, uncomfortable but bearable.

Isn't that convenient? I'll knock out two birds with one stone.

Alden smiled, but it, too, was almost sad. "We do, actually. Would you like me to escort you? It's merely a few hours ride."

Iaso's gaze clung to him, her expression unreadable. She tilted her head to the side, placing a hand over his. "It'll be like she's getting to meet her," she whispered, low enough that I could barely understand her. "She would love her, you know."

My stomach sank. They were clearly talking about me, but also someone else, another she.

I didn't ask about her, though, not yet. I couldn't handle his sadness and mine at the same time. "Yes, I would love that, Alden."

21

Elora

The cottage was more of a cabin, made of long logs interconnected at the corners, and tucked away in a clearing bordered on one side by an emerald forest and a shallow sea on the other.

Flowers bloomed in abundance, overgrown plants of every variety and color thriving beneath the warm sun. Green vines crept over the walls, each one speckled with dainty blue blooms and consuming the house like nature had claimed it.

"No one has been here in a very long time," Alden whispered.

I peeked at him to find his expression haunted, his posture slumped. He barely held onto the reins, his horse slowly coming to a stop beneath him.

Wryn may have been a Storm Bringer, blessed by the Goddess, but power like that had to have been helped in part by a mate bond between his parents, right? And if that were the case...where was she?

I glanced back at the cottage, beautiful—and abandoned. It

was clearly adored at some point but now stood neglected, and it haunted Alden. It was hers.

"What was her name?" I asked.

"Ara," he breathed. "Her name was Ara."

The ache burrowed in my chest, and I took a slow, intentional breath. "Was she Wryn's mother?"

"Yes."

I waited for him to say more, but when he didn't, I simply said, "Thank you for sharing her with me."

I couldn't imagine how excruciating it must have been for him to bring me here after so many years, but I *was* grateful. I hoped he knew that.

He turned to me and smiled faintly. "Of course. She would have loved you."

That ache became daggers.

I didn't want her to love me. Her son couldn't.

Inside the house, everything was covered in a layer of dust, but otherwise seemingly untouched. On the right side of the room, a multitude of paintings and sketchpads were scattered over every surface: the tables, chairs, easels, even propped on the windowsill. Canvas after ancient canvas was painted with faces or landscapes. Some even held fruit. The large one reclining on the glass panes held a single fruit tree—an apple tree, dotted with red that had faded to pink.

I found another and another, all depicting a similar tree in different angles. I peeked out the window to find the apple tree behind the house, already speckled with shiny, ripe fruit.

Is this why Wryn had bought the apple orchard? For his mother?

I inhaled a shaky breath, feeling my restraint slip bit by bit as I edged closer to a depiction of a young boy, eyes silver and hair brown, holding the hand of a short woman. I ran my fingers over her, down her blonde hair to the hand that held his, leaving a trail in the dust.

Wryn must have gotten his appreciation for art from her.

My eyes welled with tears. When one broke free to slide down my cheek, I blinked them back and wiped the moisture away, inhaling a shaky breath before turning to find Alden in the kitchen.

He stared at a dead potted plant sitting beneath a different window. Nothing remained but a clump of brown sticks, the dirt dried and cracked.

He lifted a finger to brush a branch, and it practically turned to dust under his light touch. His breath hitched, his chest heaving until his knees caved. He hit the ground, and I didn't move. I didn't run to him or speak or offer condolences, because he didn't need that. He didn't need me. He needed his mate, his love, the mother of his child.

A tear slipped from his eye. "I was waiting on the day you'd grow tired of me."

Silence followed, and he nodded faintly, another tear falling. When he rose to his feet, I swiveled and averted my gaze.

He cleared his throat. "I'm going to stay at the inn in the village we passed through. It's not far, so if you need anything at all, please come find me."

I nodded, unsure what to say, and his footsteps grew distant. He opened the door and chuckled, but it sounded broken, mangled.

"The garden out back seems to be flourishing without its gardener. Take whatever you desire, but if you'd like meat or flour or anything else, there's a shop in town. Just tell them to add the items to my account, and I'll pay before we leave."

"Come back tomorrow?" I asked in a rush but regretted it the moment the question left my lips. Something told me he needed help, though, encouragement or a friend—*some* reason to come back here.

He paused, clearly torn and disinclined.

"Please?"

He exhaled slowly before answering, "Sure."

With that, the soft click of the door closing echoed through the silence, and I shattered right where I was, my heartbreak the only thing I could hear, see, or feel as I collapsed to the floor.

The second my knees hit wood, I dropped my face to my hands and screamed.

I screamed and screamed and screamed. Until my throat shredded and the taste of blood met the back of my tongue. Until my voice was gone and no sound would come. Until I shook with exhaustion. Until the physical pain drowned out the intangible agony.

* * *

SLEEP NEVER CAME.

I shook out the dusty blankets before crawling into the decrepit bed. It creaked and shifted like it might fall out beneath me, but I couldn't be bothered to care. Pulling the blankets up over my shoulders, I laid my head on the rolled-up coat I used as a pillow and stared.

My eyes burned from hours of crying and lack of rest. They begged to be closed, but even when I did, sleep was evasive.

When the sun started to rise, its soft rays of yellow were framed beautifully by the window I stared out of. It lit the ocean beneath it, painting the turquoise water in various shades of yellow, followed by orange and pink, and then the sky and waves were bright blue once again.

I smiled faintly, cuddling under the comforter. No wonder Ara had this bed facing the window. I could imagine no better way to wake than with the rainbow of sunrise.

My poor throat, though, was raw. I could feel my breath sliding in and out, and I feared how it would feel to try to speak. Even a yawn felt like it was splitting my esophagus open.

After crawling out of bed, I pulled on my coat as I found my shoes and tugged them on, stumbling toward the back door as I did so.

The doorknob stuck slightly, and I had to jiggle the door to pull it open, but as soon as I did, crisp air wafted in, bringing the scent of early morning ocean and greenery. I closed my eyes and inhaled slowly, ignoring the ever-present burn in my throat.

I stepped out, closing the door behind me, and wrapped my arms around myself as I sat in a metal chair. Stones had been laid together to make a patio of sorts with several paths branching off to wind through the garden. Closest to the house were flowers but farther out were the fruit trees, bordering the normal tree line. It looked like fruit had fallen to the ground, spread by nature, and sprouted up over the years, so dozens of trees had grown to create a fruit forest—oranges, lemons, and apples.

My heart clenched. So many apples.

I could make an apple pie while we were here. I wondered if Alden would like that.

My eyes closed as I took another slow breath. Why had I asked him to come back? I always, *always* grieved alone.

Footsteps sounded from the right side of the house, and my face whipped in their direction. Alden poked his head around the corner and offered a nervous smile.

He lifted a brown paper sack. "I brought breakfast."

When he came around the corner, I noticed two mugs in his free hand and a kettle tucked in the crook of his elbow, so I hopped up to grab them.

"Th—" I dropped a mug to grab my neck as liquid fire spread through my throat. I would've screamed if that wouldn't have killed me on the spot.

The mug rolled onto the dirt but didn't shatter—thank Goddess. I picked it up and offered Alden an apologetic look, but his eyes were wide and full of concern.

"Are you all right?" he asked, motioning to the seats.

I nodded as we sat and placed everything on the metal table.

"Are you getting sick? Do you need a healer?"

I shook my head and dropped my gaze to the table. He rested a hand over mine as I started to fidget with the cups.

I glanced up reluctantly.

"You...did this, didn't you?" he asked, his eyes boring into mine. "You screamed?"

I wanted to pull away. I wanted to avert my gaze and run and hide. I wanted to force a smile on my face and shake my head no.

But he looked at me like he understood, like he didn't want to be alone in his grief.

So, I nodded once. Just once.

My first admission to another that I still grieved, even if Alden didn't know who it was for. I had never told Alivia or Godrick or Emma, because I didn't want them to hurt for me, so I dealt with it in solitude.

"I've done that before," he muttered and grabbed the kettle. He slowly poured two cups, steam swirling in the cool air between us. "Marshmallow root and white willow bark. Iaso gave me a few bags, told me you may need it."

My eyes bulged, flitting between him and the cups. How had she known? I looped my finger through the mug handle and brought it to my lips, blowing the steam away. I took a hesitant sip, closing my eyes as the warm liquid soothed my throat.

It *was* Iaso, though. Would I expect anything less? She somehow knew what everyone needed all the time. I just hoped someone did the same for her, provided what she needed. Perhaps Ewan was her person.

I took another long sip and made a mental note to be another one of her people. She needed care as much as the rest of us, even if she would never admit it.

She liked lemons, that much I knew from our trip to the market, but she didn't have a tree in her garden. I lifted my gaze to the fruit trees, counting the lemon ones in particular. With four full trees, there were enough lemons to fill an entire backpack full, which I would do, but there, just beneath one, was also a sapling.

I smiled to myself. There had to be a shovel and a pot somewhere among the gardening supplies. We would bring Iaso back a lemon tree for her greenhouse, and I could even make her a lemon custard or perhaps a cake or—

Alden held a cinnamon roll out, taking a bite of his own.

"These were her favorite," he mumbled.

I took it gratefully, stifling a wince as I bit and swallowed. If these were her favorite and he was willing to share with me, then I'd be damned if I didn't eat one with him, for her.

"Can..." I croaked, barely audible despite maximum effort, essentially screaming to make any noise at all, and Goddess be damned, it was painful as hell. "Can you...tell me...about her?"

He looked scared. More than scared—terrified, frozen, torn between bolting or outright telling me no.

I shook my head, ready to say never mind, when he exhaled audibly, his entire body slouching.

"She was...everything. I can't remember what my life was like before her, if it was a life at all, but then she found me. She smiled and I was lost. I would've done anything she asked, and I did most days, mind you." He chuckled, staring over the sea as he took another sip. "She liked to garden and paint, as you can see. She owned this place long before we met. It was her special place... *Our* special place when she finally let me move in. This is where Vaelor was born all those eons ago."

Alden started, and he didn't stop. We eventually smiled, even laughed, as he told me story after story. Ara was kind, much like Alden and Wryn. She enjoyed painting more than sketching, but the ocean was Alden's thing. They both grew up in Nautia, but somehow missed each other for far too long until she saw him entering that very inn we'd visited.

She followed him, grabbed his arm, and swirled him around. He'd been angry at first, caught off guard by the suddenness, but when he turned to find a five-foot-nothing blonde with one green eye and one blue eye smirking up at him, he'd melted on the spot.

"Well, damn it all, I thought I'd never find you," she'd scolded, and he fawned like they were the best words he'd ever heard.

I snorted into my hand as he poured me my third cup of tea, now cooled but still soothing. "Sounds...lovely."

He smiled at me, truly, revealing endearingly crooked teeth —much like Wryn's. "She was. I've never met another like her, but I...I can see why Vaelor took to you." My smile faltered, and I fidgeted with my cup. "You have the same energy as her, the same...hope, the same smile. Not the look per se, but the same infectiousness. Well, hers was. Yours is." He ran his thumb over the rim of his mug. His next words were quiet, vulnerable, and I had to lean forward to hear them. "I haven't talked about her like this since she died."

My lips parted. "Thank you...for telling...me."

He nodded, sniffling when his breath hitched. "She deserves to be talked about, to be shared, but it...hurts, for a lack of a better word, and then I avoided her for so long that I started to feel..."

"Guilty?" I offered, because I knew that feeling too well, and it was heavy, all-consuming.

He met my gaze. "Yes, guilty. Would she feel forgotten? Would she be hurt to know I hadn't said her name aloud in almost a hundred and ninety-seven long years? Would she be disappointed in me?"

His chest rose and fell quickly, his words growing breathless, and I reached a hand over to place atop his.

I shook my head, my lips pressed into a thin line. "Proud." Whatever remained of my voice faded away, and I mouthed the last few words slowly. "*She would be proud of you. For living. For telling me. For loving her.*"

His throat bobbed as he nodded, and he flipped his hand over to hold mine.

I gave him a quick squeeze. "*What would you say to her now, if she were here?*"

"That I love her." He turned to her garden. "I love you, Ara. I've loved you since the moment we met, and that has never wavered. I love you as much today as I did then, and I will until my last breath, your name the final word on my lips. Then, I'll see your beautiful face and never let you go again."

What would I tell my parents? Anything at all? What I would do when I saw them on the other side of the veil...

My smile fell, along with my gaze and heart.

Tears welled in my eyes, because when I finally made it to the other side, I wouldn't recognize them. I wouldn't see their faces and take off running. They would be strangers.

I need to be alone. I was supposed *to be alone.*

I slid my hand back from Alden, but he tightened his grip, refusing to release me. My gaze snapped to his, my brows knitted together.

He leaned over the table a few inches, wrapping his other hand around mine as he said, "You may not be ready yet, but you grieve too. I see it on your face, in your eyes, hear it in your voice, and as you are the *adopted* princess of Godrick, it's not hard to deduce you mourn your parents."

I shook my head, attempting to force a smile on my face, but my lips trembled. A tear escaped to roll down my cheek—a traitorous tear, one for me and my parents, not Alden—and I quickly wiped it away. He released my hand when I jerked it this time, harder.

I stood and strode to the door, my hand on the knob when he said, "I may not have known your parents, but I'm a parent myself, and I can tell you they're proud of you. If you were my child, I know I would be."

My reflection in the window broke me—my mouth hanging open, lips cracked, my eyes red and swollen, brimming with unshed tears and lined by dark circles, my hair knotted in a bun atop my head. I looked like pain, like unhealed grief, and I hated it.

I reared back and punched the glass. It cracked and shattered beneath my knuckles, slicing into my skin, and I gasped—not for me or the blood trickling down the shards, but for Alden, for his mate, for the door they would have opened and closed together so many times.

My cheeks burned, my hands hovering over the broken panes. *What have I done?*

I dropped to the ground to lift the pieces, stacking three in my palm as red dripped onto the stones. *What have I done? What have I done?*

I placed a large piece back where it would go and held it there while I placed another one on top of it. I braced them with my left hand while I picked up another shard with my right. The sharp edge sliced my finger, but I lifted it anyway. More red fell. More red coated the beautiful glass sparkling beneath the morning sun.

More red, more tears.

My legs shook, and I fell to one knee. My entire body shook: my hands, my chest heaving for air, even my eyes. *Fuck, why can't I see?*

My vision was blurred, but I had to fix this damned door.

I lifted another piece, but it slipped from my hand and hit the ground, where it shattered into a hundred tiny, irreparable pieces.

A choked sound left me followed by a cry that ricocheted through my chest and echoed off every facet of my heart, and then I was sobbing. My arms wound around my torso as I fell back, hitting my ass on the stone.

An arm wrapped around my shoulders. He turned and pressed me into his front side, but I didn't release myself. If I did, I feared my heart would break into pieces on the ground. It would join the broken shards—as it should.

His body was wracked with his own cries, but I couldn't stop. I couldn't soothe him or hug him or do anything. I was useless, because I couldn't stop the emotion pouring out of me, no matter how much I wanted to.

I'm sorry. I shook my head, burying my face in his chest. *I'm sorry. I'm sorry.*

The floodgates had opened on twenty-two years of isolated pain. I had finally found a friend who shared that same hurt, and it wanted to be heard, to be seen, to be felt, to be shared.

"It was just glass, Elora. Just glass."

Memories. His memories, and I shattered them.

"The door can be replaced." He sat back and lifted my hand to inspect the injuries. "You cannot be."

22

Vaelor

Drak essentially kicked me out of Rainsmyre after two weeks.

I'd helped out where I could, and we rescued two more Fae—a set of twins, a boy and a girl. We also managed to get eyes on Adrastus' boy, Rogue. He looked to be eleven or twelve, but he carried a sadness in him no child should under-stand. Not all that different to what I saw in Adon when I found him all those years ago, but rescuing this child would start a civil war with a deranged Draig.

And his poor mother...

It'd been a little over thirteen years since his attacks ceased. We were moments from ending him for the good of the realm, days, even. The plan had been laid to catch him off-guard and end his violence once and for all, but then Adrastus disappeared.

For *two* years.

We knew when he'd vanished without a trace, we were too late. We'd missed our opportunity, and worse, he'd found his mate—found and kidnapped. We still tried to find him simply to rescue her, but it took us far too long. By the time we found where he'd settled, she was gone, and his second son had been born.

My gut twisted into guilt-ridden knots as it always did when I thought of them. If we *had* killed Adrastus, that poor woman wouldn't have had to survive him—an impossible task, it seemed. She wouldn't have died, and that boy... He was forced to live with his monster of a father. It wasn't fair to either of them, and it still plagued me, but not as much as it did Drakyth.

It was only a matter of time before the boy outgrew his father, though, then he would be free, and we could swoop in to help. That was what we told ourselves, at least, the lies we tried to convince ourselves with.

In reality, we were watching a father kill his son slowly, in mind and soul before body.

Fuck.

I'd thrown myself into work after we'd returned from that short trip, doing every laborious task I could find—the most time consuming being wood splitting. Hour after hour, day after day, I cut and split, cut and split, cut and split, until Drak declared they had enough to last a year, maybe two.

After that, he shoved me away, leveled the axe at me, and told me to go home before I "ran myself into the ground with the rest of the firewood."

The muscles along my back, shoulders, and arms were sore and tender when I begrudgingly arrived back at Draig Hearth. Ewan was in Nautia for the time being, so I headed for Iaso first. I knocked, but when she didn't answer, I cracked the door open and peeked inside.

Empty.

I strolled to the wall of windows overlooking her greenhouse and found her kneeling in the soft soil, plucking leaves from a small bush. The door was already propped open, so I entered and descended the small staircase.

"No welcome back party?" I asked, forcing a playful tone.

She startled, her voluptuous hair swaying as she turned her head toward me. "Oh, Vaelor, I didn't expect to see you here."

My brows knitted. "In your greenhouse? I always come find you when I return."

She gave me a flat look and dusted her hands off before resting them in her lap. "At Draig Hearth."

"Why?" My steps slowed, my heart racing.

She started to laugh like the answer was obvious, but it died off when I didn't join her. She tilted her head before rising to her feet. "Oh, you don't know yet. All right. Elora isn't here."

I stumbled over my own feet, staggering a step and catching myself on a scrawny tree. "What?"

Did she go back to Auryna? Had she unintentionally just started a...problem between Auryna and Ravaryn?

Did I finally drive a wedge between us?

I swallowed hard against the rising tension in my chest, running my fingers over the thin bark I still leaned on. "Where?"

"Ara's cottage."

Her words could not have caught me more by surprise.

My breath caught in my throat. If she was there, Father had to have taken her. Why? Why would he do that? Why would he go there?

I couldn't imagine what or how he was doing. Would he be lost in the past again? Did he sit and stare at the wood? At the paintings? The garden? Was he eating, sleeping?

"They're doing okay." Iaso picked up her wicker basket and gave me a pat on the shoulder as she strolled by me, leaving bare footprints in the soil. An absent laugh slipped past my lips—Elora would absolutely join Iaso sans shoes. "*Both* of them."

I swiveled around to follow her. "Both?"

She glanced over her shoulder and nodded. "Both."

I let loose a breath of relief before following her back into her chambers. "You've heard from them, then?"

"Elora sent a letter," she replied.

My relief was short lived, replaced by an ugly feeling I wanted to claw out of my chest. She hadn't sent me a letter. We hadn't sent any letters in such a long time, too long, and I knew that was my fault. I ran away all those months ago, and she'd still sent me a letter, then another. I broke our tradition. I hurt her, and she didn't owe me any more letters. She didn't owe me words.

She owed me nothing, and yet she had still been reaching her hand out. She still hadn't given up on me, and what did I do?

I ran. Again.

Fuck, I'm just embarrassing myself at this point. I need...

I need to let her go home.

Iaso sent Elora a short letter, alerting her and Father of my return, but even that sent a pang of jealousy through my gut and a softer wave of nostalgia through my chest.

With that, I bid farewell and promptly left, strolling down the main halls to my chambers, past the breakfast room, down the farthest hall. Once inside, I pricked my finger and slid the droplet of blood onto the carved V hidden behind the clothes in my closet. The door materialized, and I pushed it open, stepped inside my nook, and closed the door behind me.

I released a slow breath, reclining on the door with my eyes closed. She wasn't here. She shouldn't have ever been here in the first place, but now, she wasn't here.

She wasn't in my home. She wasn't with me. I wasn't even sure she was my friend. She'd said she wanted to be, but I'd left her like I always did. Did that still ring true?

Could we be friends again if she went home? Could we go back to the way things were?

I winced and opened my eyes, hitting the wood with a single pound of my fists.

My soul didn't want that. My heart didn't want that. My body for damned sure didn't want that.

The only part of me that wanted to go back to seeing her once a year and hearing her thoughts only through written words was my mind—and even that felt like a lie.

"Damn it all," I muttered. "What *do* I want?"

I didn't have time to answer my own question before a letter materialized in my hand. My heart lurched, begging, pleading, hoping it was from Elora.

When I unfolded the paper, my breath left me in a harsh exhale, forced from my lungs. I slammed my hand on the desk, my vision blackening around the edges, tunneling on one singular word.

Sick.

Elora wanted to stay away for a few more days, because she was sick and didn't want to spread whatever she had.

A tunnel of wind and rain touched down over the ocean, the sky nearly black. A stiff wind blew through the open window, sending the stray papers flying, and I let them.

Canvases fell over. Paints spilled. Charcoal and pencils scattered across the floor.

I could do nothing to stop it.

Sweat rolled down my spine, the walls of the room closing in, and I ripped my shirt off when the room grew too small and I started suffocating.

Suffocating.

Choking.

Coughing.

Visions of a skinny hand covering a blue-tinted mouth as she coughed, her blonde hair dried and brittle, one blue eye, one green—tired and sunken in.

Sick.

Sick.

Sick.

The word echoed in my skull relentlessly, mercilessly.

Elora is sick.

I sprinted to the window and dove from it before lightning even had a chance to strike, but I didn't fall for more than half a second. It caught me like I knew it would, but it was panicked, crackling and sizzling and bright. My energy was everywhere, all at once, and I couldn't narrow my location.

It took too long, far too long, but eventually, I made it to the cottage. I dropped in the back garden, but the storm didn't stop there. Bolt after bolt struck—the ocean, the ground, the forest, an apple tree.

It burst into flames.

Fuck. Anything but the apples.

Rain fell harder, blurring even the cottage from sight as I stalked forward, but at least it soaked the trees.

Elora ripped the back door open and ran outside in nothing but her shift. She was immediately soaked as rain pelted us both, the thin white fabric revealing every part of her.

She glanced around and gasped when she spotted me. Her bare feet splashed through the puddles and mud as she sprinted over, and my steps didn't slow either.

When she halted in front of me, breathing heavily, her expression confused but expectant, I grabbed her arm, and lightning rippled across the sky, echoed in my eyes. The silver light reflected on her pale face, her eyes wide but not afraid.

"What are you doing?" she screamed over the storm, jerking her arm away.

Her voice was *hoarse.*

Terror consumed me so thoroughly, I gasped for breath, my world starting to spin, but it didn't matter. Nothing mattered but Elora, not even the bond flaring in my chest at the lack of tonic. Panic suffocated it, leaving it nearly unnoticeable.

I dragged her to the beach, so I wouldn't accidentally burn the house down when lightning struck again and again and *again.* Uncontrollable.

She fought me the entire way.

"Taking you to Iaso," I ground out through my tightening throat. My chest had never been tighter, the rain doing nothing to douse the fire ravaging my lungs.

"No." She yanked back and slid her arm from my grip, wet and slippery.

"Yes!" I grabbed her wrist and started forward again.

She yanked and yanked, pleading to stay, but she *had* to come. She had to see Iaso. *She had to.* Iaso was the realm's best healer, and she could heal Elora.

Elora could not die.

She screamed. She slapped. She sat on the ground, and still, I dragged her. She kicked at my hand, my legs, anything she could reach.

She can hate me, but she cannot die too.

Flashes of coughing and blood-speckled rags and rasping breaths.

She cannot die.

Fevers and coughing and vomiting.

You cannot die.

No longer did thunder reach my ears, just hacking coughs. Coughing and retching and blood-speckled rags and dry whispers of death. Her last breath. *"Everyone dies."*

Not Elora.

Never Elora.

My foot hit the sand, and I stuck my hand up.

"Vaelor!" she screamed.

The world went still—the rain, wind, lightning, my body, mind, heart. Time itself slowed as she called out my name.

My name.

I lowered my hand slowly but didn't release her as I dropped to my knees and met her gaze, rain still falling but lighter.

"You cannot die too," I whispered, broken and strangled.

"Oh," she breathed, shaking her head fervently. She took my cheeks in her palms. "Oh, Vaelor."

With that, she threw her arms around my neck and squeezed. I couldn't breathe, but that was all right. I hadn't been able to breathe since the moment she sent that letter, and now, she was holding me. Elora held me, and I could feel her chest rising and falling in even breaths, her heart racing in her chest against my bare one.

Alive.

Elora is alive.

I wrapped my arms around her waist and buried my head in the crook of her neck, inhaling cinnamon vanilla. "I can't lose you too."

Her voice cracked when she whispered, "You're not losing me. Not today, not tomorrow, not ever."

"You have to come back to Draig Hearth. Iaso can heal you. She can help. She can—"

"I'm not sick."

I stilled. "What?"

When she started to unwind her arms from around my neck, my first instinct was to hold them there. I wanted to feel her, embrace her, hold her. I wanted *her* to hold *me*.

But she wasn't sick.

Instead of relief finding me, anger poured through my veins.

She moved her hands back to my cheeks. "I didn't want to come back yet, and Iaso had sent me a letter saying you returned. I thought if I..." She shook her head, water dripping from her lashes. "I didn't know hearing I was sick would scare you like this. I didn't think—"

Clenching my jaw, I gripped her wrists and pulled her hands from my face. "No, you didn't *think,* Elora."

She ripped her hands from mine. "I—"

"You *never* think."

I jerked to my feet, and she remained kneeling in the sand, her feet neatly tucked beneath her ass. She was so fucking perfect and it only enraged me further. I wanted to slip my thumb past those full, red lips and feel her warmth. I *wanted* to bend her over my knee until she was a sobbing, wanton mess, slick for my cock while spewing apologies.

But I did neither. "You only feel, and you subject everyone around you to exactly how you feel too."

Her chin trembled for a moment, her throat bobbing before her expression hardened. She slapped the sand before rising to her feet, her entire body on display beneath the soaked white linen.

My gaze fell to the two rose-colored buds revealed by her dress, and every thought in my head came to a screeching halt. I'd never seen her nipples before. I wanted them in my mouth, in my hands, pinched, licked, sucked—

She stepped closer and pointed a finger at me.

"You know what? Sure. Fine. You're right. I do wear every emotion clear as day on my face, but at least I'm not a *coward* like you." She jabbed her finger in the center of my chest over my heart, and my fists clenched at my sides, rage renewed. "I'd rather wear my damned heart on my sleeve than lock it in a cage like yours. You think you're protecting it, being cautious or logical or whatever excuse you tell yourself at the end of the day, but you're not. You're subjecting yourself to permanent heartbreak, permanent loneliness, and it's *sad.*"

She shook her head and took a step back, then another, but

on instinct, my hand jerked out and grabbed her waist. A muscle feathered in her jaw, her chin held high, as I pulled her closer inch by inch.

"Better to be alone than in pain, than to lose someone," I seethed, wanting to grip her tighter, to slide my hands over every soaked inch of her, soft and malleable beneath my touch.

"Is it?" she whispered. "No...No, I don't believe that. I don't even think you believe that. I think you know exactly how miserable it is. I think your soul begs for more, and your mind can't stand it—or just can't accept it."

She gently wrapped her fingers around my wrist and pulled my hand away from her side before stepping away again to distance herself.

My heart thundered, torn between anger, lust, regret, and resignation, between leaving and grabbing her again, between screaming profanities and whispering filthy words that made her cheeks flush.

She tilted her head, her brows furrowing. "I believe its best to have, at the very least, *felt* love and perhaps lose it, too, than to live the life you're choosing." She took another wide step back, and my feet remained planted where they were. "Perhaps this is me losing it now." My throat constricted, my eyes following her feet, counting every step. *She's leaving.* "Perhaps I'm alone in that, in this feeling, but I'm grateful for it regardless, because at least I know I've lived. I'm not chained by fear. I don't *let* myself be chained." Another step. Another. Another. She was too far, her heel touching the yard once again. "I feel sorry for you, Vaelor. I'm sorry that the closest thing you'll ever feel to love is what you put into your kingdom. My only regret is that it cannot love you back. Not in the way I can...could. Not in the way I could have."

My eyes snapped to hers.

She loves me. She's in *love with me.*

She'd said those words before, but I'd been too blinded to

truly hear them, to feel the power in them, and now, she said them in past tense.

She could have loved me.

Could have.

She loved me, and I hurt her.

She loved me, and I left her.

She loved me, and she was walking away, her back to me as she inched closer and closer to that back door. But she wasn't running, not in the way I did. She was leaving, which felt *much* worse. She was giving up.

Why did that damned door feel like more? Like if I let her walk inside and close it behind her that she'd close the door on me, too?

She should. She should leave me out here and slam the door behind her, slam it so hard the glass rattled and frames fell off the wall, because she deserved better. She deserved someone who had never hurt her or taken her for granted, who knew what they wanted outright and didn't fight demons she couldn't see. Hell, I couldn't even see them, but I sure felt them, clawing at the confines of my chest constantly.

Let her go.

She reached the path.

Let her go.

She stepped onto the patio.

Let. Her. Go.

She was within steps of leaving me, leaving us behind.

"No," I whispered. Blood pounding in my ears drowned out the rain, tingling in my veins, panic winding through my chest. "No, no, no."

Before I had a second to consider the repercussions, I sprinted after her. She swiveled on her heel, gasping when I neared her, but I didn't stop. We collided, my hands finding her cheeks as my lips crashed to hers without restraint—with passion, with release, with love.

I didn't hold back. I didn't hide. I didn't repress. I kissed her like she was the moon and I was the sea, like we'd been watching and longing for each other for eons, only to now discover we were within reach. I devoured her like she was the light I was tethered to, the force that pulled me, moved me, because damn it all, she *was*.

She slowly melted, her hands finding my chest, a moan slipping past her lips and into mine. I groaned and deepened everything. One hand slid to her jaw while the other moved to her lower back, pressing her to me so not a single part of her body wasn't touching mine. My tongue slid along the seam of her lips, and she gasped, her mouth parting, and I slipped in.

I wanted *all* of her.

I was tired of fighting. I was tired of being afraid.

I wanted to be brave. With her. Because of her. *Like* her.

I broke the kiss, and her eyes fluttered open to meet mine, her chest heaving. Her body molded to me, and I never wanted her anywhere else. This was where she belonged—in my arms. Today. Tonight. Tomorrow. Forever, in every life, every time, every realm.

"Free me," I whispered as I ran a thumb along her bottom lip. "Free me of this cage, Elora, because I need you."

She smiled, beautiful and radiant and genuine and directed at me. After so long, that damned smile was mine, and my heart sang for it. She lifted her hands back to my cheeks and pulled me down to her as she arched back, drop after raindrop rolling down her face, her hair, her body. My rain consumed her, just as she had consumed me all those years ago.

"You don't need me to free you," she whispered. She pulled my hand from her chin and placed my fingers to the pulse point on her throat. Her heart beat erratically but repeatedly—unending. "Love me and release *yourself.* Love me because we're alive, and this life is meant to be *lived.* Free yourself and live with me, because I need you too, the real you. Not Wryn. Not the cold Vaelor I've known these past few weeks. The one who wrote me letters and taught me how to paint and laughed and shared and surprised me for my birthday. *Love me.*"

It was as if the wool had been pulled from over my eyes, a weight lifted off my chest, like I sucked in air for the first time, because she wasn't asking me to simply love her. She was asking me to stop fighting it and *allow* myself to love her, freely and openly and wildly—the way she deserved.

Everyone dies, but not everyone lives.

I decided, right then and there, within her hold, with her glorious smile and sky-blue eyes and thumping heart, that I *would* live. With her. Because of her. Because even a second of this had to be worth it. It *had* to be. I couldn't imagine anything or anyone ever being more worth it.

I slipped my hand farther around her throat until my entire hand wrapped around it, and I walked her back step by step. Her grin grew devilish, deliciously wicked—the embodiment of temptation.

That was what she had always been, right? Temptation, but I hadn't realized just how much she offered. Lust, yes, but love? Happiness? Freedom?

She offered me the world, and I had the audacity to refuse her. Not anymore. I was done making a fool of myself.

"I do love you, Elora." I kissed her soft lips, her cheek, her jaw. "I've been in love with you since the moment you kicked your shoes off in that damned orchard."

My mouth trailed down her neck to where it met her shoulder, and something sparked within me, hotter than anything I'd ever felt. My chest burned, my cock ached, and my heart felt like it might burst.

Suddenly, I was overwhelmed.

I nipped at her skin, and she gasped, arching farther into me. I bit harder, and her whimper reached my ears. She sank her nails into my back but didn't stop me.

"I want to break your skin, taste you, and fill you with my storms. I want to spark your soul and mark you permanently so the entire realm knows you're mine, and I'm *yours*." Lightning cracked across the sky on that last word. It struck the ground behind me, but I didn't care, and neither did she. She didn't startle or flinch. She didn't even pull her gaze from mine.

Lightning struck again and again as the urge consumed me, and when she nodded, her lips parted, I smirked and ran my thumb along her bottom lip again. "Do you know what that would mean, Elora? Truly?"

She shook her head, waiting on bated breath.

"It would mean you'd never be free of me. No matter how far you go, no matter how many years pass, you would *never* be free, but I would be yours, utterly and completely yours, to hold, to kiss, to use, to fuck, to own."

Slowly, I pulled her dress up and slid my finger up her thigh. She shivered, chills following my touch, but when I reached her cunt, everything turned blistering. Her knees threatened to give out, but I caught her with a groan. She was already soaked.

"But that would also mean you're *mine*. This"—I sank two fingers into her, and she arched with a gasp—"would be mine, today and always. I'll know when you need your *mate*, dear, sweet Elora, and I'll have no objection to fucking you into oblivion every single time I get a hint of your arousal."

I needed her to fully understand before she said yes, because I had a feeling when she unleashed me, I would never be restrained again—not with her.

She wouldn't just be mine. I would be hers, permanently, in more ways than I already was, and damn, did I want that. I wanted her to have me, body, soul, and heart. I wanted to be consumed by her. I wanted to give my damned life to her because she deserved it more.

"I want to be yours, Elora," I whispered. "Will you have me?"

She smirked, looking up and tapping her chin like she had to consider it.

A growl built in my throat, and I tightened my grip around hers, thrusting a third finger into her. "I'd say this needy little cunt wants me *desperately,* sun ray, wouldn't you?"

PART II

THE ENDING

"We would drown together."

23

Elora

Goddess, his *mouth.*

My cheeks heated, but what else could I have done but nod? Because he sure as hell wasn't wrong.

The tightly leashed, respectful Vaelor had disappeared before my very eyes, morphed into this beast of a man, one my body screamed to get *well* acquainted with.

His smile turned devilish, and the blush spread down my neck but didn't stop there. My skin felt too hot, too tight, like if he didn't touch me and douse the flames, I was going to combust.

As if my thoughts were written on my forehead, his hand resumed its motion. When his fingers curled inside me, my eyes threatened to roll back, my legs trembling.

But it wasn't his fingers I wanted tonight—well, not *only* his fingers.

I slid my hand down between us and palmed the front of his trousers, biting back a gasp at the size of him. He ground into my hand with a groan, and the sound wound through me, straight to my core. I clenched around his fingers, and he moved faster.

"Oh..." I moaned, breathless as I continued to stroke his cock through the fabric. "Oh, Goddess."

"Goddess?" he whispered into my neck, sending a wave of chills over my skin. He was everywhere, touching, tasting, feeling, consuming. "Sun ray, if you must call out to a deity, call out *my* name, because I'm the only one who will answer you." He pressed his lips to the hollow of my throat. "The only one who will savor you." Another teasing kiss. "The only one who will feel this cunt around my fingers, my tongue, my cock."

My breath hitched, and his lips found the swell of my breast. *Take it off, rip it, shred it.* I needed the fabric between his mouth and my breasts fucking gone, burned, destroyed.

He gripped the neckline of my thin dress, and I nearly melted when his gaze found mine, molten silver. The corner of his mouth ticked up, and he tore the fabric effortlessly.

I'd never been more thankful to be in a shift than I was at this moment.

With my breasts exposed, he held my gaze as he lowered to his knees and brought my nipple into his warm mouth. A loud moan left my lips of its own volition, my hands tangling in his hair, but he released me too soon. The bud hardened in the chilled air as he kissed his way to the other. "If you must pray, pray to *me,* the king on his knees for you."

"Vaelor..." His name left me on a pant, and Goddess damn me, the heat in his eyes at the sound of it could've brought me to my knees—or burst us both into flames, but fuck, at least we'd die in bliss.

My head fell back to the wall as he licked and sucked and swirled his tongue. I repeated his name over and over, the only word left in my head, breathless and begging—a prayer, as he said. Although, it felt like he was worshiping my body instead, kneeling at my altar while his mouth proved his utmost devotion.

Suddenly, he slipped his fingers from me and slid his hands around my thighs. I yelped when he stood, lifting me with him, and my legs wrapped around his waist on instinct.

A laugh bubbled in my throat. "I could've walked."

He nodded as he opened the back door and stepped over the threshold. "You could've."

Our soaked clothes dripped on the floor as he kicked the door shut and carried me to the bedroom, my heart racing harder with each step. My chest heaved, my nerves frayed but excited.

I wanted this. I wanted him.

Still, nervousness bit at me and he seemed to notice as he laid me gently on the bed. He moved up my body until our faces were mere inches from each other. His head tilted to the side as he slid his hand into my hair, his touch soft as he cupped the nape of my neck.

"I love you," he whispered. "I'm sorry it took me so long to admit that, but damn it all, I do, Elora. I love you so much."

My eyes burned, and I swallowed hard against the rising knot in my throat. My fingers wound in his hair as I replied between kisses, "I love you too."

He braced himself on one hand and lifted up, trailing his fingers down my neck to slide my hair back and reveal the hollow of my throat. "I want to be yours, and I want you to be mine, but I won't mark you without hearing you say the words. I need to know you want this too because it's a choice—*your* choice."

My heart swelled, and a tear slipped down the side of my face. With one palm on his cheek and the other over his hand at my neck, I whispered, "I've wanted you for a very long time, Vaelor, and this is just one more way to have you. I *want* you. I always have and I always will. Please."

His irises crackled, and butterflies released in my belly—hot, tingling, *needy* little butterflies. He licked his lips when I slowly pulled his hand away, and his gaze locked onto my throat. When he lowered, his irises grew brighter, blinding, casting the entire room in silver.

My chest rose and fell quicker with each passing second, and when he skimmed his lips over my skin, I gasped.

"Relax, love," he murmured and kissed the spot again. "Breathe."

I inhaled slowly and tried to relax, but he was about to *bite* me—break my skin with his fucking teeth. How could anyone be calm knowing that? But I couldn't deny how enticing the idea was, how depraved and delicious it sounded.

His teeth grazed along my skin, and I closed my eyes, winding my arms around him. Another breath, and he sank his teeth in with excruciating slowness.

I felt everything, all at once, pain instantly drowned out by ecstasy in its truest form.

My muscles tensed, my mouth falling open and back arching, as his lightning raced through my veins, caressing and claiming every part of me, every inch, before settling in my core and setting me on *fire.*

He growled, his hand lowering between us as he did exactly what I needed. He yanked his trousers off and slid the head of his cock along my soaked entrance. My knees fell to the side, hips lifting, and he pulled his teeth from my skin.

"I can smell you, your need, and my, my..." He clicked his tongue and inhaled deeply before pressing a warm, wet kiss over the stinging wound. He kept teasing his cock at my entrance, teasing and teasing and teasing, and I wanted to fucking scream.

My hips hitched, my nails digging into his back. "Aren't you a needy little thing?"

"Vaelor!" I shouted in frustration, which rewarded me with an inch—a wide, stretching inch that sucked the breath from my lungs.

He let out a slow hum and grabbed my jaw to tilt my face to his, forcing me to meet his molten gaze. His lips were coated in red—*my* red. That should've disturbed me but instead, I felt myself growing impossibly wetter, hotter.

He flashed me a wicked grin and wrapped a hand around my throat as he growled, "Fucking *mine*," then fused his mouth to mine, his tongue and cock thrusting into me all at once.

He swallowed my moan, and I was *lost.*

"Yours," I panted, helpless to say anything else. My legs wrapped around his back, and he slid his hands under my ass to lift me while he sat back, pulling me with him. When he eased me down onto his cock, my head fell back as my breath left me. I was impossibly full. "So...*yours.*"

With my hands rested on his shoulders and knees planted on either side of his thighs, I lifted myself and slid back down on him, taking every inch, and the sound that left him was so deliciously erotic, stars sparked in my vision.

I wanted more of *that.* I wanted to hear him, watch him fall apart beneath me. I wanted him to lose control, to explode, to destroy me for anyone else. I wanted to destroy *him* for anyone else, to make him so utterly mine that no one else existed.

My eyes fell to his mouth, still coated in my blood, the mark his teeth left still stinging, and I grinned.

He already was mine. Permanently.

"Fuck me, love." His large hands swallowed my waist as he started to move me again; I hadn't even realized I'd stopped. "Let me watch you chase your pleasure, because you look fucking magnificent doing it."

I repeated the motion on his cock, and he hit that sensitive spot inside me, sending a shock wave through my body. Once I got the angle right, I did exactly what he commanded—chased my damn pleasure with the cock I'd wanted for way too long.

"This is mine." I held the side of his face, running my thumb along his mouth. I held his gaze, lips parted and hips rolling, and he smirked. "My mouth." I sank on his length, taking him as deep as I could. "My cock." I kissed him and held him there, tasting and licking and nibbling until I wound tighter. My breaths grew uneven, movements sloppy. "My mate."

He groaned and wound an arm around my waist. In one swift motion, he flipped us so I was on my back again, and he didn't miss a beat. When he thrust into me, it was powerful, much harder *and* faster than my movements.

Better, I decided. *Fucking better.*

With one brutal thrust after the other, I shattered around him—stars and flames and tidal waves, all of it.

I fell apart, clenching around his cock as he pounded into me and dragged out my orgasm as long as possible. Only when I was quivering and gasping beneath him did he wrap his fingers around my throat and hammer into my overly sensitive pussy. I screamed at the onslaught of pleasure, feeling oddly free—more so than I ever had before. This had all been my choice. More so, I fought for this, for him, for us.

He held my life in his hands, lungs burning and vision darkening, but I'd never felt more satisfied, more safe, more loved.

Fuck, I love him.

When I thought I couldn't handle anymore, like I would truly crumble beneath him, he sealed his mouth to mine and slowed, throbbing in me as he came. I sucked in breath after breath, inhaling his scent so deeply, it was all I could smell: warm sea storms, leather, and...sex.

He pressed his forehead to mine, breathing heavily, and

cupped my cheek, his touch soft like summer rain. "Are you all right, love?"

I chuckled, despite the warmth blooming in my chest. "More than all right, *love.*"

He smiled, his lopsided grin too handsome, too perfect.

* * *

I WAS BLISSFULLY warm as Vaelor ran a finger up and down my arm, my leg thrown over his, my head on his chest. After cleaning up and drinking a tea that Vaelor said would prevent a pregnancy, we'd laid down and hadn't moved in hours, felt no need to. No sleep came, but I didn't need that either.

I'd been waiting years for this, to be able to hold him, bask in him, simply be with him with no restraints, time or otherwise, and I wanted to savor it.

Now, the room was silvery blue with early morning moonlight, hazy and calm, the waves lapping along the shore outside the open window. The sun would rise soon, but I wasn't ready for our little bubble to pop. In this moment, we could've been the only people in existence.

"Can I...tell you about my parents?" I wasn't sure why the words bubbled up, why they needed to be said right now, ruining our moment of peace, but I couldn't stop them.

His hand stilled before resuming. "Of course."

"Not Godrick and Emma." I bit my lip and fought the urge to bury my face in my hands. "My blood parents."

He gave my arm a light squeeze. "I knew who you meant."

"I-I've never told anyone before." My cheeks burned, and I closed my eyes, pressing my ear to his chest. His heart beat steadily, and I took a deep breath in an attempt to calm my own racing pulse.

He wrapped his arms around me entirely, holding me,

surrounding me in a way that soothed my soul. He always had, because he was warm and safe and mine, and I could tell him. I could finally share them.

No amount of solace could soothe the slight shake in my voice, though.

"I don't remember their faces," was the first thing I said, and then the words flowed from me in unstoppable waves like they'd been waiting decades to be spoken. "I was a toddler when it happened. Godrick had been on the path to a peace treaty meeting of all things when I stumbled onto the dirt path in front of him, no more than two years old, crying, soaked to the bone, and bleeding from a cut above my eye."

My fingers probed my right eyebrow, feeling the scar hidden beneath the small hairs. It never went away completely—my reminder that none of it was a nightmare.

"It didn't take him long to find our carriage at the bottom of the ravine, halfway underwater. My parents died that night. They were dead before he ever reached them, but the door had been kicked open, the wood around the latch shattered, and my... Well, Godrick said it looked like my father had shoved me out before I could die with them."

Vaelor *listened,* his hold steady and body still. He didn't offer condolences or "you're lucky," or "it'll be all right," and I was immensely grateful. I didn't want to hear any of the meaningless sentiments, because that was exactly all they were—meaning-less. People didn't know what to say or how to react to death, especially traumatic death, but Vaelor understood. I might not know how his mother passed, but I could guess.

"The accident is etched into my memory: being thrown about the carriage, rolling over and over until we crashed into the rocky ravine, the ice, the *water.*" A shiver ran up my spine. "All of that I remember clearly, hauntingly so, but not their faces." I winced, a burn starting in the back of my throat, and Vaelor ever so slightly tightened his hold. "That's what bothers me most and makes me feel so...guilty. They died, and I don't even remember their faces. My father used his dying act to shove me from the carriage so I wouldn't die with them, and I can't remember his face. I can't even....I can't remember what color his eyes were. Were they blue like mine? Or brown or green? I can't even place one color over the other when I try."

I snuggled deeper into his bare chest and noticed his skin was wet beneath my face. I quickly wiped my cheeks, not knowing when I'd started crying, and bit back an apology.

"I only have two memories of them, actually, two sounds: one being just...horrible screams and snapping wood and crunching metal." My hands trembled where they lay on his chest, and he rested one hand over them, holding them both in one of his while the other remained firmly locked around my waist. "And then my mother's voice singing a nursery rhyme. I can hear her, the inflection in her tone, the soft whisper and smile in her voice, but I can never make out the words."

I hummed the sound, tears rolling freely down my cheeks, but he didn't seem to mind.

With my ear pressed to his chest, I heard his heartbeat jump, and I stilled into silence. He inhaled slowly and whisper-sung words that twisted my gut in knots. Sobs broke free, but he continued. I needed him to; I needed to connect her voice to the words, and these were it. I knew it in my bones.

When he finished, I cried like I'd never cried in my life, my tears seemingly endless, and he held me the entire time. Until the screams became wails, wails became sobs, sobs cries, cries hiccups, hiccups sniffles. Until the weight eased in my chest, exhausted but relieved.

For the first time in over twenty years, I felt better, lighter, like he somehow yanked me above the surface of that damned river that had been unknowingly drowning me all these years so I could finally breathe—I hadn't even realized I'd been holding my breath since that night.

He didn't have to say anything. I didn't need his words. I had needed to say my own that had been shoved so far down, I wasn't sure I would ever be able to say them aloud, but then, he created a space that felt so safe, my story begged to be heard, and he did exactly that—he listened. He felt. He understood.

And as it turned out, that was all I ever needed.

"My mother died of an illness," he whispered a few minutes after I'd settled. "Two hundred years ago, and I'm still clearly... affected by it."

He took a long breath and tightened his arms once again like he needed to know I was here now. "Before she died, she'd told me, 'Everyone dies.' I knew how she meant it, but those two words haunted me until they found their way into my very being, until they were the only two words my soul could hear, over and over and over. Everyone dies. Don't fall in love, because everyone dies. Keep your circle small, your friends close, and your healer closer, because *everyone* dies."

I'll die.

My heart broke because I would die on him. I knew that. He knew that. "Vaelor..."

"Don't."

"But—"

"Don't say it."

I snapped my mouth shut and snuggled into him, my arm wrapping around his torso.

"You were right," he said, resuming his motion along my arm, sliding up and down. "You've always been right. Life isn't worth living if all you ever feel is fear. *This* is what makes all the bitterness worth it—perhaps even makes the good sweeter in comparison."

My smile was shaky because he was right. Love did make life worth living, but the nagging thought still remained. I didn't want him to have to experience that. I didn't want to be the source of his suffering, his agony, his...grief.

Being the cause of this pain made me want to vomit. Would he be okay one day without me? A small part of me answered no, because I didn't think he would be, but I hoped he didn't stop living after me. I hoped he kept his heart open, that he learned to love and laugh freely.

I hoped he'd leave his fear here at the cottage once and for all, because no one, not even the mighty Storm Bringer, could stop time, and I was human. Death would knock on my door much sooner than his, and that was unavoidable. *Time* was unavoidable.

It was selfish of me to say everything I did, to push him, kiss him, fuck him, to lie here with him even now, but damn, I loved him. I loved him so much, and it made me selfish—stupid and reckless and foolish and so damned selfish—but I wanted to give him every single second of whatever time I had left in this realm. I needed to, because not doing so felt like asking my lungs to breathe without air, my heart to beat without blood. It would have gone against fate itself, against nature. I *needed* him to survive.

And he loved me too, enough to claim me, to devote himself to me, despite knowing the loss he would inevitably suffer. The scabbed wound on my throat was proof of that.

I was selfish, and he was selfless, and I had to be okay with that, because I couldn't live without him, and he wouldn't live without me, not right now, not yet.

We lay in silence for hours, in love and hurt and relief and maybe even a bit of fear, but we were together.

He was mine, and I was his, and that was it.

There was no question. No doubt. No regret.

Our hearts were bound, souls entangled, and fate would never have it any other way.

24

Vaelor

Elora was sound asleep—and wonderfully naked—
when I slipped out of bed the next morning.

I *had* to pause in appreciation of her. The sun
thought so too, it seemed, as it kissed her bare skin, pale and
freckled, practically glowing against the emerald bedspread
pulled down to her hips.

Leaning over, I slid her long, red hair over her shoulder to
reveal my mark, scabbed but permanent. It would heal but
never leave. My chest squeezed at the sight, energy racing under
my skin, urging to spark, to lick, to consume.

I had never felt anything so right. The stars had aligned
beautifully when they made her for me and me for her. Fate had
never made a more perfect pairing, and I knew that in my bones.
The world knew it, the Goddess, the stars, fate. To deny it would
be to deny the truth.

In the corner of the room was a small table of discarded art
supplies: charcoal, cracked and crumbling from the ages, and a

pile of sketch pads, seemingly untouched by the years or my
mother as the pages were blank.

A small area of the desk had been cleared, the art supplies
replaced by a stack of letters with a quill lying on top as a
makeshift paperweight. Quietly, I slid the quill over and lifted a
page, smiling at the name signed at the bottom: Alivia.

So my efforts hadn't been in vain.

After replacing it and the quill, I grabbed some supplies and
returned to the chair across from Elora.

She needed to be sketched, just as much as I needed to
sketch her—far too ethereal to not be preserved on parchment,
a Goddess among men sent to bless my eyes and mine alone.

She was fire and blue skies, fierce and gentle, kind and head-
strong, passionate and lost in a world that didn't deserve her.

I marked her form onto the parchment: her lines and curves,
her freckles, her locks and closed eyes, her faint, sleepy smile,
but no medium could ever capture what made her
extraordinary. I knew that as I had tried many, many times.
Every time I witnessed her features in a new light, viewed from a
different angle or lifted in a different emotion, my soul *insisted* I
depict her over and over. My nook was chock full of her, but the
portraits were never right.

I couldn't capture her laugh. I couldn't draw her heart or
mind or the way she teased. I couldn't infuse her cinnamon
vanilla scent into the parchment or recreate the way her auburn
hair sparked under the sunlight. I couldn't put her on paper in
the same way she existed before my eyes, and it was maddening.

But I never stopped trying. My hands would never allow for that. They itched to continue, to paint and sketch, to touch and explore.

It would never be enough.

I would never have enough. I wanted to be consumed by her, in thought and body and heart and soul *and* art.

Every part of me, hers.

The chest-tightening, breath-stealing panic was still present when I thought of the future, so I simply...didn't think of it, and when I couldn't escape it, I gazed at her. I watched her chest rise and fall, counting her even breaths.

I was so damned tired of being afraid, and I wanted to let myself have this, have her without living every moment grieving the loss that hadn't happened.

She was *here*.

She was alive, and she was mine—finally. After years of want, of longing and denial, she was mine, and I'd be damned if I let something as simple as fear tear her from me now.

It was as if her blood on my tongue had seeped some of her bravery into me as well, her soul strengthening mine in the ways it needed, filling gaps and holes. Where I was broken, she healed. I just hoped I could do the same for her.

I'd been honored when she'd shared her parents' deaths with me because I knew the weight that held. Speaking it aloud was difficult, dragging up and verbalizing memories that our hearts naturally wanted to keep buried. It was hard and painful but necessary—something my father still had yet to do.

But buried wounds could not heal. They needed to be aired out; otherwise, they would only fester, and an infection of the soul was lethal.

Even I hadn't been entirely successful in healing—clearly, though I was trying. We were both trying, and that was all we could do.

When I was semi-satisfied with the sketch, I laid it on the nightstand and strolled to the bedroom door. It was closed, shutting us off from the rest of the house, but it was time I saw it.

We'd been too...occupied last night for me to look around, but I knew what I would see with the light of day pouring in every window: dust and decay, abandonment. This house had not been touched since she'd passed, and the fact that it still stood, much less was livable, was a miracle.

I exhaled slowly and pulled the door open.

I didn't make a single step over the threshold before my jaw fell slack, Elora's warmth filling my chest all over again.

There was no dust, no decay. It didn't appear abandoned at all. In fact, the only sign of damage was the back door boarded with slats of wood, replacing the glass that had once been there.

The cottage was small and open. From the bedroom door, I could see all the way to the other side of the house, and every single inch between me and the kitchen on the far end was clean, every surface dusted, the floors and walls wiped. The curtains were pulled open with new potted plants sitting beneath them—namely, a freshly sprouted woman's revenge.

My throat tightened more with each hesitant step I took through the room. In the corner, my mother's canvases had been organized, dusted, and lined into neat piles. A few had been hung on the walls, the largest being our painting of an apple tree.

I swallowed hard as I neared it and ran my finger over the old paint to feel the strokes and bumps—the marks my mother's hand had made. I'd been young when we'd painted this; so young that all I was able to do was paint the red blobs she turned into apples.

It had been hung on the wall beside the window that framed that very tree—young at the time but now, massive and thriving.

My body was torn between crying and laughing when the front door swung open. I whirled around to see Father entering with a smile and a basket of ingredients.

He stopped mid-step when he found me instead of Elora, whom I assumed he expected. Closing the door, he sighed. "I guess it's about time we visited, hmm?"

My eyes widened. He had never been even partially okay when Mother was involved, but here he was, entering her cottage and *smiling*.

My chest constricted, and I had to force air into my lungs, but where it usually only did so in panic, this was...different. This was warm rather than icy, swelling rather than tightening.

"Yeah, I'd say so," I replied.

He placed the basket on the table, and we sat in the seats on either side. I peeked inside and lifted a brow at him.

"Elora is teaching me how to make cinnamon rolls," he said, his cheeks tinting pink.

"Mama's favorite?" I asked with a breath laugh.

He nodded, shifting his gaze about the room, taking in every detail. "She's really fixed this place up."

I tensed, expecting the look to return to his eyes, for him to fall into his grief again. "Father..."

"I think Elora broke something, or perhaps healed something in me," he whispered, and I fell back in my seat, speechless. "We've decided grief never shrinks. It never leaves or lessens, but that's all right because our world—our life grows larger to make room for it and more. Ara is never gone from here." He tapped his chest. "But that doesn't mean I have to wait with one foot in the grave for the day my body finally decides to join her."

Two hundred years he'd been grieving in silence. For two hundred years, the briefest mention of Mother sent him right back, and two weeks with Elora had cracked him wide open and then stitched him back together.

I blinked away the burn in my eyes, my chest heaving.

I had never loved her more than I did in this moment.

He looked at me, eyes brimming with tears, and I noticed his face was slightly sunburned. Glancing down, I found dirt beneath his fingernails. He'd been working in Mother's garden.

Damn it all, Elora is...everything.

"I'm not betraying her by living, and I'm sorry it took me so long to realize that. I'm sorry, son, so sorry."

I offered him a shaky smile and shook my head. "Don't apologize for loving her."

He nodded and chuckled, a broken sound that shook loose

his welling tears. They slipped past his lashes, and he turned away to wipe his eyes with his palms.

He sighed and stood to carry the basket to the kitchen counter where he pulled out and lined up the ingredients, including a short, handwritten list from Elora. "She didn't tell me whose death she still mourned, but their loss must be deep too. She understands. As much as I wished she didn't know this pain, she does."

"I know," I whispered. For someone who was the embodiment of sunshine, she knew pain and loss in a way I would have never expected.

"Who's ready for a baking lesson?" Elora's voice startled us both, and we whipped around like two schoolboys caught doing something we shouldn't. Her eyes widened, shifting between the two of us. "Did I interrupt something?"

"No." I snapped from my stupor, striding across the room to throw my arms around her in a tight embrace. She giggled and swatted at my sides, but I merely tightened my hold.

When I whispered, "Thank you," she softened and wrapped her arms around my waist in return.

"For what?" she whispered back.

"*Everything.*" I kissed the top of her head and released one arm to swivel her toward the kitchen. "And yes, love, we're ready to learn."

Unfortunately, it turned out we weren't as ready as we thought. The only cinnamon rolls that made it out alive were Elora's. Mine somehow came out flatter than when they went in, and Father's were salty—excessively so. In fact, it tasted like the only sugar that made it in was the sprinkling on top.

Thank the Goddess, Elora was able to roll twice as many as we had in the same amount of time because we were starving by the time the scent of warm cinnamon filled the house.

She'd chuckled at our pitiful attempts, then fully cackled at our expressions. "Second time's the charm."

Father wiped his forehead, smearing the white powder into his hair. "I thought it was the third time's the charm?"

She lifted a brow. "Do you want it to be the third?"

"I want it to be the first," he grumbled with a chuckle as he tossed his rolls in the trash.

Elora braced her hands on the counter and lifted herself up to sit. Pulled like a moth to a flame, I inched closer until I reclined on my elbows beside her. A soft giddiness had settled in my chest for the first time in years, and I didn't stop to question it. My smile was effortless, easy, inescapable.

My arm skimmed her leg, and she shifted a tad closer.

"Imagine Mama seeing this. She'd be...amused, to say the least." As soon as the words slipped from my mouth, I paused, afraid Father would sink. I lifted my eyes to him, body tense.

His arms fell to the side as he looked down at himself, an apron tied around his waist, coated in a layer of flour. I didn't even dare to breathe while I waited for some kind of reaction, good or bad, but then, he *laughed*.

My mouth curved into a smile as Father doubled over to brace his hands on his knees. He laughed and laughed until he gasped for breath, clutching at his abdomen. I couldn't help but join him, and amid the mirth, Elora placed a hand on my cheek and turned me to face her.

With flushed cheeks and misty eyes, she kissed my forehead once before whispering, "He's happy."

We both swiveled to Father when he said, "She would have laughed at us much sooner than Elora, shamelessly and adoringly."

This was my father, and I was so relieved to finally, *finally* have him back, to be able to speak of my mother and hopefully reminisce one day. I was ready to hear stories, share memories, and speak her back into existence—if only in our hearts. She didn't deserve to be clumped in with pain and fear. Mother didn't even belong in the vicinity of those.

Much like Elora, she'd been made of warmth and smiles, of bravery and love. It was time her memory felt like *her*, even if it was tinted with nostalgia and a strange form of homesickness.

What had Father said? *"Grief never shrinks."* Our lives only grew to accommodate more.

My arm wound around Elora's waist, her long hair tickling my forearm, and my heart swelled, willingly burning in her flames.

But it was all snuffed out when a letter materialized in the fist of my free hand. Suppressing a sigh, I discreetly slid my arm from around her.

I exited the room with the excuse of relieving myself before unfolding the letter with a sinking pit in my gut. No matter what words the parchment held, I knew I'd have to leave. Drak didn't send letters for any other reason.

But my eyes slid closed, my head falling back as soon as I read it, because it wasn't from Drakyth at all.

It was from Rya, which meant it would be a long day ahead, and I needed to leave *now*.

"Fuck," I whispered under my breath. Energy sparked the dry page, and it burned quickly.

With another steeling breath, I turned the knob and opened the door to find Father and Elora eating the last two rolls. Under better circumstances, I would've teased them for not waiting on me, but I couldn't even bring myself to smile as I was leaving much, *much* sooner than I wanted.

"I just received correspondence from my general." My heart sank at the lies falling on Elora's ears. "Apparently, there was a spat between a few men, and he wants me to deal out punishment."

She swallowed her bite, kicking her dangling feet, and cocked a brow as she asked, "And your general can't do that himself?"

"You'd think so, wouldn't you?" I avoided her gaze as I answered, grabbing a tunic from the back of a chair. I slid it overhead and strode to the door. Turning back with my hand on the knob, I added, "I'll see you both soon."

"See you soon," Father echoed, but Elora hopped down from the counter.

I walked out before she could say anything else, pretending not to notice her moving toward me, but of course, she had no quarrel reopening the door and following me out.

She shut the door behind her and jogged after me. "Why don't I believe you?"

I stumbled over my own damned foot and internally groaned.

She laughed and her following footsteps stopped. "That's what I thought."

I glanced back at her, my brows pulling together. "Please understand I wouldn't be leaving if it wasn't important."

Her expression softened before she closed the remaining distance between us and craned her neck to look up at me. "Vaelor, I can't do anymore secrets."

My heart broke, shattered. I'd kept nothing but secrets for years, and here I was, forcing them on her once again. Perhaps I could have told her of the Sanctuary, but this wasn't that. This wasn't rescuing children or providing safe haven. This was entirely different, and I didn't want her to have to witness this.

I placed a palm on her cheek, and she closed her eyes, holding my hand there with both of hers. "I'm sorry, love."

Her eyes snapped open, and I saw...betrayal. She clenched her jaw and dropped her hands away.

"You will not lie to me again, Vaelor."

"I won't lie to you, but neither can I tell you the truth." I took a step back, followed by another, knowing this looked like running. She must be thinking that, feeling it, and I wanted to retch at the thought. "I have to go, sun ray, but please forgive me. I *will* return to you as soon as I can."

She matched me step for step, the hurt her eyes sparking into rage. "No. No, you *gave* yourself to me, and—"

Her words stopped when lightning raced across the sky.

"I'm sorry, love," I whispered and lifted my gaze and hand to the sky—which was why I didn't see her sprint at me full force.

Lightning struck at the same moment her hand wrapped around my wrist. Her scream drowned out the crackling energy, and I gripped her forearm as tightly as I could.

25

Vaelor

As soon as we landed at the Oasis, she crumpled to the ground, limp and unconscious, and I lunged forward to catch her head before it cracked on the hard ground.

"Fuck," I whispered under my breath, slamming my hand into the dirt.

"Did you receive—" Fauna's rushing steps stopped when she saw us. "Is that Elora?"

"Yes," I seethed. Even staring at her face as she was now, I wanted to scold her. I wanted to bend her over my knee and bring my hand down on her ass over and over until it was red and heated beneath my palm. When she was healed and safe, I would do exactly that.

That was dangerous—so fucking dangerous. If my grip on her had slipped, she would have been lost to the skies, her physical form gone.

She would have been stuck on the other side of the veil,

essentially dead but worse—a living soul left in the realm of the dead.

"Here's the blood." Fauna handed me a vial. "Do you want to leave her here?"

"No." The word left me on reflex. I should leave her here. It would be easier, safer, but if Elora was so dead set on finding out, willing to risk her *life*, then so be it. "No, I'll bring her. Do you have one of Iaso's tonics?"

Fauna nodded and darted for her office.

The rage held me upright for now, but if I were to carry us both to Canyon without replenishing my well, nothing would keep me awake. I'd hit the ground unconscious, just like Elora.

"Grab two if you have them," I shouted to Fauna.

When she returned, I quickly downed one before dropping to a knee and tilting Elora's head back to pour a tonic into her mouth slowly. "I'm not sure if it'll help her, but if she's already like this after one trip, I have no idea how long she'll be out in Canyon."

I handed the vials back, placed the other vial of blood in my pocket, and slid my hands under Elora to lift her. Holding her tightly against my body, I gave Fauna a sharp nod, and lightning struck again.

We landed outside Canyon's borders within seconds to find Augustus waiting, his blue hair so dark, it appeared nearly black. He did a double take when he saw Elora hanging limply in my arms.

"I'll explain later," I said, groaning deeply when I realized Elora hadn't completed Canyon's oath. Damn it all, I should have left her in Nautia. "Is she draining him already?"

"Yes," Augustus replied as I followed him down the narrow alley leading to the spelled entrance, stone walls reaching high into the sky on either side.

"The process has already begun." Mors stepped from the

other side of the spell wall. His wispy white hair was braided back, his white eyes reflecting orange from the flickering candle in his hand.

"Can she take the oath without being awake?" I asked him. Because Mors was the oldest being in Canyon, other than his wife and her sister, he would know if anyone did.

He sniffed, stepping closer. My hands tightened around her, but I let him. When he neared her face, he moved her hair to reveal the mark before lifting his gaze to meet mine in question. He didn't say anything, but I nodded regardless.

"Your souls are merged, and yours has said the oath. All she must do is share her blood. The words are not necessary this day."

He stepped back and pulled a dagger from his robes. He lifted her hand, and her body didn't so much as flinch as Mors slid the tip along her palm. He lifted her hand to me, and I blew the blood, which turned to dust and sank into the six-pointed sun etched into the wall. It glowed a burning red above us before the wall disappeared entirely.

We followed Mors and Augustus to Rya's room, deep within Canyon, down the winding caves carved from the stone. The room was lit with dozens of candles, bright enough to reveal the dead man hanging upside down with his throat slit, the trembling woman in the corner, and Rya as she swiveled from her table upon our entrance.

I laid Elora down on a bench covered in furs, handed Rya the vial of blood from the creature of night, and turned to the woman. I crouched down before her, shielding her line of sight from her husband's body. Her eyes flashed to mine, wild and wide, as she continued to rock back and forth with her arms wrapped around her legs.

"Are you sure this is what you want?" I whispered.

"Y-yes," she said with a quick nod.

"He won't remember you," I said slowly.

She stopped rocking, letting loose a long breath. "But he'll feel me. He'll know he loved me in this life, and that's all I need. We can make new memories, but I can't make a new him."

"That...is a very good point." That was the reason all loved ones asked to do this. They couldn't bear to lose their partners, but they sacrificed much to do so. Her husband would never be the same, and she knew that—or thought she did. For her sake, I hoped so.

She gave me a shaky smile and leaned forward to whisper, "Although, I didn't think the process would be quite so...gruesome."

"I know." I nodded, glancing back over my shoulder to find the bucket of blood only halfway full beneath him. "Would you like to step out while we finish the process? I'll retrieve you before he wakes."

Her eyes darted back to her husband, and she winced, resuming her rocking. I shifted a step to the right to shield her from the sight once again.

"Would that make me weak?" she whispered, more to herself than me.

"No. When he died, you could have fallen to the floor. You could have fallen apart, but instead, you acted quickly. You found Rya and started the process before it was too late. You've been nothing but strong, and if he loves you as much as you love him, I think he'd want you to step away and rest. I don't think he'd want you to see this."

Her face crumbled while I spoke, tears falling, forehead wrinkling, lips trembling. She inhaled sharply and nodded. When I extended a hand, she took it, and I pulled her to her feet before guiding her to the room next door—a sleeping chamber stocked with mead and whiskey. I showed her where everything was, but she collapsed on the bed before I had even closed the door behind me.

It wasn't long after that the man's body had been sat upright against the wall, the wound on his throat stitched nearly all the way closed.

Rya lifted the necessary concoction: the blood of the creature of night mixed with the blood of many Fae. She never specified how many people had to contribute to create the "blood of many," and I didn't ask. As long as she got it willingly, I didn't care either way, but that was why they did this in Canyon, because blood couldn't be spilled with ill intent here. It had to be given.

She dipped a long tube in the bowl and sucked the other end until the dark liquid started to run through before she slid the tube into the man's neck.

The blood would replace the Fae's essence, overloading his system with so many different identities that the body itself no longer registered as one person. He would have no scent, no memories, no pupils or irises, no distinguishable markers other than the face he was born with and the feelings of his past life.

He wouldn't remember who his wife was, but his soul would remember the love he felt for her. That could never be removed or forgotten, regardless of what form he took.

Rya's daughter joined us in the other room, quiet as always. I didn't know her name, as they never shared it. I had never even heard her voice, but her hair was recognizable—violet, her eyes two orbs of amethyst.

She stayed silent, her expression flat. I'd never seen her any other way. I had always gotten the impression she disliked her role, but she never complained or refused. Her mother had given her ample opportunity to resign as the soul weaver, but she always returned.

"You must decide—do you want to do this? Once she starts,

she must finish," Augustus asked the one only Rya and Mors could see.

Their small family was all gifted by death in some way, and they used it beautifully. Death magic, while typically shunned, wasn't always dark and terrifying, even if it appeared so. Augustus could speak and hear the souls while his wife could see them. Their daughter... Well, she weaved, just as her moniker implied.

Augustus nodded along as he listened to the soul before he turned to his daughter and wife. "He's sure."

"Does he understand what it means, though?" Mors asked. "That this is what he will be?"

He turned to the invisible man and motioned to his eyes and long canines, his blackened shadows escaping his fingertips to swirl up his forearms. His face flickered and rippled, shifting from his own to mine, Rya's, the man's wife, then to the soul's—a mirror image of the one staring at us with dead eyes, reclined on the wall and drained of color.

"You will become a Puer Mortis. You will be no one and everyone, and you will *never* die. You will watch the sun set on the end of the world with me, along with every other undead. You will no longer crave food, but blood, although it will not sustain you. Rather, it will destroy you. You will crave your downfall for centuries, and it will not cease until you consume enough souls—animal, human, or Fae. Do you *truly* understand this?"

I knew Mors was only asking because he hadn't understood when he was turned. He had been the first of his kind, turned by his wife, so the rules and consequences were unknown, and he'd had to learn to navigate them all without help.

Augustus' head swiveled to the soul, listening. "He understands. Anything to hold his wife again."

All eyes shifted to their daughter, and she nodded. She

reached forward and plucked a glowing string out of thin air, visible only in the reflection of her purple eyes—the soul's life thread. Her other hand disappeared into the man's chest and wrenched his heart out. It wasn't his physical heart, but a glowing one, the counterpart to his life thread, intangible to everyone but her.

With a deep breath, she took her needle, threaded the invisible string, and began stitching it into the man's heart. Augustus flinched, then winced and strode from the room. The soul must be screaming as the weaver sewed him back into his body, and by the time she finished, he would no longer know who or what he was.

It didn't take long, but it was always taxing on her. Neither she nor the newly-formed Puer Mortis woke for over twelve hours—and horrifically, neither did Elora.

It wasn't until late in the night that she finally stirred, and naturally, when she woke to see a dead man with a throat stitched back together, she screamed. The shrill sound echoed through the cave system, and the creature's eyes snapped open —whiter than Mors, nearly glowing. He sucked in a ragged breath, and his wife rushed to his side, shushing him.

I slapped a hand over Elora's mouth as she continued to scream, squirming and kicking under my hold until I dragged her from the room. She mumbled something into my hand before biting my finger, and I dropped her with a stifled groan. She fell to the ground and shuffled away, her brows furrowed and mouth downturned in anger.

"Elora, stop," I whispered forcibly as I grabbed her ankle and yanked her back. She started to shout again, and I covered her mouth, flipping her until her back was pressed into my chest. I lowered my mouth to her ear to whisper, "If you bite me again, I will bite you back."

Her breath hitched, and she stilled. I walked her into

another sleeping chamber and kicked the door shut before I led her to the bed. Her hips hit the mattress, and I bent her forward until her front was pressed into it as I leaned overtop her.

"Now do you see why I didn't want you to know?" I nipped her earlobe, then her neck, moving lower.

When I sank my teeth into the mate mark, she moaned into my hand and arched her back. I ground my hips into her backside, and she whimpered.

"You could've hurt yourself—or worse, *died*." I enunciated the word as anger pulsed through me once again. I bit harder, re-breaking the skin of her mark, and lapped at the drops of blood. "You don't get to endanger what is *mine*, do you understand?"

She nearly sobbed and nodded, wiggling and squirming beneath me, grinding her hips into my hardening cock.

"Do you? Because I think I should make *sure* you know. I want it to be fucking instinct. Your safety comes before all else."

I shifted to the side, keeping one hand over her mouth while my other caressed her backside before sliding down to hike her dress up. With it bunched around her waist, she was bared to me —no undergarments. I clicked my tongue and thrust two fingers into her *hard*, curling them into the spot that drove her mad, moving faster, mercilessly, until she writhed and screamed beneath me.

The only sounds in the room were *her*: her slickness, her moans, her heaving breaths.

Fucking beautiful.

When she was on the edge, her pussy clamping around me, her movements erratic, I ripped my fingers from her. She whipped her face to me, mouth hanging open like she wanted to protest, but froze, cheeks burning, when I brought my fingers to my mouth and sucked the taste of her from them. She whimpered before burying her face in the mattress, and I let her, merely kissing the top of her head as I lifted my hand and came down on her ass in a hard crack. She stiffened, and a scream tore from her, somewhere between a cry and a moan, stifled by my hand and the blanket.

She didn't try to flee, though, her only movements that of her heaving chest. She laid beneath me, brave and accepting of her fate, and I already wanted to praise her for it.

"You do not take risks." *Slap.* "You do not jeopardize *my* mate's life." *Slap.* "You do not run headfirst into the unknown." *Slap. Slap. Slap.*

Her skin was red and heated when I stopped to massage her ass with my palm and made a mental note to apply a soothing salve later. I slid my hand free of her mouth to move down her body and kneel behind her, widening her legs to reveal her pretty cunt, soaked and dripping.

"Do you understand?" I asked, kneading both of her swollen cheeks.

"Y-Yes," she cried and inched her legs open farther. "I'm s-sorry, Vaelor."

Leaning forward, I kissed her glowing cheek once, then the other, pressing my lips to every inch of her as I moved closer and closer to where she needed me. "Tell me you won't do it again."

"I won't. I won't. I—" She threw her head back and fisted the blanket as I swiped my tongue over her clit.

When I sucked that sweet little bud into my mouth, she stuttered and started spewing apologies, promises, anything she thought I wanted to hear, and I fucking *loved* it, her begging music to my ears.

"That's my good girl," I groaned into her and devoured what I'd been craving since last night.

26

Elora

Vaelor had explained the Puer Mortis, but the horrifying sight would haunt my damned nightmares, I was sure of it.

I'd chided him several times, and while he did apologize for me having to wake up to that sight, he'd also finish with something along the lines of, "If I was willing to risk *his* mate's life to find out, then I was going to find out every unnerving detail."

We'd had this conversation at least three times, and they'd all ended the exact same way: I'd roll my eyes at him talking about me in third person like I wasn't here, he'd ask me if I needed a reminder on exactly who I belonged to, my cheeks would *burn*, and he would, in fact, remind me in every delicious way.

But for Goddess' sake, they could have at least faced me away. He did regret that much, that I opened my eyes to the creature rather than bringing me in later.

Either way, I *had* seen it, and I would never forget it.

While I couldn't imagine going through something like that

or subjecting someone I love to it, I would never question another, because love differed for everyone. Some loves transcended this realm, this time, souls so tied and inseparable that they refused to leave the other, even in death, and Puer Mortis were proof of that. Why else would a soul cling to the veil rather than transition smoothly?

Vaelor had said that was one of the necessary components to create one: the soul must be "clinging to the veil" by refusing to leave the realm of the living. They became ghosts—unseen, unheard, and untouchable to everyone but the family who created the creatures.

There they would remain, split between worlds, until they were either stitched back into their body or rigor mortis set in— whichever came first. At that point, they'd missed their chance and would be forced to the other side.

Every aspect of the procedure was nightmarish, but to them, *nothing* was more horrible than being separated from their soul's counterpart, so I understood.

Love trumped all, death included, and everyone else be damned apparently because Puer Mortis *ate* souls. I couldn't even fathom what that meant, but Vaelor said they could survive on animals.

After that...experience, we'd spent days in Canyon, bouncing between the sleeping chamber, the inn, any shadowed corners or isolated hallways. An insatiable need had arisen in Vaelor since he allowed himself to want me, and while I was thoroughly and utterly spent—over and over and over—I *reveled* in it.

Vaelor had awoken something in me too, a darkness I hadn't realized was there, one he yanked from me: a dark need to be possessed and fucked for his own pleasure. I wanted to be used, although it never ended there. He made sure I came too many times to count, dragging them from me even when I felt like there was nothing left, even when I was so sensitive, it nearly hurt, even when I could no longer lift my limbs and I was holding onto consciousness for dear life.

But I wanted to be taken, and take he did. Repeatedly. Incessantly. Beautifully.

He was beautiful when he was free—raw and powerful and unrestrained.

He laced his fingers through mine, undoubtedly smelling the desire arising from my depraved thoughts, and tugged me through the crowded alleyway.

"Where are we going?" I asked, nervousness fluttering like butterflies in my belly.

He glanced over his shoulder, that heart-stopping grin curving his lips. "You'll see, sun ray."

I licked my lips, my mouth suddenly dry. My heart thumped in my throat when he turned and led me deeper and deeper into the stone. The tunnel grew darker the farther we went until the candles, sporadically lit, became more common, but the light wasn't a normal flame. It was blue, the normal flickering orange replaced with what looked like...rippling water.

Water?

My fingers tightened around Vaelor's as my feet slowed before coming to a stop when the entire cave reflected that rippling water. He turned to me and lifted his arm over my head without releasing my hand, essentially binding me as he edged me back. I hit the stone wall with a faint gasp, and he slid his fingers up the column of my throat, grazing his mark before he tilted my chin up.

"If you want to leave at any point, just say the word, and we leave, all right?"

My eyes bounced between his two silver ones before I swallowed hard and nodded.

"I need to hear that you'll tell me, love," he whispered, his thumb gliding along my bottom lip.

Warmth swelled in my chest, loosening panic's grip. "I'll tell you."

He smiled and pressed his lips to mine, his kiss slow. I whimpered when he nipped my lower lip, but a low chuckle slipped into my mouth, the wicked sound going straight to my core. He inhaled slowly, and heat spread over my skin.

He brushed his lips along mine as he whispered, "I could take you right here, couldn't I?"

My heart lurched, my thoughts fragmented and words lost, but he had his answer when he lowered to the mate mark and inhaled again. With a deep groan, he dipped his hand beneath my dress and skimmed his fingers up my inner thigh to cup my bare core.

His eyes flashed at my lack of undergarments, and a wave of satisfaction rolled through me. "I could fuck you right here against the wall for anyone to see, and you'd let me, wouldn't you?"

He didn't give me a chance to respond before his lips recaptured mine, demanding this time, as I moaned against his mouth and nodded fiercely. I was at his mercy—exactly where I wanted to be. Two fingers thrust into me, and I bowed off the wall into him, my sharp gasp echoing down the empty hallway.

"I love the way you react to me." He moved his hand to my throat and tightened his fingers as he leaned back, holding me against the wall. With my dress bunched around my waist, he watched his fingers slide in and out of me with hungry eyes. "The way your body reacts to *any* part of me—fingers, tongue, cock. You take whatever I give you so greedily, and it's fucking beautiful."

I didn't know what prompted my next words. Perhaps it was because there was more euphoric delirium flowing through my veins than blood, but I couldn't stop them. "Do...Do humans bite their mates too?"

His heated gaze snapped to mine and let loose another cacophony of flaming butterflies in my lower belly. He stepped closer again, forcing me to crane my neck to look at him as that horribly perverse smirk returned. His entire face was cast in ripping cerulean light, and his metallic eyes caught it *beautifully*, turning a soft silver blue.

"Do you want to bite me, dear, sweet Elora?"

I returned his smirk and ground my hips into his hand, which earned an approving groan from him. "There are a great many things I would like to do to you, *Vaelor*."

Hearing his real name from my lips always did things to him, and this time was no different. He nearly shuttered as I enunciated it, my voice low and sultry.

"Is that so?" His breath sent shivers over my skin.

I grinned, biting my lip as I nodded. His answering smile was so beautiful, so genuine, I couldn't help but cup his cheeks and pull him down to me as I stood on my tiptoes. I needed to kiss that smile, to feel his lips against mine when he felt this free, this happy.

And his kiss felt as freeing as he looked.

My freedom at the tip of my fingers.

His own at the tip of his.

When he broke the kiss, I whimpered, but he pulled his fingers from my pussy and slid three back in. My body arched, my head falling back on the wall with a moan, louder and breathless. His chest rumbled with a low laugh before he ran the thumb of his free hand along my jaw, my bottom lip, my cheekbone.

I met his gaze and fell into molten silver, so hot it could've melted me on the spot.

He *looked* at me, the same way he did back in that ballroom all those months ago. My heart fluttered, the flush growing in my cheeks, but I studied him in return, as best I could while he continued to move his hand between my thighs. I took in every plane of his face, the stubble along his chin and the waves in his hair, the fresh tan on his skin and his hard body beneath his unbuttoned white shirt. With his sleeves rolled up, the veins in his forearms were on full display, the muscles rippling with each thrust of his fingers.

My eyes shot back to his when I found his palm slick with my own desire.

He flashed his wicked grin, stoking the ever-growing fire in my chest, and a breath slipped past my parted lips. The very air around us felt electrified, my skin tingling.

He truly was carved by the Goddess, specifically for me. I hoped he felt the same way when he looked upon me—impossibly enamored—because I knew, without a single doubt, that I stared into my fate's eyes when I met his gaze.

Vaelor Wrynwood *was* my fate and I his.

"An artist and his muse," he whispered.

With that, he stepped back, pulling his hands from my skin, specifically from one soaked and aching part, and I furrowed my brows, protest on the tip of my tongue. My eyes widened when he slid his fingers into *my* mouth. I squeaked and froze.

"I thought you deserved a taste too." He swirled his fingers over my tongue until I sucked them, and his eyes darkened. "Exquisite, hmm?"

He pulled them out to grip my jaw with his wet fingers, and his lips crashed to mine hungrily, a growl rumbling through him as if he'd been starved until this moment. His tongue slipped into my mouth, exploring and tasting, while his other hand gripped my waist, my back pressed into the wall as he pushed himself farther into me like he couldn't get close enough.

When he finally released me, I sucked in a breath, giddy and feverish—intoxicated.

"Sweet, *sweet* Elora, how will I ever get enough of you?"

"Never," I mumbled. "You'll never get enough."

He cupped the nape of my neck, craning my face to his. "And neither will you."

I shook my head, and he slid his hand from my neck down my spine, sending a wave of chills over my skin. When his hand found my lower back, he motioned me forward, deeper into the cave.

I sucked in a breath as we rounded the next corner.

Water.

Lots of water.

Dark water.

A pool, reflecting on the stone walls, steam rising in waves.

I hadn't realized I was gasping until Vaelor planted himself between the water and me, his palms on my cheeks. He'd lowered himself to my eye level, his voice soft and steady as he said, "You are safe, love. You're in control. You decide what we do here, how far we go."

I couldn't speak. I couldn't nod. I could barely breathe. A faint wisp of betrayal wound around my heart, and it took several breaths before I could muster, "Why...Why would you bring me here, Vaelor?"

He dropped to one knee so I was looking down at him. "Because you helped me overcome my fear. It's because of you that I can be...happy, for the first time in many, *many* decades. You saved me, Elora."

My eyes stung, and I placed a hand on his cheek.

Fear was a visceral feeling, overriding any rationale, any thought, any want or need or desire. It was an all-consuming beast that took utter control of its victims, and to think of Vaelor facing this every time he looked at me, every time I forced him to speak with me, every time he touched me, held me, kissed me...

A tear slipped past my lashes. "My brave artist."

He wiped it away with his thumb before pulling me to sit on his knee, winding an arm around my waist. "It's your turn to face your fears, my brave soldier, if you're ready."

I nodded slowly. Twenty-two years was long enough, wasn't it? Still, I didn't look away from him, afraid that if I did, I'd lose all sense of courage.

I wrapped my arms around his neck and buried my face in his chest, my words barely audible. "Will you carry me into the water?"

"Of course." He kissed the top of my head before gently setting me on my feet and lifting my gown over my head. He dropped it to the ground and removed his own clothing, leaving us both bare.

I flinched when his fingers skimmed along my skin, moving down to my ass. When he lifted me, I buried my face in his neck and wrapped my legs around his waist.

As he walked into the humid room, my muscles tensed so tightly, I feared they might snap. Flashes of falling and crashing and tumbling, submerging and sinking, dark water and icy agony bombarded my mind, the feeling so palpable, I had to force myself back to the present, to Vaelor's warmth around me.

Despite the flashbacks, I kept my eyes screwed shut, my breathing and pulse erratic. Each step was torture, each and every step bringing me closer to water, to ice, to death.

It wasn't logical. I knew it wasn't, but fear was never logical.

This was *water*. This was that river. This was that night.

I was going to die.

We were going to die.

"Sun ray," he whispered.

I shook my head, but he stopped walking. The stillness

somehow set me further on edge, like if he didn't hurry and sink us beneath the surface, I *would* run or burst into tears or—

"Do you want to sit here for a moment?" My eyes peeled open slowly to see his tanned skin. "Perhaps we could just...look at the pool? We could listen and watch, observe until your nerves settle."

I paused and felt him, his warm and solid body against mine, his arms beneath me and love surrounding me, consuming every inch of my heart, soothing my soul. I said nothing as I laid my head on his shoulder and breathed, slow and steady, and he didn't rush me.

We stood there for Goddess knew how long, but eventually, I shook my head. "No, let's go in. I want to be brave with you."

He tightened his hold and took the last few steps to the pool. My heart threatened to beat out of my chest, but I inhaled and exhaled slowly, forcing the air in and out of my lungs, reminding myself I was in Vaelor's hold.

When he stepped into the water, though, the slight splash ignited the panic. I wrenched around him, my body so taut, my limbs trembled. I had to be hurting him, but he held strong and took each step with caution, as if giving me time to adjust.

When the liquid touched my foot, a sob broke free, muffled by Vaelor's chest. Still, he didn't stop.

Inch by inch, we were swallowed until the surface lapped at my waist. It took *several* agonizing minutes, maybe hours, days for all I knew, before the tears stopped and terror was replaced by exhaustion.

At some point, Vaelor had taken a seat on an underwater bench, and I rested weightlessly on his lap, still wrapped in his embrace—my safe haven.

Finally, with swollen, tired eyes, I lifted my face to see our surroundings, and my gut instantly knotted. The water was dark inside the cave, lit only by blue-flame candles, and I couldn't see beneath it. I couldn't see my hips, my legs, my feet.

My breath shook, but I forced myself to look as I moved my stiff legs. I deeply disliked the feel of water swaying around me, but Vaelor's skin was slick against mine, solid and *here*—alive, with me.

Swallowing hard, I unwound my arms from around his neck and turned on his lap to recline my head on his chest. I crossed my arms to rest my hands on my shoulders, but he held them instead, his thumbs drawing circles on my palms.

This water was warm, not freezing.

It was a still pool, not a fast-moving river.

I wasn't drowning, in water or fear.

I wasn't...dying.

I was in water, and I wasn't dying.

Partially submerged and *not dying.*

I'm not dying.

A shaky laugh suddenly escaped me, and I sagged into Vaelor's body with relief. Sucking in a breath, I lifted my hand to cover my mouth, but it was wet on my lips. I pulled back to stare at it before glancing at the other one, finding it underwater, resting on Vaelor's. They both had been, and I hadn't even noticed.

Vaelor traced those damned circles on my hands until I relaxed enough for him to pull my arms under the surface too.

Goddess bless him.

With one deep, slow breath, I sank into him, and thus, the water. It surpassed my nipples, and I closed my eyes as my head reclined again, moving with his steady breaths.

His finger slid up my forearm to the crease of my elbow, the seemingly innocent touch sending a shiver down my spine. "I'm so proud of you, you know that? Always so brave."

My heart fluttered—among other things.

His hand continued upwards, tracing my bicep, my shoulder, my collarbone. When he slid it across my chest to the other side, his arm barred over me while his other hand slid along my leg.

His teasing fingers skimmed along the inside of my knee, my thigh, closer, closer, closer...

My knees fell open, my legs on either side of his thighs, spreading me wide for him as his hand finally swiped over my now-aching pussy, the need returning tenfold.

It was astonishing, the way my body responded to his lightest touch—utterly insatiable.

A growl reverberated from his throat when he sank two fingers into me, the sound mingling with my moan, both echoing off the water and stone.

"Beautiful," he hummed. "I want those sounds, your *beautiful* moans, to fill this cavern, love." Adding a third finger, he curled them inside me to hit that sensitive spot he loved to torment, and I bowed against him, clawing at his forearm still wrapped over my chest, holding me against him. "Sing for me."

Already wracked with exhaustion and edged for what seemed like hours, I shattered within minutes, yet he didn't stop. I shook my head when he pulled his fingers from me slowly and swirled them around my swollen clit.

"Vaelor...I can't," I panted, writhing against him.

He held me firmly locked against his large body as he dipped his head to whisper, "You can and you *will*, love."

My brows furrowed as my head fell back to his chest, still shaking back and forth. When he thrust his hips so his cock slid between my thighs and along my pussy, I snapped my legs shut with another breathless moan, and he groaned, each thrust in rhythm with his fingers, teasing my entrance.

"You're so perfect, dear, sweet Elora, truly made for *me*." His last word came in tandem with another thrust, but this time, his cock buried inside me, and I screamed, tears springing to my eyes.

It was *too* good, too much, and I wanted to combust. I *wanted* to explode or transcend or break into pieces before him—it felt like I would.

He didn't give me a moment to adjust. Hell, I didn't even suck in a breath before he pulled out and slammed back in hard enough to spark stars in my vision. His hands moved from my chest and clit to grab my waist, and my breathing quickened, my heart hammering.

"Spread your legs."

I did so immediately, and he rewarded me with a kiss over the mark on my throat. I whimpered at the touch, and he kissed it again as he lifted me off his cock until just the tip remained, my legs dangling on either side of his, spreading me wide and entirely at his mercy.

"I love you," he whispered and *bit.*

His teeth broke my skin as he thrust into me, bottoming out —then, it was endless, merciless, and I could hardly breathe, let alone do anything else. My head fell back, eyes closed as I basked in *him.*

There wasn't an intelligible word in my head as he moved with delicious expertise—other than *fuck,* which seemed to be stuck on repeat.

He moved faster, deeper, hungrier than he ever had, holding me at the right height for my core to swallow every inch of him as his teeth marked me again and again. I was sure blood flowed from the wound, but I couldn't be bothered to care—not as his sparks licked at every surface of my body.

Suddenly, with his cock buried inside me, he stood and turned, lying me face down on the stone edge, cold beneath my sensitive nipples. My knees hit the bench, and I lifted my hips to meet his, which hadn't stopped moving, thrusting, pounding, reducing me to nothing but a puddle—a pleasure-filled, screaming, wanton puddle.

But then, an actual spark slid along my spine, and I gasped. When I jerked up to turn, he pressed a hand between my shoulder blades and lowered me back down.

My chest rose and fell quickly as the shimmering electricity lit the stone below us with pale blue light before it slid down my arms and around my wrist.

"Vaelor?"

His lightning tightened like rope, slipping over the back of my hands and between my fingers before sinking into the stone. My heart raced as I jerked at them, but they didn't budge. I was shackled to the ground, fingers splayed and palms flat.

His low chuckle was my only warning. Another spark kissed my clit and *vibrated.*

I'm going to die.

There was no air, no thoughts, no realm.

Just us and this pool.

His cock, his magic—he would kill me, and I would die with a love-drunk smile on my damned face.

"You're not going to die, Elora," he growled behind me, his voice husky and breathless. I hadn't realized my thoughts escaped my lips, but again, I couldn't be bothered to care. I looked over my shoulder and met his gaze—silver and molten, sizzling and powerful. He *was* power, tall and towering, his muscled abdomen rippling with each thrust, rivulets of water rolling down his body. "Not today. Not *ever.*"

I nodded helplessly, melting into moan after moan as I held his gaze, refusing to look away from such beauty, because damn it all, he *was* beautiful.

"I love you," I sobbed. "I love you. I love you. I love you."

One of his hands released my waist to wrap around my face

and turn me to him as he leaned over me. His mouth met mine in another devastating kiss, hot and insatiable.

"I love you too, sun ray." His hand lowered to my throat as he whispered, "Shatter for me."

More sparks wound their way to my nipples, and I threw my head back, unable to do anything against his relentless onslaught of pleasure. He was everywhere all at once, determined to drown me in *him*—and for the first time in my life, drowning didn't seem like such a bad thing.

It dawned on me then, like this hadn't been the case for weeks, months, *years*: I was completely and utterly lost to him. My heart was consumed with wanderlust and his soul the only thing I cared to explore.

A blinding orgasm ripped through me, and my nails dug into the stone, pulling at the binding. Tears poured down my cheeks, sobs and moans and screams slipping past my lips until he slammed into me one final time, spilling into me with a groan of his own.

When we finally caught our breath, he pulled away and his magic dissipated into thin air. He scooped me up and sat back on the bench with me in his lap, kissing my forehead.

The rest of the evening was spent in soft adoration. He held me, kissed me, smiled and whispered, every word and action loving, gentle. He washed my hair and skin, and I did the same for him. Everything about it, about us was warm.

I was warm, inside and out, my chest a glowing ember he'd ignited—one I knew in the depths of my soul would burn until my last breath, and even then, I believed it'd follow me into the afterlife too.

27

Elora

When we met Rya and Augustus for breakfast after several days spent in our lust-fueled haze, my cheeks immediately heated, but the meal was fast, their conversation falling into the hum of tavern chatter while I dreamed of Vaelor's hands and tongue and dirty words.

Goddess, he'd reduced me to nothing more than a wanton mess. No matter where we were, how many times he filled me, loved me, kissed me, my body always craved more.

He was utterly inescapable.

My cheeks burned deeper, and he gripped my leg under the table, rubbing his thumb along my inner thigh, telling me he knew I was aroused. The flush spread down my neck, and I exhaled slowly.

After Rya and Augustus bid us farewell, Vaelor threw a leg over the bench so he straddled it, facing me with an elbow rested on the table.

"You're a needy little thing, you know that?"

My eyes flashed to him, my mouth opening and closing like a floundering fish. "*Me?*"

He slid his hand behind my nape as he nuzzled into the crook of my neck to inhale deeper. "Well, it's not my arousal driving me fucking mad."

"It *is* you," I muttered, nearly unintelligible as he left a trail of kisses down my throat.

"As long as it's only me," he whispered, that damned possessive edge back in his tone.

"It's only ever been you."

I felt his smile against my skin as he paused for a split second before biting his mark again. My heart pounded, and I clenched my jaw, stifling a moan and gripping the edge of the bench.

When he released his teeth, I shoved at his chest and whispered, "We're at breakfast for fuck's sake."

He didn't budge an inch. "So?"

"*So?*" My eyes bulged from my skull. "I don't think your people want to see their king doing...whatever it is you're doing."

He didn't move, though, not his hands, his mouth, his nearness. The only hint of movement was the curve of his lips as he grinned. I shoved at him again, but he grabbed both my wrists in one of his hands, holding them in my lap under the table, the other still firmly locked around the nape of my neck.

He moved to my ear. "If you try to push me away again, I will bend you over this table and show my people exactly how much I love my mate."

Heat ripped through me so ferociously, I snapped my thighs together, and he didn't miss the movement. The bastard never did. He chuckled, his breath tickling my skin.

"Although, maybe you'd rather I just bend you over my knee. I know how much you love that," he whispered so low, even I could barely hear him.

My chest heaved, but the rest of me remained as still as stone. "I've created a monster."

He laughed this time, a deep, genuine sound. "You *freed* a monster," he corrected. "You *own* a monster. You *love* a monster. But not created. No, fate did that for you."

A different warmth spread through me, because he wasn't wrong. "How can you be two completely different people?"

"What do you mean?"

"How can you be regal and thoughtful and..." My breath hitched when he pressed his lips to the mark again. "And just when you're around everyone else, then be *this* when you're with me?"

"Because this person, this 'depraved beast' as you so eloquently put it last night, is yours and yours alone. No one else has ever or will ever see this part of me, but I think you love that, don't you? Being the only one able to drive me to the brink of insanity?"

I absolutely did. He satisfied every desire I had or ever could have—truly made for me, literally, in every sense.

"Answer me." His grip tightened around my nape and forced me to look at him.

"Yes." My voice sounded as breathless as I felt. "Yes, I like owning this part of you. And you, my depraved beast, love knowing I'm yours, don't you? You like that you're the only person to have ever tasted me? Touched me? *Fucked* me?"

I was provoking him, I knew I was, but I couldn't help it. The flash in his eyes, the wicked tilt of his lips, the tightening hold made it all too tempting, and hell, I had not one ounce of resistance left in my body.

His grip moved to my chin, tilting my face up to him as he scooted impossibly closer. "You're absolutely right."

Then, his lips met mine, softer than I expected, sentimental, and my heart melted. My hands found his chest, feeling his heart racing beneath my palm—alive in every way, unrestrained by anything other than his devotion to me.

"I love you," I whispered against his lips.

He smiled and slid his fingers through my hair. "I love you too, sun ray."

If my heart swelled anymore, it was going to burst.

"I have somewhere I want to show you. It's..." He paused and took a deep breath. "No one else at Draig Hearth knows of its existence, but no more secrets. No more lies."

My heart would definitely burst soon, but I simply nodded. "No more lies."

"I want you to know every part of me, every inch, every thought." His gaze moved to my hair as he brushed his fingers through it again. "I want to burn in your flames."

* * *

WE STOOD hand in hand in front of a mansion, old but well maintained, beautiful in an ancient, secret-holding kind of way.

The sun set behind it, casting the dark house in its glowing embers as we strolled closer.

"Why are we..." I started but stopped when a mammoth of a man stepped from the massive door, his body framed on either side by blood-red *wings.* My heart lurched, and I tightened my hold on Vaelor's hand.

I might not know much about Fae, but I did know the only Fae with wings were Draigs, and Draigs were...mean, for lack of a better word.

My feet slowed before planting where they were. Vaelor took a step or two before realizing and turning back to me.

He gave my hand a quick squeeze. "Do you trust me?"

My gaze slid from Vaelor to the Draig and back. "More than anyone."

He ate the distance between us, cupped my jaw to tilt my face to his, and whispered, "Then trust I would never take you anywhere, to meet anyone who could hurt you."

I nodded, despite the fear still swirling in my gut. He grinned, revealing endearingly crooked teeth, and kissed my lips once, twice, three times, and I melted slightly in his hold.

"Are you here to introduce me or force me to watch you fornicate on my lawn?"

I gasped, yanking back from Vaelor with wide eyes and burning cheeks. Vaelor's mouth pressed into a tight line as he glanced over to the Draig, who was *much* closer now. I stepped into Vaelor's side, and he wrapped an arm around my waist.

"Do you want to meet Elora, or did you want me to severe your head from your shoulders?" Vaelor replied, and my face whipped to him, mouth agape.

"And how would you manage that? I'd swallow you whole before you had the chance."

My stomach twisted as my eyes flitted back to the Draig standing directly in front of us, and I pressed farther into Vaelor's side.

I knew Draigs could shift into dragons, but I didn't expect their normal Fae size to also be so large. Vaelor wasn't much shorter, maybe an inch or two, but the Draig was wide and burly —like perhaps he could swallow us both without having to shift into his beast at all.

I decidedly had no interest in seeing how large that beast was.

"Well, at least then I could fry you from the inside."

Why are we here again? I'm going to faint.

My gaze darted back and forth between the two of them, my heart pounding, but then the Draig cracked a smile. Vaelor mirrored it before they relaxed and sank into easy laughter. I let lose a small breath, but when they both looked to me, I stopped breathing all together.

"This is Drakyth Draki." Vaelor motioned to the Draig who grinned and stuck a hand out.

I stepped forward to shake his hand, but Vaelor's grip tightened on my waist, anchoring me against him.

Vaelor's gaze fell to his extended hand, and Drakyth's skin lit silver as Vaelor's irises glowed with sizzling energy. Lifting to meet his dark gaze, Vaelor slid his own hand in and shook Drakyth's. "That wasn't an empty threat."

I sucked in a sharp breath. *I'm going to faint, Vaelor.*

Drakyth's mouth tilted up in a mischievous smirk as he looked to me. "He's possessive. I didn't expect that."

As the shock subsided, I stifled my smile, but there wasn't a thing I could do about the flush spreading up my neck. I...liked that. I liked that I made Vaelor, the tightly leashed, regal, kind man, feral.

"Don't touch Elora. Understood." Drakyth stepped back with his hands up in front of him.

I didn't know what came over me, but I stepped forward and grabbed Drakyth's hand, giving it a firm shake. "Nice to meet you."

Drakyth winked before he jerked his hand back like I'd burned him and leapt off the ground with a thrust of his wings. I gasped and staggered back a step but understood quickly when a bolt of lightning struck the ground exactly where Drakyth had stood.

I screamed, my mouth hanging open wider than it ever had as I swiveled on my heel toward Vaelor. "Are you mad? You could have killed him—or me!"

"It wouldn't have hit you," he said, lethally calm. He held my gaze as he stepped closer, and I craned my neck to look up at him when he invaded my space.

My ass was going to regret this later. I could nearly feel the sting of his palm already—which only made my core burn. I shifted on my feet and crossed my arms.

"If you don't want others to die at your hand, then *don't touch them.*"

My breath left me. "You...You..."

He grinned, his eyes heated, molten silver. "Cat got your tongue, love?"

"You would've electrocuted him, because I shook his hand?"

He shrugged and looped an arm around my shoulders, swiveling me toward the front door. "It would take a lot more than a lightning strike to kill him."

Drakyth hit him with his shoulder. "Doesn't mean it wouldn't have hurt, dick." Leaning around Vaelor, Drakyth pretended to whisper as he said, "Don't worry, El. I don't mind helping you provoke him. That was the first time I've ever seen him lose control. Ever."

"El?" Vaelor asked.

"El, Ellie, Elora." Drakyth waved his hand through the air. "Does it truly matter?"

"El is fine," I said in a rush, stifling the laugh bubbling up. When Vaelor glared down at me, I closed my eyes, biting my lip, my form shaking. Drakyth's snort echoed from the other side of Vaelor, and we both burst into laughter. "I like Drakyth."

"I'll kill him," Vaelor seethed.

Drakyth *wheezed,* bending over and bracing himself on his knees, breathless. I started to wait on him, but Vaelor pulled me forward toward the house.

Drakyth waved a hand for us to go on. "I like you, too, El. Goddess, I'm just glad I found a way under his skin of steel."

When we entered through the front door, I nudged Vaelor's side. "Skin of steel, hmm?"

His hand found my backside as he led me toward a room off

to the left. "You're going to wish you had skin of steel when we get to our room later."

My eyes widened, and I bit my tongue as the flush spread over my entire body, my heart thumping wildly.

"Although, I'm fairly certain you'll get exactly what you wanted from that interaction."

I didn't have time to consider his words before a man around my age stood from the chair he sat in. With tanned skin, rusty red eyes, and black hair, he looked to be related to Drakyth, but he turned to Vaelor and said, "Father!"

"Father?" I mumbled under my breath.

This was the time, I knew it. My eyes were actually going to fall out of my head, or my jaw would hit the floor, or my heart would leap from my chest. *Something* was bound to happen from the icy wave of shock that poured over me. I blinked rapidly as the man strode across the room with a smug grin. Just before he threw his arms around Vaelor, Vaelor stuck a hand out and stopped the man by placing a hand over his face, holding him at arm's length.

"What is wrong with you two today?" Vaelor ran his free hand through his hair and turned to me.

The other man knocked Vaelor's hand away and threw a single arm over his shoulders before looking at me. "Did I give you a good scare?"

"You gave me something." I rested a hand over my racing heart before asking Vaelor, "So, you don't have a son?"

"No, love." His eyes cut to the man hanging on his side. "I don't have a son."

"You having a child wouldn't have bothered me. I mean, you're like a million years old." The man and I both chuckled while Vaelor only cracked a smile. "It would have bothered me more that you kept him a secret all this time. Well, you having a child who looks to be my age would be...strange."

I internally winced—or maybe not so internally, as they both laughed.

The man, Goddess bless him, reached out and patted me on the shoulder. "Aw, it'd be like having a brother."

I froze, my eyes flashing to Vaelor's to find his sharp focus on my shoulder. He reached forward and wrenched the man's hand off by his wrist—albeit much more gently than with Drakyth.

"Don't," was all Vaelor said.

I sighed. "So, anyone want to introduce us?"

"This is Adonis, Drakyth's grandson, but we just call him Adon." Vaelor motioned to Adon, who bowed dramatically.

He tipped his face up with a shit-eating grin. "At your service, milady."

I curtsied, holding back laughs. "Nice to meet you."

Vaelor let out a long breath and plopped down on a couch, legs spread with one arm thrown over the back. I sat at his side, and he wrapped that arm over my shoulders.

Adon sat on a stool across from us and leaned forward with his elbows on his knees, hands clasped. "You're the first person Vaelor has brought here for a visit."

He'd said no one from Draig Hearth knew about this place, but that still caught me off guard. I looked between the two of them, and Vaelor nodded.

"Where is here?" I asked, turning back to Adon.

His smile turned genuine, then, sentimental. "The Sanctuary."

They spent the next hour explaining it all, starting with how Vaelor found Adon and the eleven other children. It branched from there, and the letter system was created. Everything was hush hush and word of mouth. They were sure the villages suspected, but no one ever asked, and he never told. All correspondence was burned, and not a single person in Vaelor's life knew about this place, not even Fauna.

I thought if one person knew, it'd be her, since she was involved in the creation of Puer Mortis. She was the one who stored and provided the necessary vials of blood from the creature of night, but apparently not. Even his friends in Canyon weren't privy to the secrets of the Sanctuary. Everyone he loved was kept in the dark, because he feared that one day, someone would be rescued, and the abuser would grow angry enough to retaliate.

It was better if they didn't know, safer.

"But you told me?" I asked.

Vaelor paused, his expression torn. His fingers discreetly found the pulse on the hollow of my throat, and he stared for longer than normal. Counting, I realized. "I want you in every part of my life. I want you to *know* me. No secrets. No lies."

I rested my hand overtop his and pulled it to my mouth, giving him a light kiss on the palm. "No secrets."

Vaelor had an entire second life outside his role as king—or rather, he took his role as king above and beyond. His people were his to protect, and he meant it with every fiber of his being.

"How many people have you rescued?" I asked Vaelor.

"It all started with this asshole. I'd had the idea for a while, but Drak didn't agree until I brought Adon here. The damned kid gave me a run for my money, though. Made me chase him all over Rainsmyre." Adon grinned again, his form shaking with laughter, but his eyes showed fondness. Vaelor might not be his father, but Adon sure respected him as one. "How many years have we been doing this?"

Adon answered without a second thought. "Nine."

"Nine years," Vaelor repeated. He tilted his head, his eyes lifting to the ceiling as he mulled over numbers in his head. "They don't all stay for obvious reasons. Children do, but adults eventually leave when they feel ready. Everyone but this one. He's stuck to us like a parasite." Even as Vaelor said the words, his affection was clear, and it warmed my heart to see him this way.

I would love to see him with our own child one day.

My smile slid from my face, and I cleared my throat, shoving that very sudden, very random thought from my head.

"That's not a number." I nudged his side with my elbow.

Vaelor glanced at Adon. "Perhaps near one hundred, give or take?"

"One hundred and twelve." Adon nodded once, beaming. "And not a single one has returned to whatever situation led them here."

A mother and two children, young girls with short hair, entered through the front door. One girl carried a basket of daffodils, while the other carried a basket of pastries. The woman glanced in our direction and stilled before a broad grin stretched across her face.

But then, three more children entered behind them, all younger than her two daughters, each one carrying their own basket of flowers. They tugged at the woman's dress, and she sank to her knees, wrapping her arms around them all.

"Are we ready for treats?" She wiggled her brows at them, and they squealed and took off running toward what I assumed was the kitchen.

She dipped her head to Vaelor, and he returned the greeting before she turned and followed the children.

I couldn't pull my gaze from where they'd stood. My eyes burned, my throat tight, holding back tears with all my might. If Godrick hadn't found me, would I have ended up here? Or somewhere like it?

Goddess, I hoped so.

"This is..." My hand found Vaelor's and gripped it tight. "Everything, my love. *You* are everything."

A single tear slipped past my lashes, and I released a shaky laugh, quickly wiping it away. He slid his fingers into my hair and rested his forehead on mine. His scent filled my lungs, leather and warmth and sea storms.

Everything about him, from his hands to his smile to his heart to his scent, felt safe, and he was exactly that—safe, for me and all of his people.

Ravaryn was beyond blessed to have him as a king, but I knew in my bones I was more blessed than any. Fate might be a fickle thing, but it seemed she smiled on me, and I would never, *ever* stop thanking my lucky stars for Vaelor Wrynwood.

Adon cleared his throat at the same moment Drakyth walked in. I giggled, pulling back, as Vaelor hurled a pillow at him. Adon flung back off the stool with a loud thump and a grunt, and Drakyth howled with laughter once again. Vaelor joined him this time, and I covered my mouth with my hand, watching the three of them with a chest full of mirth.

Perhaps Vaelor didn't need a friend all those years ago.

Perhaps it was me who needed him.

Or perhaps we needed each other to fill the gaps we couldn't reach, to hear words not fit for any other's ears, to stitch wounds we didn't cause, to smile and laugh and hold, to understand deeply, thoroughly, completely.

Perhaps our souls saw their counterparts in the other, and we were only a matter of when, not if.

We were fated, written in the stars, across time.

Infinite.

This feeling, so large and all-consuming, was infinite, everlasting and bottomless, warm and bright—a star. I held a star in my chest where my heart should have been.

I rubbed at my sternum absentmindedly with one hand while my other quickly wiped away a stray tear that slipped past my lashes.

No, not just any star.

Vaelor Wrynwood, my best friend, my love, my everything, plucked the sun from the sky and placed it in my chest "to accompany my eyes," as he once said.

28

EIGHT MONTHS LATER

Vaelor

"I swear to the Goddess herself, if you let anything happen to him, I will hunt you down and kill you myself," Elora said, her voice stern but shaky.

Drakyth leaned down to meet her gaze. "I will guard his back with my life, El."

El. I groaned internally. I had never been an overly possessive person, but Elora changed me into a beast. I wanted her all to myself—her gaze and words, her name, her nearness, and especially her smiles.

But I knew, without a doubt, that she was mine, and I was hers, so I let it slide. However, she hadn't so much as shaken another's hand in my presence since the time she met Drakyth.

My hand had worn her ass out that night while she screamed and came—*repeatedly*. The little nymph liked it, and it didn't take long for me to wrench the words from her mouth.

The memory stirred in my cock, and I adjusted myself.

"You're sure about this?" she whispered only to me, placing her hands on my shoulder as she stood on her toes. Her brows were furrowed, worry pressing into every feature of her beautiful face.

I ran a thumb between her brows, smoothing the crease before lowering to run it along her bottom lip. "It's time, sun ray. The boy has suffered long enough."

"Tell me again. I need to hear it again."

She didn't need to elaborate. I knew exactly what she wanted to hear for the tenth time. "The Sanctuary is hidden. Adon will be there, ready for him when we arrive. The boy was left alone. Adrastus is gone, but we don't know how long exactly. Maybe hours, maybe days, but we have to go *now*, love."

She inhaled a shaky breath, nodding, and plastered a smile on her face. I cupped her jaw and leaned down to bite that damned lip. She gasped but melted in my hold.

"No lies means no fake smiles," I whispered into her mouth.

"I'm scared," she whispered back.

My hand slid into her hair and pulled her head back an inch. "I know."

"But," she sighed, "he's just a child, and he needs out. He needs the Sanctuary. He needs to be with the family who won't hurt him."

"Such a kind heart." I pressed my lips to her forehead.

Elora had encouraged this rescue after hearing of my guilt, of the nightmares that occasionally frequented me in my sleep, and once we convinced Drakyth, we spent months planning. Adrastus was watched and followed tirelessly, at least one person tracking his every movement until we understood his schedule.

But the boy would turn thirteen within the next year, which meant his shift was coming, and we couldn't let him go through that with Adrastus. He deserved to shift with someone who would be gentle, who could lead and teach with compassion. He needed his grandfather.

This rescue, however, would be much more difficult than any other before. We had to get in, get the kid out, and disappear into the night without a trace while Drakyth waited for his son, Adrastus.

We had the chains ready—iron imbued with a spell. Once locked in, Adrastus would no longer be able to shift. He would be locked away, and the realm would be safe once again. That boy would be safe.

"We should have done this years ago," Drakyth said. "Thank you for pushing us, Elora. It seems we just needed a kick in the ass."

"We have to be careful, silent. No evidence left behind," I said, and Drakyth nodded once, gripping his two swords by the hilts in their sheaths at his hips. "Less than half his staff is loyal to him, but they *all* fear him, so we can't be seen."

"We won't be." He dipped his chin to Elora.

"I'll see you soon, Drak," she said, her brows furrowing again.

My heart hurt, and I wound an arm around her shoulders to pull her into a hug as Drakyth stepped off to the side with his back to us. Elora never said goodbyes when she was scared. She said it felt too final, too much like an ending. "See you soon" meant there would be another time, and she clung to hope in that way.

I slid my finger under her chin and tipped her head back to press my lips to hers, long and deep.

"I love you," she mumbled into my mouth, then cupped my cheeks to pull me down and place another peck on my lips, the corner of my mouth, my chin, my cheek, my jaw. Everywhere.

"I love you too." *More than I can ever say.*

Her blue eyes had turned to the deepest ocean under the dim moonlight, brimmed with gut-wrenching tears. I hated that they were for me in any capacity. My thumb wiped along her cheek, anticipating their fall.

"Return to me," she whispered.

"Every day, my love. You know I'll return to you. Every. Single. Day."

She nodded once before turning to Drak. "Remember what I said. I *will* kill you."

Drak glanced over his shoulder with a faint smile. "Understood."

With that, I downed two of Iaso's tonics for good measure, grabbed his arm in a death vice, and held Elora's gaze as she backed away.

A tear slipped down her cheek.

Lightning struck, and she disappeared.

We dropped outside of Adrastus' estate, near Blackburn but forcibly isolated from the town. Even the air around the manor was eerily quiet, unsettlingly so. No birds, no wind, nothing.

It was large but plain, with no surrounding vegetation or color, not even grass—a prison. The windows were dark, no visible candles lit inside, leaving the moon overhead as the only light.

I released Drak's arm, both of us tense and silent. Trepidation covered us like a suffocating fog as we stepped into the surrounding forest. With the tonic we'd taken to hide our scents and night hiding us within its darkness, we'd be essentially invisible, even to a Draig, had he been here.

We weren't taking any chances. Not this time, not tonight. I had a mate to return to, and this boy had a home waiting on him. For the first time, he would taste comfort.

We crept along the property to the back door. Drakyth stepped out first and quickly unlatched it, peeking his head inside before waving me forward. We slipped in, and he closed the door silently behind us.

There wasn't a single candle lit, the room utterly black, and uneasiness settled in my gut. Where were the workers? The maids? The cooks?

It was late, but it wasn't past midnight. There should still be *someone* awake.

I didn't dare breathe those words aloud, though.

While Drakyth and I continued our work with the Sanctuary, it had been Adon who studied Adrastus and his son intently, watching and learning as much as he could, even down to the blueprints that laid out every passageway of the house. He'd handed those over to Drakyth who learned them like the back of his hand.

I followed him to the right and ducked into a servants' hall, narrow and impossibly dark. I kept one hand on his back, carefully avoiding his wings because they were sensitive in ways I had *no* interest in, while my other hand trailed along the wall. We climbed a spiral staircase to the second floor where we passed one door, two, three, and stopped at the fourth.

"This should be his," he whispered so low, I thought it might have been nothing more than a draft.

I patted his back once since he couldn't see me, and the sound of the doorknob turning filled the silence. My heart thundered, thumping in my ears, as I waited on bated breath.

The room inside was lit with silver moonlight, the window open and curtains blowing in the breeze.

It *was* a prison.

The only thing in the room was a small bed. That was it. Not a desk, not a rug or artwork or toys. Nothing.

A bed with a single blanket and no pillow—and no child.

The room was utterly empty.

Drak let loose a breath, shaking his head. "Where..."

He stepped into the room and glanced around.

Shluck.

He flinched before going still, an arrow protruding from his side. I jerked forward and ripped him back by his shoulder.

As soon as he staggered into the passageway, I slammed the door shut at the same moment that something—or some*one*—rammed it full force.

With gritted teeth, I ripped the arrow from Drak's side, and he grunted behind closed lips.

Whoever was on the other side of the door pounded on it as I tossed the arrow to the side. The banging of fists echoed down the hall as we sprinted back the way we came, taking the steps three at a time. When we hit the bottom floor, heavy footsteps sounded above us, and we ran faster.

I slammed the door to the servants' hall open, and we spilled into the back entryway, no longer worried about silence. The footsteps of our attacker paused before a loud thump hit on the same floor as us and started again.

Fuck, they jumped levels.

Another arrow loosed and sank into the wall, an inch from Drakyth's face, but not before it sliced through his brow. Blood poured over his eye, and he wiped it away with the back of his hand, his wings rippling with anger.

I shoved him out the back door. "Go!"

He hesitated with a torn glance back at me but shot to the sky with a grunt, wiping his eye again. The moonlight revealed his side soaked in red, his hand pressing into the bleeding wound. His wings moved slowly, each flap contorting his face in pain, but they moved, and that was all that mattered.

Another arrow zipped past me, my shoulder stinging. It sliced through my shirt and skin, and warmth seeped down my arm as I sprinted to the tree line.

I was too close to the house, and that boy had to be in there somewhere. If I left from here, I risked burning him to the ground with that damned house.

Just a little farther—

Another arrow planted itself in my calf.

I hit the ground with a thud.

Another sank in my shoulder, shattering my shoulder blade. A guttural roar tore from me, but it was drowned out by the loud crack of lightning.

The last thing I saw was fire catching. Flames licked the ground, consuming my pooling blood like fuel. It spread toward the house, and when it met wood, it grew bigger, wider, *hungrier.*

Only one person stepped from the home.

One person met my gaze.

Blood red eyes, large wings, and a wolfish grin.

"A house for a house, Vaelor."

29

Elora

A month had passed.

Four weeks.

Thirty days.

A full month since Vaelor and Drakyth nearly fell into Adrastus' trap, and I hadn't stopped looking over my shoulder.

Well, not mine. Vaelor's.

He'd been bleeding profusely and limping when he returned. Thank the Goddess Iaso had been here. She'd almost left for a trip to see Ewan in Nautia, but I talked her into staying a day or two extra for "girl time."

Lies.

It was all lies, and they were bitter on my tongue when Vaelor came into view, injured—then more lies to cover that.

They'd been ambushed. Adrastus had known they were watching and waiting, and he'd managed to catch wind of their plan. He faked his departure, removing his son from the estate instead, but how had he known?

We still hadn't answered that question, and that doubt-filled fear kept me looking over Vaelor's shoulder, waiting for the moment that Adrastus would appear behind him.

And the nightmares.

Goddess, the damned nightmares.

Night after night, I envisioned *someone* being murdered by Adrastus, whether that was Drakyth, Adon, Vaelor, me, or even his own child. I never saw a face on his son, but it was a twelve-year-old boy with wings, pale from lack of sun. I could hear his terror, or sometimes, it was worse: his resignation, his relief.

I wasn't sure why I'd grown protective over a child I had never laid eyes on, but I had. Maybe it was simply because he was a child forced into the hands of a monster. Maybe it was because I knew childhood pain—not in the same way, but I could empathize, because mine could have been the same. The years after my accident were only good because of Godrick, and this boy deserved that too. Maybe it was just another one of fate's tricks, a string, a connection, or maybe it was because of a much greater reason, one no one else knew of. Yet.

I couldn't stand the thought of a child—*a damned child*—locked away in the room Vaelor had described. No friends, no toys, no smiles, no hugs, no laughter, no life.

Everyone deserved a chance to live. *Everyone.*

The metallic tang of blood met my tongue, and I ripped my finger from my mouth. My nail beds were shredded, my cuticles cracked and bleeding as they'd taken the brunt of my anxiety.

Until Adrastus was imprisoned and the boy was safe, it wasn't going to go away. I knew that. Vaelor knew that, and thus, one more reason he wanted to bring it all to an end.

He was more determined to finish what he'd started than ever, which was why we were here in Canyon: to buy arrows tipped with that spellbound iron.

Vaelor held an arrow up, inspecting the tip as sweat rolled

down his forehead. My own shirt was starting to cling to my form.

The blacksmith's hearth was *hot,* yet she somehow seemed unphased. There wasn't even a sheen of sweat on her back, revealed by the strange blouse that cut low enough for her flaming bird tattoo to peek through.

My eyes widened when she turned, holding a dagger glowing bright orange *without* gloves.

"And the spell was already encased?" Vaelor asked.

"Yep." She dropped the weapon in a bucket of water, and it hissed and bubbled around the burning metal. She turned to us, wiping her hands on her apron before bracing them on the table. "The iron was imbued before the tips were dipped."

Vaelor released a deep sigh and glanced at Drak. "Think it'll work?"

He took the arrow and inspected it before collecting the other twelve. "As long as they aren't pulled out, it should keep him down until I can get the chains on him." He looked at the blacksmith. "Thank you, Edana."

She nodded once. "Your other commissions will be done by the end of the day, too. Do you have the gemstones?"

Vaelor reached into his pocket and pulled out three blue stones, two larger ones and one dainty. He placed them on the table, and where two stones touched, a faint light emanated.

I leaned over for a closer look. "I've never seen anything like that."

"Storm's eye." Edana scooped them up and tucked them in a satchel.

"They harbor energy from those who can give it," Vaelor explained. He slipped his hand into mine and bid farewell to Drak and the blacksmith.

"Harbor energy? For what?" I asked as he tugged me down the crowded alley.

"My magic's well is nearly limitless if I want it to be, but I don't like taking, which is why I use Iaso's tonic. Storm bringers can pull energy from other things, other people, but it doesn't feel right to me. The energy just feels wrong inside my body, foreign."

"Okay..." I nodded, not understanding where he was going with this.

"*I* can do that. I can refill my own well if need be, but others can't. Iaso, Ewan, Drak, Adon... None of them." He sighed, placing a hand on my lower back to guide me. "If I channel enough into them, they can be used to refill a magic well—mine *or* another's. I commissioned three because those were the only stones I could find for now."

We exited through Canyon's spell boundary, and I did a double take when I found Drakyth standing there. *How did he beat us?*

I didn't have a second to ask before he ran forward and scooped me up. My first instinct was to kick and fight because Vaelor was absolutely about to strike him down.

"Calm down, love," Vaelor shouted from way too far below.

My eyes snapped open, and my chest seized. I latched onto Drakyth, my body frozen against him. "I'm not on the ground."

Drakyth shook with laughter. "No, you're not."

When he finally set me on my feet, I sucked in a deep breath and staggered away from him, bracing a hand on my abdomen. My stomach curdled, and my eyes glued to Drak's face, afraid that if I looked away, nausea would force dinner back up.

I hadn't realized I had a fear of heights until now, but I most certainly did as I finally looked away from Drakyth. My breath left me in a harsh whoosh. The desert surrounding Canyon was visible in every direction, all the way to the shimmering horizon.

High.

We're high.

I could see for *miles* from atop this plateau. "Why would—"

My head whipped left and right before I spun, looking for Drakyth, which set off a wave of dizziness. I stepped over to a nearby crystal tower and clung to it.

Gone. He's gone.

Great.

The stone was cool beneath my palms, despite the desert heat, and I closed my eyes for a moment, taking slow, deep breaths.

Wait.

I opened my eyes.

This is a damned crystal tower?

Curiosity piqued enough to dampen the fear, and I finally took in my surroundings. My jaw fell slack, and I stood straighter, releasing my death grip on the stone.

Crystals were everywhere, large and silver, sparkling beneath the setting sun, all touching or protruding from a pool of water.

Arms wrapped around my midsection, and I relaxed at his scent. It soothed me to my very soul; it always had, and I knew it always would.

Vaelor hummed and placed his chin on top of my head. "The two larger stones are for daggers while the small one... That one is for a ring."

My heart skipped a beat, my chest rising and falling quicker.

"For you." He spun me in his hold so I faced him.

"For me?" I whispered.

He tipped my face to him and glided his lips along mine. "For you."

"I don't have a magic well to be refilled."

"Maybe not, but it would make me feel better if you wore it. I want to be able to give to you if you ever need it."

A soft chuckle escaped my tightening throat, my eyes burning. My damned eyes always burned, always cried. Why did every emotion have to come through in tears?

"And..." He dropped to one knee, and my breath hitched. "Fae may not have traditional marriages, but you're not Fae, are you, dear, sweet Elora?"

I shook my head, covering my mouth.

"Then please, do me the highest of honors and marry me, because I'm nothing if not yours."

I dropped to my knees and nodded fervently when words eluded me.

"Is that a yes, love?" He cupped the back of my head to tilt my face to his as he pressed his lips to my cheeks, kissing away the tears.

"Y-yes." I wound my arms around his neck. "Did you ever doubt that?"

"No." He chuckled, but my laugh came out choked and broken. "But if we're to be married, I..."

At his hesitation, I pulled back to meet his eyes. "What?"

He sighed and sank back to sit on the ground, pulling me into his lap as he did so. "I asked Augustus to speak with the souls, and we've found a way to...to connect our lifespans."

I shoved myself out of his hold and sat on my knees to stare at him, to see if those words had truly come from his mouth, or if I'd imagined them, but he held my gaze with suppressed hope.

I sucked in a deep breath against the tension in my chest, excitement filling it too viciously to allow air too. "So, you wouldn't...I wouldn't..."

"No, sun ray, you wouldn't." His grin was brilliant, breath-stealing, putting the sunset to shame. "You would live with me, *as long* as me."

I launched myself at him, and his rich laughter filled my heart with warmth. I wrapped my arms around his neck, my breaths coming out shaky, my body torn between laughing and crying. "How?"

"Well, that part is more difficult."

My heart sank. Of course, the other shoe had to drop at some point.

"It's an ancient soul binding spell, a marriage ceremony of sorts, forgotten to time. It has to happen here, actually." He motioned to the pool, and I looked over my shoulder at it. The sinking sun cast the pool in burning red, steam rising from it in soft waves. "We prick our fingers on one of these crystals, drop the blood into the pool, and if the Goddess deems our love true, she'll link our fates, even more than they already are."

"That doesn't seem so bad."

His throat bobbed. "If one person's love isn't true, they both die."

That should've scared me, but it didn't, not at all.

I crawled back into his lap, straddling his legs. "Is that what you're worried about?"

"Elora..."

"Because I'm not. I want to marry you in every way, human and Fae. I want my heart and soul and life all tied to you, because I fear my world no longer revolves around the sun. I have no doubts, not a single one, Vaelor. *We* are true."

His smile grew at my words, his heart thundering beneath my palms on his chest, strong and steady and *alive*.

"I don't have any reservations, except..." I bit my lip and glanced down as I lifted his hand and placed it on my lower belly. "One."

His brows furrowed before understanding dawned on him, his silver eyes widening. He wrapped his other arm around my waist as he sat up straighter, holding me against him.

"Are you... Elora, you're..."

My cheeks flushed. "I'm pregnant, Vaelor. I don't know how. I've taken the tonics, but I guess they're not infallible."

"We'll wait." He nuzzled his nose against mine before pressing a gentle kiss to my lips and lifting me by my waist to set me on my feet, leaving him at eye level with my womb. His hands rested on my hips as he pulled me forward and kissed my belly. "We'll wait for our babe to be born, and then, you'll be mine for the rest of our *very* long lives."

He stilled suddenly. His head cocked to the side, brows furrowed.

My smile faltered. "Vaelor?"

He pressed his hand a little firmer onto my belly, but he didn't answer.

"Are you okay?"

His eyes snapped up to meet mine, and Goddess help me, they brimmed with tears. "A girl."

"W-what?"

"She's a girl. I can feel her in there, her tiny little heartbeat enough energy for me to pick up."

I closed my eyes as another tear fell, my smile so wide my cheeks ached. "A girl."

"A girl," he repeated. Holding my hand, he tugged me down to his lap and wrapped his arms around me, enveloping me in *him*, his warmth, his scent, his love. "My girls."

30

Elora

Vaelor sat straight up in bed, eyes crackling when his head jerked to the door, his chest rising and falling quickly.

I scrambled to my knees, my shift bunching around my waist, the autumn breeze blowing through the open window and sending unnerving chills over me.

"W-what is it?" I asked, searching his face, but he saw straight through me, his face pale and tight.

No, he was looking *past* me, past the door, down the hall, the feelers of his magic reaching well beyond our chambers.

My breaths came quick, uneven, when he didn't respond. His jaw clenched as he pressed his palm over my womb, and he *kissed* me. He kissed me like it was the first and last time, deeply, reaching and touching and caressing every inch of my soul.

My lips trembled. *This isn't right.*

He nudged me back softly, pushing until I stood at the edge of the bed before he broke his lips from mine. "Go into the closet, love."

"W-why? What's happening?" I grabbed his hands, but he pulled away, his glowing eyes glued to the door. "Look away from the door. Look at me, Vaelor. Look at me."

He closed his eyes before finally, *finally* looking at me, his expression broken.

"No... No, this is a nightmare." I shook my head and pinched my arm. "Wake up." I pinched harder. Harder. Harder. "Wake up. Wake up. Wake—"

His eyes snapped back to the door, and he shoved me away from the bed as he crawled out. "Go, Elora."

I stumbled back, gasping, hyperventilating, shattering, dying. "Vaelor..."

"Now!" He stood with his back to me, blocking the closet.

I stumbled inside on weak legs, sobbing silently, my cheeks soaked. "It's just a nightmare, though. Just a nightmare."

I grabbed a pin from the top shelf and pricked my finger with trembling hands and blurry eyes. Tears speckled the floor at my feet as a droplet of blood formed. I turned to Vaelor, and he stilled when I planted a kiss between his bare shoulder blades.

"I love you," I whispered before tracing the E he'd carved for me and slipping inside his nook.

I lifted the slat barely wide enough to look through when the chamber door slammed open, and I watched.

I watched everything, numb, barely breathing as silent tears slid down my cheeks.

So numb. Immobile. Frozen in time.

I could hear nothing. I could do nothing. I could only watch.

Red wings and red eyes and red blood.

Red blood.

Blood.

Running and pooling and flowing where it shouldn't.

And then, silver eyes.

Silver eyes met mine.

Silver eyes that no longer glowed, no longer sparked.

He lifted a hand to me, and everything shattered. Splintered.

My world, my reality, my heart was crushed into a million pieces.

Dust.

My heart was dust, scattered among broken, confused stars, but I ripped the door open anyway. My legs trembled when I stepped out of the closet into warm liquid. My gaze fell to see my bare foot in a pool of red, and my knees gave out. I collapsed on a choked sob, and my palms found that red too.

I crawled to him.

My feet. My hands. My knees.

Covered in Vaelor.

"It's just a nightmare," I mumbled as my stained hands hovered over him. "We'll wake up."

"Sun ray..." His voice was strained, and my gaze snapped to his face, ashen.

I touched a hand to his cheek, and his skin was cold. Too cold.

My hand slid into his hair, and a trail of dark red followed its path.

His breath hitched, a gargling sound leaving his lips. "I love...you, Elora. I have always...loved you."

"I love you, Vaelor." I kissed his forehead. His nose. His cheeks. His lips. "I love you and our baby, and we're going to wake up. You'll be okay because it's just a nightmare."

"Deam meus...es...tu missus." His words floated around me like a breeze, like a whisper, like his last breath.

I pulled back, but his eyes were closed.

"Open your eyes, Vaelor." My body shook, and I cupped his cheeks. "Open your eyes. Open your eyes! Open—"

His chest wasn't rising and falling. My eyes darted over him, around him, aimlessly searching. I watched his chest to count his breaths like he did mine when he was scared, but nothing. I touched his throat to feel his pulse. Nothing.

"Wake up, Vaelor. Wake up..." A silent sob wracked me so viciously, my vision went black, and I fell back, landing in more of him, more of his sticky warmth. "It's just a nightmare."

A hand touched my shoulder. I didn't move.

An arm tried to turn me. I didn't move.

I waited.

I waited and waited and waited for Vaelor to wake up, for me to wake up.

But the blood cooled, and Vaelor didn't move.

The blood cooled, and his chest didn't rise.

The blood cooled, and he didn't hold me. He didn't reach for me. He didn't say my name.

The blood cooled, and he didn't wake up.

Because this wasn't a nightmare.

It wasn't a nightmare, and I was coated in Vaelor's blood, and Vaelor was dead.

Dead.

Dead.

"Vaelor is dead." The words were barely a whisper until they weren't. Until I screamed.

A hand clamped over my mouth, but I didn't stop. I screamed like my heart was being ripped from my body— because it was. I screamed like I'd watched the world end— because I had, and now I was simply waiting for the rest of us to crumble around him: me, the castle, Ravaryn, the realm.

I screamed until my throat was shredded and blood coated my tongue too.

A figure sat in front of me, blocking Vaelor from sight, and I shoved them out of the way with everything I had. I scrambled forward and collapsed on his chest.

He didn't smell of sea storms or leather or warmth anymore.

He smelled metallic.

Because Vaelor Wrynwood was dead.

"Elora," a voice said.

I scrunched my eyes, shaking my head as I held onto Vaelor's body. He'd told me of the veil, of the other side, and I knew he wasn't here, not in this body, but I couldn't let go. I screamed into his chest, sobbing, wailing, *begging* him to hear me, to return.

"You promised, Vaelor. You promised…"

You promised to return to me every day, every fucking day, so return to me.

"Please." My voice cracked, choked and blistering in my raw throat. "Please. Please."

Now, I understood that wife, willing to do horrible things to bring her husband back.

I understood why Alden grieved for two hundred years, waiting day by day with one foot in the grave for the moment he would see her again.

I understood why Vaelor was terrified, why he was willing to sacrifice centuries to fear and restraint.

I understood pain—slicing, suffocating, deafening, *drowning* pain with no end.

"I'm going to die, Vaelor," I mumbled. I sucked in breath after breath, but no air came, and I didn't fight it. Not when my vision tunneled on his face and my chest burned, not when stars sparked in my sight and I pretended they were Vaelor's raindrops. Because physical pain was easier, more manageable. "I'm drowning."

Suddenly, I was thrust back under that icy water. His body was cold, his blood cold, his damned heart—once so warm it felt like the sun inside my chest—cold, and I was drowning, my sticky hands trembling, tingling, fingers numb.

I'm going to join you because this will kill me. This will end the world and destroy the realm and shatter everything.

How could it not?

"Listen," the voice said again, this time with more...power.

A dark fog settled over my mind. My sobs eased, and I looked up to find rusty red irises staring back.

Adon knelt on the other side of Vaelor, his eyes wild and bloodshot, panicked. "I didn't—I wouldn't have—"

"Did you do this?" My voice was hoarse and broken, barely audible. It felt like white-hot daggers in my throat, but I screamed the words so they'd come out like whispers. "Did you do this, Adon?"

He shook his head. "No. No, I didn't know. I didn't... Adrastus said he just wanted his throne. He was going to imprison Vaelor, and my family would take the crown again. I-I didn't know. He s-said—"

"You killed him." My voice was hollow. My chest was hollow. My soul was hollow, and I was numb.

"W-what?" Adon's eyes snapped to me. "No."

My lips trembled. "You brought Adrastus here, didn't you?"

Adon scrambled back, fisting his hair, shaking his head over and over. He muttered words I didn't care enough to hear.

I stared at Vaelor's face, pale and lifeless.

Dead.

Adon's voice grew louder, but still, I didn't listen, not until he used some kind of magic in his voice and forced me to hear him.

"Forget." His expression was manic, his nostrils flared and face red. Sweat beaded on his forehead, disrupted by a drop of blood sliding down his temple. His hands, coated in Vaelor, had soaked his hair too.

Vaelor was everywhere he shouldn't be.

"Fuck, h-how do I do this? Fuck. Fuck!" He fisted his hair again, ripping out a few strands before lunging for me. *"Forget."*

"No." I shoved at his chest, but he came right back and gripped my arms. "No, Adon! Do not take him from me."

I kicked and fought and bit and clawed. His fingers dug into my skin, tightening until I thought my arms would snap. Still, I didn't listen. I didn't stop.

"Forget," he said again, and that dark fog slithered over me like death, cold and icy and unnerving and *dead*.

"Do not take him from me, Adon! Do not take him!" I needed to remember. I needed to remember everything, every painful detail: his smile, his laugh, his kindness, his love and compassion and scent, his *death*, so I could tell our daughter. I had already forgotten my parents. I would not forget him too.

I could not.

Forgetting him would be to forget the other half of myself.

"Forget I was here."

I stilled in his hold, his vile fog infiltrating my mind until I could see nothing but darkness.

"Forget we ever tried to rescue Rogue Draki."

A silent tear slid down my cheek.

"Forget you ever met me or Drakyth or saw the Sanctuary. Adrastus killed Vaelor *alone*. No one else was here."

I finally met his gaze, and he flinched.

"Find Vaelor's healer and his father and leave, Elora. Go to Auryna. Marry."

And just like that, every part of me that mattered withered and died.

31

Elora

Days passed in a blur.

I didn't remember any of it. Not changing my clothes or bathing or leaving Draig Hearth. I didn't remember Iaso erasing Vaelor's mark from my neck with one of her Goddess-forsaken medicines, but I felt it—or the lack thereof, replaced by a deep, *deep* ache in my chest, drowned in numbness. I didn't remember crossing the border with Alden or sleeping or eating, but we were here, standing hand in hand outside of Godrick's castle.

Why is Alden here? How is he here?

He should be curled into a ball. He should be unreachable, like me. His words fell on deaf ears, his comfort, his panic techniques, all useless.

Nothing would ease this ache.

Nothing would fill the emptiness in my chest.

I hadn't smiled since Vaelor smiled back at me. I hadn't taken an easy breath or had a thought that didn't contain his face, bleeding and pale and *dead*.

He was dead.

Dead. The word echoed in my skull every day, all day, every night, in every nightmare, in every cry. I thought those might be the only three words I knew anymore: *Vaelor is dead.*

Three words that had single-handedly shattered my entire person.

There was nothing left, and I finally understood Alden. Maybe that was why he helped me, because when he looked in my eyes, he saw his reflection.

He'd placed a glamour over his Fae ears, leaving him seemingly human, and I didn't like it, but I didn't like a lot of things any longer. What was the point?

Everyone dies, right? Everything and everyone?

Everyone fucking dies.

Truer words had never been spoken, and that was only confirmed when I walked in through the front door alone. I didn't look back to wave at Alden as he watched from afar. I didn't say goodbye or hug him or offer him a smile.

I did nothing, because I could do nothing. Merely walking took every ounce of energy I had.

As I entered, the guards' faces fell in shock, but they waved me forward, their eyes dropping to my feet.

Barefoot.

I hadn't put on a pair of shoes since Vaelor died. I'd felt his blood beneath these feet.

Now, I needed every texture, every ground, every floor to grate that warm, wet feeling from my memory. Nothing had worked so far—not grass, gravel, tile, hot coals, or forest floor— and I was losing hope anything ever would.

I followed the directions of guards, making it all the way to a...funeral before I realized anything was different.

Black was everywhere: black flowers, black banners, black

rugs. Candles were lit on every surface, benches on either side of the long, dark carpet leading to the casket.

Alivia and Godrick leaned over whoever lay inside.

I walked forward on numb legs, and they turned when gasps rippled through the mourning crowd. Alivia found me first, her face swollen and blotchy, clutching a wet handkerchief in her gloved hand. My feet stopped when she sprinted. She collided with me in a tight embrace, nearly knocking us both to the ground.

She sobbed into my shoulder. "M-mother. She...She died. She's dead. A sickness."

I didn't return the hug. I didn't speak. I just stared at the casket. I could barely make out Mother's profile, pale and *dead*.

Dead.

Everyone dies.

Alivia's breath hitched as she pulled back and led me forward. Godrick's face looked...blank, absent, and I knew he understood too.

He knew this pain, felt it, lived it, drowned in it.

We would drown together.

EPILOGUE

Fear won that day in Ravaryn and finally snuffed out Elora's light.

After the funeral, Alivia begged Elora to stay, but she didn't. She couldn't.

"I just need time," Elora had said, her voice as hollow as her insides.

She walked out of the castle barefoot, in a strange silver silk gown she refused to remove, and for a reason not even she could explain, she took Evander with her, agreeing to his marriage proposal. They wed quickly, and that "time" she asked for turned to months, years blurring into decades.

The memories of everyone she once loved—Godrick, Alivia, Emma, Vaelor, everyone—all died on Elora's lips, as she never spoke their names again. Not to Evander, not to Ara, not to anyone. The only person from her past who made it to her present was Evander.

With the death of Vaelor came the death of her optimism, the death of her hope.

Where once stood Elora Stirling, the carefree adopted

princess turned secret captive of Vaelor Wrynwood, now stood Elora Starrin, the quiet, tightly sealed wife of General Evander.

Ara's safety became her sole concern, and Elora refused to be in contact with anyone who had ever seen Vaelor.

She couldn't bring herself to, as she was laced with a deep-rooted fear they'd recognize him in their daughter. She swore to herself no one would ever know, save for Alden, Ewan, and Iaso —not even Evander or Alivia. The woman who once trusted the world now trusted no one because fear had consumed her. It swallowed her whole, and she allowed it.

Evander hadn't understood why they needed to move away upon her return, or why she wouldn't speak of their childhood any longer, but he respected her wishes. All he'd ever wanted was to marry her, and he made the sacrifice to have her as a wife —even if she was an entirely different person than the one he'd known just a year ago.

After eight long months of near silence, he stopped asking questions entirely. Elora never gave any answers, and then, Ara was born. His one and only daughter wrapped him around her finger, and he never once questioned the speed at which Elora fell pregnant, aloud or otherwise.

Alivia and Elora never spoke again, neither reaching out to the other. The two who were once inseparable missed everything of importance—their weddings, one of love and the other of necessity, the births of their daughters, a mere year apart. When the news of Godrick's abdication reached them, Elora considered reaching out to Alivia, sending a short letter or a simple flower or even an apple pie, but she didn't, and then she never had the chance.

When Alivia's daughter, also named Alivia but known as Livvy, was only seven years old, her mother, Alivia Stirling, was murdered. Godrick disappeared not long after, and it was suspected he was killed too—for money or greed or perhaps he was just in the wrong place at the wrong time. Perhaps Adonis came back for him, for both of them, but it was never proven. Their deaths were never investigated.

They all fell through the cracks of time and faded into the background of greater things such as the rising tension with Ravaryn and the talk of war on the horizon—later becoming the Ten Year War.

Each death was another nail in the coffin that held Elora's heart, and she dealt with each agonizing moment in silence behind a brave, unwavering mask.

While Ara was carefully shielded from their past, Evander knew her former family, and he knew the pain their deaths caused her, but they never spoke of it. There were no shared looks or kind words or sympathy. She would never allow it, even if Evander had wanted to.

However, by Ara's eighth birthday, Adonis had called Evander back to the Capitol to be his general and sunken his grimy claws so deep into Evander's mind that he never even considered offering his condolences.

His mind had been warped into a strategic war zone, leaving only enough room for King Adon, Auryna, and his armies. Evander Starrin, the kind man and loving father, was killed long before his body ever was.

Livvy never learned of her family's long royal history; she never discovered she was nearly the crown princess, next in line to rule after her mother. She, like many others, was lost to tragedy—forgotten and thrown to the wolves, the most prominent wolf being her own father. Lyren lost himself to drink in the grief of his wife's death and twisted into the cold, cruel beast Livvy knew and hated.

As for Elora...

Her only light was Ara. With eyes so gray, they matched the stormy sky, Elora took solace in them—her sole tether to

Vaelor—but Ara would never know his eyes, never know his face.

It seemed fate had decided that since Elora couldn't remember her father's face, neither would Ara.

For nearly twenty-seven years, she never dared to speak Vaelor's name aloud. He was a secret she would take to her grave for the safety of their daughter, to keep her from Adrastus, from anyone who would seek to harm her.

For twenty-seven long years, Elora Wrynwood hid beneath Elora Starrin as one of the Goddess' most valiant soldiers— braver than many, more selfless than most, more determined than all.

She was prepared to sacrifice everything, and she did.

While the peaceful realm she once viewed through beautiful, rose-tinted glasses fell around her, rebuilding itself on the blood and bones of its people, Elora was orphaned once again, left with nothing but her daughter, her dreams long turned to ash, and the silent memories of an epic love.

Deam meus es tu missus.
You are my Goddess-sent.

ABOUT THE AUTHOR

J.D. Linton is the debut author of The Last Storm, book one in the Rogue x Ara series.

She's married to her high school sweetheart and a mother of one. She enjoys reading and writing spicy fantasy romance, and as with most writing mamas, she's also a midnight writer—up all day with her real baby and up all night with her fictional babies.

When not writing, you can find her reading, making a million Tiktoks, or at the park with her son.

Writing has truly changed her life, and she's even more thankful for the incredible community it brought with it.

ALSO BY J.D. LINTON

The Last Storm

The Last Draig

For the Love of Fritters & Frights

Printed in Great Britain
by Amazon